"It's all here: family, friends, foes, and human frailties. An emotional treat from beginning to end."

—ALAN JACKSON, coauthor of *Pretty Maids All in a Row*

"Riveting, relevant, realistic—these are all words that describe Michelle Buckman's timely novel *My Beautiful Disaster*. This compelling story of a young woman's journey from 'disaster' to restoration is a must-read for twenty-first-century teen girls."

—JANICE A. THOMPSON, author of *Parenting Teens: A Field Guide*

"I didn't intend to read the book straight through, but I did. I didn't think I would be drawn into the lives of a bunch of teenagers, but I was. This book has characters so richly drawn that it is impossible not to relate to them. Michelle can take on difficult subjects without allowing them to becoming offensive, delivering a powerful and compelling message that can interest and reach today's youth with a message more vital today than ever. *My Beautiful Disaster* is beautifully done."

—TERRY BURNS, author of the MYSTERIOUS WAYS series

"I personally love discovering a new writer, and I've found a gem in Michelle Buckman. Buckman joins the ranks of Melody Carlson and Bill Myers for writing relevant teen fiction that doesn't mince words and isn't afraid to deal with the grit and grime our teens face in our world today."

—DEENA PETERSON, reviewer, A Peek at My Bookshelf

Also by Michelle Buckman

THE PATHWAY COLLECTION

Maggie Come Lately (TH1NK/NavPress)

THE PATHWAY COLLECTION

My Beautiful Disaster

A Novel

MICHELLE BUCKMAN

www.thinkbooks.com

TH1NK
P.O. Box 35001
Colorado Springs, Colorado 80935

Published in association with Yates & Yates, LLP, Attorneys and Counselors, Orange, California.

TH1NK is an imprint of NavPress.
TH1NK and the TH1NK logo are registered trademarks of NavPress. Absence of ® in connection with
marks of NavPress or other parties does not indicate an absence of registration of those marks.

ISBN-13: 978-1-60006-083-0
ISBN-10: 1-60006-083-8

Cover design by The DesignWorks Group, David Uttley/www.thedesignworksgroup.com
Cover photo by Steve Gardner, Pixel Works Studios
Creative Team: Nicci Hubert, Jamie Chavez, Reagen Reed, Arvid Wallen, Kathy Guist

Unless otherwise identified, all Scripture quotations in this publication are taken from *The New American
Bible* (Catholic Edition/Memorial Edition; Illustrated), Memorial Bible Publishers, Inc., Box 23304,
Nashville TN 37202; Copyright: Today, Inc. 1976 All rights reserved; Text copyright 1970 by the
Confraternity of Christian Doctrine, Washington DC.

Buckman, Michelle.
  My beautiful disaster : a novel / Michelle Buckman.
    p. cm. -- (The pathway collection)
  ISBN-13: 978-1-60006-083-0
  ISBN-10: 1-60006-083-8
  1. Teenage girls--Fiction. 2. Teenage pregnancy--Fiction. I. Title.
  PS3602.U28M9 2007
  813'.6--dc22
                              2007022979

Printed in the United States of America

1 2 3 4 5 6 7 8 9 10 / 10 09 08 07

In loving memory of my parents

Chapter One

MY NAME IS Dixie.

I'm not gorgeous or anything, but I started hanging out with the hottest girls in school my sophomore year, so I reached the status of being popular by default. Or at least I *was* popular. That rank has changed.

Some people say I've made a mess of my life. I don't know. Maybe my stepsister Maggie's description is more accurate. She's a huge Kelly Clarkson fan, so it didn't surprise me when Maggie dragged up some of her lyrics to describe me. She says my life is a "beautiful disaster." You be the judge.

Maggie and I were friends long before we became stepsisters. We met on the first day of kindergarten. Maggie's skinny body was topped with a mop of bright red Irish curls, and I was round with baby fat and strung with two straight blonde braids. We sat at the same little table and drank juice and ate cookies together, stuck our hands in Play-Doh, and fought over the dinosaur puzzle. After that no one could separate us. We took every class together. We shared ChapStick, hairbrushes, and one bout of lice in elementary school. We bought our first bras together when we were twelve. We tried out for cheerleading together even though we knew we wouldn't make the squad. We walked for March of Dimes and ran track together in ninth grade. We finished each other's sentences and each other's sandwiches. We slept at each other's houses, talked all night, and cried on each other's shoulders many a time. We did everything together.

Then we became sisters. My mother married Maggie's father.

You would think that would have made us closer. I mean, we were already closer than sisters, but something happened when we moved in under the same roof and had to share a bedroom. Or maybe it was already happening before then, and living together made us face it straight on.

You see, Maggie and I weren't exactly popular at school in our early years. In fact we were pretty much invisible. We blended into the walls and floors. Nobody took any notice of us. No one invited us to parties or commented on our clothes or asked what we thought of the latest Reese Witherspoon movie. We weren't as bad as the losers or the nerdy kids who kept their noses in their laptops all the time; we just weren't important to anyone. All that changed when Maggie got on the news one day. I would tell you more about that, but that's her story, and this is mine.

What matters is that suddenly everyone noticed us. We had boyfriends and invitations to parties and everything. The weird thing is that after years of yearning to be popular, Maggie rejected it all. She became *known*, recognized, but remained more or less a loner. I'd had enough of that life. I embraced my new visibility and left her behind.

By the middle of tenth grade, I was hanging out with Heather and Tammy, two cheerleaders who held the school in the palms of their hands. Maggie and I still hung out in classes, since Heather and Tammy weren't in any honors courses, but after school we went our separate ways—she to study with Webb, a boy from our neighborhood, while I met up with Heather and Tammy and hit the mall or went to their houses or to the pizza parlor or whatever. Despite that, Maggie and I were still okay with each other. We were still friends, just with differing interests. Maggie barely noticed anyway since she was so hung up on Webb. I think she was glad I had someone else to hang out with. So things were fine between us at that point. And it wasn't the idea of our parents getting married that threw a kink in things because it was pretty much our doing. Maggie's daddy was dating a lady Maggie couldn't stand, so we introduced my mama to him as a decoy. Well, I should say *re*-introduced. From stories Mama had told us, we knew that they had been in high school together and that they dated at least once back then, but how Mama ended up marrying my daddy, Richard Chambers, and Maggie's dad ended up marrying Mallory had some undercurrents that Mama wouldn't share with me or Maggie.

Anyway, whatever happened between our parents in high school was rekindled when Maggie and I got the two of them together. That was back when we were in tenth grade. During the summer between eleventh and twelfth grade, they got married and we became sisters. Which brings me to our senior year. By January, Maggie was sick of sharing a bedroom with me, and Heather and Tammy and I got Asby Jones, popular juvenile delinquent, to make us fake IDs so we could go to a bar to hear a new group called Blind Reality that Heather kept raving about. That is where my beautiful disaster began.

Chapter Two

MY HOMETOWN WAS about the size of a city mall. I couldn't go anywhere without someone knowing me and seeing what I was up to, but luckily the bar was in Columbia, which meant no one would recognize us there, or look at our fake IDs and know our mamas and our aunts and our grandmas, or call up Sheriff Tate to come drag us home.

I hadn't ever done anything like that before—sneaking into a bar—and my heart was in my throat all the way there because I knew it was wrong. I wasn't an angel, but I'd never before done anything illegal, other than drinking underage at parties. That didn't seem as scary as trying to get into the bar with a fake ID. There was a sense of excitement and adventure that carried me along and made me ignore my usual sense of ethics. No one from my church would be there, I knew that for sure, so it wasn't likely to get back to Reverend John that the teen leader of his youth group was out on the town with friends.

I had some major pangs of guilt when Heather first suggested the excursion, but Heather . . . well, I tended to do whatever she suggested for fear of being shunned if I didn't, because she absolutely *made* my social life, and I wouldn't be anyone if I weren't hanging with her. Besides, it's not like we were going there to drink. She just wanted us to hear the band. What harm could come of that?

After all our worries, the guy at the door barely even glanced at our IDs, and we entered the bar without incident; but it immediately struck me as foreign territory, a place I didn't belong.

The first thing that surprised me was that it wasn't full of smoke the way bars are always portrayed in movies—crowds of people lounging at tables and leaning on the bar in a haze of cigarette smoke. This place had gone politically correct and confined the smokers to a separate area to the far left of the entrance, as well as an outside lounge beyond, which consisted of a small square of cement surrounded by a ten-foot fence and half a dozen metal tables. That was fine with me because I had no intention of smoking. There were some dumb teenage antics I went along with, but smoking wasn't one of them. I watched my father die of lung cancer when I was thirteen, and it wasn't a pretty sight. He couldn't talk. He could barely swallow. I had to help him steer his walker into the bathroom, sit him in a chair in the shower, and bathe him—me a little girl and him a grown man—as his body wasted away and the life in his eyes died under the strain of pain that handfuls of pills didn't mask. So I told Heather and Tammy straight off that it was no deal smoking around me. I wasn't an idiot.

The lack of smoke didn't diminish the partylike atmosphere. The lights were dimmed to twilight level, just enough to make me squint, as if it would bring things into better focus. Special lights embedded into the ceiling cast a soft glow across the bell-shaped glasses hanging from wooden racks above the mahogany bar, and glistened on the brass rod running around the edge of the counter. The bartender, a hunky guy, considering he was probably in his thirties, was busy pulling bottles from the rack lining the mirrored wall, his hands moving with practiced confidence as he mixed three different drinks. He swung around to place them in front of two middle-aged businessmen dressed in khakis and white button-downs, and their female companion, a lady who had obviously never studied the art of adjusting her wardrobe from work to eveningwear. She still had on her tailored coat, and her hair was pulled into a severe ponytail that emphasized her flat face and pointed nose. She definitely needed to let her hair down, take off the coat, and add a scarf or something to soften the neckline of her blouse . . . things I'd learned from Heather and Tammy over the previous couple of years.

All but one of the barstools were occupied, men and women lined up munching on peanuts, sipping drinks, and making small talk, with their disjointed reflections peering back at them from between the liquor bottles. The rest of the bar wasn't elbow-to-elbow crowded, but most of the wooden tables seated at least a couple of people, sometimes more, their heads bent in concentration to hear each other over the general din of conversation.

Tammy poked me as we entered to let me know the two guys near the door were eyeing the three of us. The closest one was blond with a huge fuzzy mustache that looked like some freaky mammoth caterpillar had taken up residence on his face. The other was better looking, the clean-cut type that looked like he had money, but way too old in my opinion. Tammy liked older guys, though, so she was probably thrilled. She had never actually dated a grown man, but that was her goal. She thought high school guys were pathetic. Both men had their eyes glued to us, maybe out of boredom and lack of anything to talk about, or maybe they were calculating our ages and had a thing for high school girls. Heather was worth a look, that's for sure. She stood five-ten even when she was barefoot, with legs to die for. And that night, even though it was only about forty degrees outside, she had on this miniskirt that showed them off to the max, with spiky heels that raised her to about six-two. (I would love to have seen Maggie try to walk in those heels. She would have fallen flat on her face.) Heather had flat-ironed her hair and sprayed it with sheen so that it shone like spun silk and swished across her shoulders when she turned her head. Tammy, with a darker and more classic look, wore a conservative top, hoping it made her look older, not promiscuous . . . but she had on tight jeans that didn't leave a whole lot to the imagination. Being shorter than either of them, and rounder, but not fat, I wore a matching pants and shirt outfit that emphasized my waist and my curves. It made me look older than usual. Nothing on the level of Tammy and Heather, though. So if guys were looking at us, I doubted their sights were set on me.

I followed the other girls through the crowd to an empty table, totally aware of every step I took as the heels of my boots clicked against the ancient hardwood floor. My hips brushed against the arms of unsuspecting men huddled over their beers; if they looked up, they'd catch the sparkle in my eye—I was out at a bar with a fake ID and a night of fun ahead of me.

Heather wanted to sit right up front so she could see the singer, Ariana—some girl she'd met at a modeling competition. Apparently Ariana had asked Heather to come listen to them play. She just wanted to be able to say she knew the singer, like that would be some thrill, considering no one in the world had ever heard of this dorky group. I figured they wouldn't be all that good.

The band was setting up. Heather slid into a seat and pointed at the black-haired beauty setting out microphones. "That's her.

That's Ariana," she said, and went into the long tale of how they'd met. Heather was known for telling elaborate stories when she had an audience, like in the middle of class with everyone watching. She was one of the few kids who could get away with it; the teachers loved her.

As she talked, I watched Ariana. I had to admit that she looked like a model. She had high cheekbones and flawless skin the color of the caramels I used to get in my trick-or-treat bag every Halloween when I was kid. She moved like a cat, her hips swaying to the movement of her long, slim legs. Instinctively, I knew it was her beauty that attracted Heather. She liked being around beautiful people. Tammy didn't. She didn't like to be outshone. She popped up out of her seat. "I'm going to get a drink."

"Sure, just draw attention to us again, like getting in the door wasn't enough of a risk," Heather hissed with uncharacteristic seriousness; she usually played the ditz, using sappy stories and her beauty to get what she wanted. "Sit down," she said.

Tammy blinked at her tone but remained standing. "Isn't that the point of coming to a bar?"

"No. It's to hear the band."

Tammy rolled her eyes. "I can at least get a Coke." She flounced off, a peacock needing to preen her feathers.

Heather jabbered away about how cool Ariana's silky black outfit was, while I watched the band set up. I'd never seen such a thing before, even though my stepbrother, Tony, played guitar. He seemed to confine his playing to his bedroom and had never played in a band that I could remember. I wondered if he would have enjoyed being there onstage and whether or not he knew how to set up amps and such. I'd known him as long as I'd known Maggie, and yet I suddenly realized I didn't know much about him at all. I wished Maggie were there so I could ask her why he wasn't in a band.

I shook the thought away with a smile. Maybe a part of me missed hanging out with Maggie more than I cared to admit. She always had such deep interest in other people.

The drummer, a clean-cut guy with an easy smile and quick movements, appeared intent on his task. All the drums had to be set up just so, along with a huge set of cymbals. He moved so quickly I imagined him as a kid, like some of the guys in elementary school who couldn't sit still; he had probably banged pots and pans on the kitchen floor as a toddler, always moving, always making noise and driving his mother nuts.

Another guy, tall and lanky like a giraffe, messed with a sax, putting the mouthpiece on and trying a few notes. On the far side, a square fat girl sat at an electric keyboard and stared at the crowd with disinterest.

There were two guitar players. One, "Don" I heard him called, was leaning against the wall plucking at metal strings. His face was so plagued with pimples it made my face hurt to look at him.

The other guitar player had his back to me most of the time as he moved from place to place checking wires, flipping switches, arranging speakers and amps. He moved offstage and returned with a white electric guitar, his hair flopping over his face as he looked down to plug in the cord and check the connection and volume. When he finally turned around, my heart stopped. He was the best-looking guy I'd ever seen: tall, lean, muscular. His face was rectangular, with a chin that jutted out firm and square, and hair that hung loose around his face — not to his shoulders, but definitely long. I imagined attending the prom with him as my date; I would be the envy of every girl in school. I felt like the life was sucked out of me, then filled back up with some new glow and purpose attached—I had to get a date with him.

Unfortunately, he didn't even see me.

After tuning up a few minutes, the group didn't waste any time getting the show started. The guitarist, the good-looking one, stepped up to the microphone and welcomed the crowd. His voice was rich and deep, and when he started singing, it resonated with a huskiness that made me think of a mysterious character in a movie, a secret agent who hissed out plans in dark alleys. It sent a chill up my spine.

The longer I sat listening to him, the more enthralled I became. At one point I pulled my attention away from him long enough to scan the crowd and saw he had a connection with his audience. Only a few people were talking, but even though most were watching and listening, mesmerized, I was sure no one felt as drawn to his presence as I did.

When the band took a break, Heather and Tammy rushed up the side steps onto the stage to speak to Ariana. Tammy flashed her eyes at my singer. After all, he wasn't a high school student; I guessed he was probably twenty-one. But even so, I knew Tammy wouldn't be after him with any serious intent. She wanted a businessman, firmly established, with money to burn. Heather smiled that coy smile that almost puts a price tag on her body, even though she'd never dated any guy long enough to get that close. (Three dates. Both of them said that was their limit, then on to the next guy, just passing time till *real life* delivered what they wanted.) Me, I stayed in my seat watching him. Two other girls walked up to the edge of the stage and flirted outrageously. He took it all in stride, used to the attention, taking it as his due.

I knew if I wanted him to notice me, I had to bide my time and wait for the right opportunity.

He looked toward the bar, anticipating a drink, but remained where he was, careful not to offend his growing fan base. His eyes flickered over me, just a slight pause in surveying the room. I smiled ever so slightly, but he didn't really see me, and I stayed in my seat and looked away. I was content to let the tension build for a while. I intended to see him again when the competition wasn't around and he had time to really look my way. I didn't stand a chance if I was lodged between Heather and Tammy.

Onstage, Ariana was making introductions.

"Vince," Heather said, her eyelashes fluttering like a spring butterfly, "you are fantastic."

Vince. His name was Vince.

Chapter Three

HEATHER COULDN'T TALK about anything else for days. She told everyone at school that Ariana's band was the greatest. I personally think she just wanted to toot her own horn, to announce to everyone that the lead singer was her friend, but no one was impressed. It's not like Ariana was an American Idol or anything; she was just some girl singing with a local band. I didn't mind Heather's rattling on about it, though, because the band was topmost in my mind, too, but for different reasons. I couldn't quit thinking of Vince. So when Heather arrived at school on Tuesday morning talking about going to the band's rehearsal that evening, my ears pricked up as I shifted my book bag to the opposite shoulder.

"I guess I could tag along with you, if you want," I said with the most nonchalant air I could manage.

"Really? That would be great. You want to follow me there? They practice at Mike's house."

"Who's Mike?"

"The drummer. I thought you knew that. Kind of a geek, but he's wicked on the drums, don't you think?"

Tammy was primping in front of the mirror she pulled from

her pocketbook. "What's with you two? They aren't all that fantastic."

"Yes, they are," insisted Heather. "Ariana is absolutely fab! Sure as the devil, she'll be famous someday, you just wait and see. In fact, we're talking about going to the modeling and talent convention — you know, that one that's held in Atlanta. Everybody goes to it. They have bunches of agents there looking for new talent. It's going to be in a couple months. I can't wait."

Tammy slammed her locker door. "Go for it."

Heather knew that tone. Tammy was settling into jealousy mode. "You can join us at the convention if you want."

"Like that's going to happen. I have tons of talent, you know." Sarcasm dripped from her words.

Heather played up to her. "Come on, Tammy. You would be a great model. And think of all the shopping we could do in Atlanta."

"I have no desire to be a model."

I ignored them. They constantly had to boost each other's egos. Sometimes it made me crazy. The truth was that even though I'd hung with them for two years, I really wasn't brainless, so their need to constantly assure themselves that they were, like, perfect or something, got annoying. The best strategy was to change the subject. "Let's go to Hardee's after school and get milk shakes."

Heather and Tammy watched everything they ate, but chocolate milk shakes were their one great weakness. "Sounds good to me," Tammy said.

The first bell rang, and I took off down the hall to physics as they turned into art appreciation. I knew Tammy would spend the next hour thinking about milk shakes, Heather would be dreaming about stardom, and I would be sketching pictures of Vince to the drone of Mr. McCallister's boring lecture.

Going to hear Blind Reality practice would have been boring if I wasn't so hung up on Vince. They kept going over bits and pieces of songs, reworking parts until they had it down, then practicing it a time or two straight through before going to the next song. Mostly I concentrated on Vince, on watching him move, on absorbing his voice, wondering if he would ever notice me. But I kept myself hidden in the shadows, sitting on an old lawn chair at the side of the garage where the practices were held, where Mike had probably played his drums since getting his first set at age five or something. There was enough space cleared out for the band, but the garage looked as if it hadn't ever held a car, as cluttered as it was with gardening stuff, a lawn mower, bikes, and tools. I felt lost among the rakes and shovels propped around me.

Heather hung out at the next two practices, but I had art club after school one day, then a yearbook staff meeting. We'd voted on senior superlatives that week, and they all had to be added to the senior pages. Tammy and Webb both got Most Attractive. Heather and Sean Black both got Best Dressed. I could have slid in as Third Most Popular, but that wasn't a choice, and I'd blown my chances of Most Intellectual the day I started hanging out with Heather. That went to Maggie and Sam Taylor, as well as Most Dependable. But I did nab Most Likely to Succeed—me, the girl without a life plan. Anyway, there was a lot of work to do on the yearbook that week, and I had youth group at church on Wednesday, along with tests to study for in the evening, so I didn't go to another band practice until the following Monday, after a weekend of parties and shopping and spending the night with Heather, while daydreaming that I might have a chance with Vince. But he was all business on Monday, and Heather was only interested in talking to Ariana afterwards. Vince disappeared with his guitar, while I stood there against the wall like a gardening tool.

The next Monday, I decided I would give it a try once more.

I didn't ride with Heather but drove separately and arrived fifteen minutes after the band's normal start-up. The garage was silent, and I worried a moment that perhaps they had cancelled practice, except there were several cars in the driveway, including Heather's.

I slipped in the door and stood along the edge to see what was going on. Heather was perched on a bench beside Ariana, the two of them chatting about something. No one had formally introduced me to the band members, but listening from my quiet place in the shadows, I'd come to know who was who. Judy, the pudgy girl with glasses, was Mike's father's boss's kid; she sat slumped over like a toad, half-asleep behind her keyboard with a book in her lap. Mike was messing with his drums. The skinny sax player was Josh. He sat off to one side, cleaning his instrument, blowing on it, then polishing it with a soft rag. Don, the pimply-faced guitar player, wasn't there.

I eased into the lawn chair without a word to any of them. I preferred to watch things from a distance. I'm not exactly shy, but Maggie had taught me that I could learn a lot more about people by observing them than by walking right up and talking to them, and at that point I was still enjoying just being the observer.

As my eyes adjusted from the bright sunlight to the dimly lit interior, I spotted Vince off in the corner, his back to the rest of us, talking into his cell phone in agitated tones. He slammed it shut and turned around. His face was red and his eyes looked bloodshot. "I can't believe it. He quit on us. I don't get it." He punched at a stack of boxes, knocking the top one over so it clattered against an old fan, which dominoed into a couple bikes. Vince didn't seem to care. He kicked at the bottom box and cussed.

Ariana turned from Heather to Vince. "Don quit?"

"Yes." He cussed again. "I'll fix him. That's for sure."

No one else seemed too ruffled over it. Judy kept her nose in the novel she was reading. Mike twiddled his drumsticks.

Ariana asked, "Why did he quit?"

Vince's face contorted into what I guess was intended as a sneer but looked a bit more sinister as he mimicked Don's voice. "Says he's decided performing every weekend isn't what he wants after all."

One of Mike's drumsticks clattered to the floor. "But we just lined up our biggest gigs ever. And we have the festival to do this Saturday. Is he nuts?"

"He must be," Ariana said.

"The point is we're short a guitar player. Who are we going to call?"

Judy blinked as if just coming awake. "Do we need a second guitar?"

"Yes, especially when I sing," Vince said. Anger resonated in his voice, as if it were Judy's fault for even asking. "I can't do both.

We've got to know someone we can call."

"How about the kid from that talent show last year?" Mike asked.

"He stank."

"I know a girl—" Ariana started, but Vince interrupted her.

"No. No more girls or it'll be a girls' band. We need a guy. Come on, y'all. Think."

"There's Ted Swenson," Heather said, sitting up with importance. "He's only in eighth grade, but he's pretty cool. I remember he played in the school talent show last year, but I'm sure he still plays. I could call him if you want. I've got his sister's cell phone number right here," she said pulling her Razr out of her little pink pocketbook. "She's not really a *friend* or anything, but her mama works in the nail salon, so she's absolutely fab at doing nails. I just adore the way she can put little designs on my nail—"

Vince frowned.

"Oh, well then." Heather snapped her cell phone shut and put it away.

I let silent frustration float around a moment, debating my words before I finally spoke up. "I know someone."

I don't think they had even noticed that I was there until that moment, because everyone turned at the sound of my voice, their eyes wide with surprise. I stood up and moved to the open door, the sun on my back, my face in the shadows. My skin flushed. Other than that one glimpse in the bar, Vince probably hadn't even looked at me before. When I took a step farther into the room, out of the bright sun, his eyes lit on me like an eager puppy looking for a treat, and then traveled the length of my body as if taking in all of me at once. He moved toward me, making the air catch in my chest at getting his full attention.

"You're one of Ariana's friends?"

Heather eased off her seat on the bench. "She came with me to that performance a few weeks ago, remember?"

"With Tammy," added Ariana.

Judy yawned. "Where have you been, superstar man? She's been sitting there listening to us without saying a word for a couple weeks."

Josh went back to rubbing his sax. "Didn't think you could speak."

I stuck my hand out to Vince like a total dork. "Dixie Chambers."

He took my hand and quickly kissed it. "If you really know a guitarist, I want to kiss more than your hand."

That made me swallow my voice for a few seconds until I regained my senses. "My stepbrother plays."

"Is he any good?"

"He's taken lessons since he was five or something." I was glowing under the attention. I felt like the more good things I could say about Tony, the better I appeared. "He can play anything. He has three guitars."

Mike struck his drums and frowned. "Sure."

"He's not in a band?"

I watched Vince's face as he spoke. He had lips like—I don't know—rose petals, if that doesn't sound wimpy. Like what a sappy romance would call *luscious*. He smiled, those gorgeous lips slightly parted as he weighed my every word. His eyes were focused on my face, and my hand was still in his. I hoped it wouldn't start perspiring. "No, he's not in a band. He just likes playing."

He lifted my hand to his lips and kissed it again, then turned my palm upward and laid his phone in it. "Call him. If he says yes, I plan to kiss your mouth too."

I'd lived with Maggie too long; I said something I didn't mean: "You won't kiss these lips until I say you can."

That made him laugh. He stepped closer. He stood a head taller than me and looked down, his breath fresh and minty. He touched my hair. "You mean you don't want me to kiss you?"

Who would have figured Maggie might know a few secrets of seduction, even if that wasn't how she intended her advice? I smiled like a conniving fox. "I didn't say I didn't want you to kiss me. I just said it would be on my terms." I pulled the cell phone up between us and dialed home.

Tony wasn't there. Cindy, my kid sister, answered the phone. I envisioned her lying on the floor of the family room with Whizzer, the family's German shepherd mutt, rolling around as she talked to me; Cindy was nine but still acted more like seven, full of giggles and ridiculous ideas. But it was impossible not to love her, sweet, dimpled, curly blonde that she was, and it made me smile to hear her voice. She reminded me that Tony was at the grocery store—working. He had taken a job at Piggly Wiggly at the beginning of the year and worked three evenings a week. Under Vince's spell, I'd forgotten that Maggie and I had dropped him off a few hours earlier, on the way home from school. I had even promised to pick him up later. With three teenagers in the family, we all shared one car, which was a sight better than two years earlier, when we had to borrow our parents' cars, but still aggravating at times.

I glanced at my watch. It was about time for him to get off. "I can pick him up from work and bring him over, but it will take me a while. We live quite a ways away."

"Fine," Vince replied. "We'll wait."

I handed him back his phone. He clutched my hand for a moment before releasing me.

He had no worry about my returning.

Tony stared at me blankly when I explained about the band. "You're kidding, right?"

"No. Aren't you excited?"

It was an honest question. Tony walked around with a permanent bland expression on his face that tended to mask his emotions. I never knew what he was thinking, or if he ever really thought about anything at all. He certainly didn't worry about appearances. He never tucked in his shirts. His shoelaces flopped around untied. And his unruly brown hair rarely saw the bristle-end of a brush. At least nowadays he showered.

"In case you haven't noticed, I don't play in public."

"But you can. You're great. And girls will flock around you when they see you playing up there." It was true. Tony would fit right into a band. He was shy and too short for most high school girls, but no one would be able to tell that up on stage. Besides, he had a gorgeous wide smile, and having unbrushed hair kind of suited a rock-and-roll guitarist. Girls in the audience would really go for him. "You'll end up with a girlfriend in a week."

"I seriously doubt that."

"Yes, you will. Girls will be all over you, especially when they hear how good you are."

"I don't like playing in front of people."

"You play in front of us all the time."

"Not in front of people I don't know."

"Are you telling me all those times I've caught you jumping around your room, strumming that thing, and blasting the windows out that you're not dreaming of being onstage?"

He frowned and turned away to look out the side window. At the next stoplight, I drummed my fingers across the steering wheel. "Please, Tony, for me."

"What's it got to do with you?"

"This guy, Vince. It's his band."

"You want me to play in public so you can add another boyfriend to your list?"

Tony was kind of bitter about boyfriends because his one and only girlfriend, Polly, had dumped him for a Swedish guy that arrived midyear as an exchange student. Polly walked around with a constant grin on her face now, much to Tony's despair. I don't know why he was in the dumps over her. She had a horrible haircut and absolutely no sense of fashion.

"It's not like that. Vince is just a really nice guy. I want to help him out."

He didn't look convinced.

"There's this great-looking girl, Ariana. Maybe you could ask her out."

"The girl you mentioned last week? You said she's like nineteen or something. What would she want with me?"

"You never know." The light turned green. I hesitated. He had to agree so I could go straight. If he refused, I had to turn. "Please, Tony. Just try it?"

"All the cookie-dough ice cream I want for an entire month."

Ice cream or Vince? No question there. "Absolutely. It's a deal."

I pulled into traffic.

"Where are you going?"

"I'm taking you there."

"I need my guitar, brainless."

I laughed and took the next left.

Chapter Four

TONY WALKED INTO the garage like a lost waif, with his guitar case hanging dejectedly at his side. Vince strode up and shook his hand. "Hey, man. Am I ever glad to see you. Vince Evans."

Vince Evans. It was the first time I'd heard his full name. I repeated it three times and then added it to mine. *Dixie Evans.* Stupid, I know, but that was how caught up I was just looking at him.

Tony shuffled his feet a few times, but warmed up to Vince as they talked, and finally relaxed and grinned his Cheshire grin. "No problem, man. I haven't played with a band before, so don't get your hopes up."

"If you're as good as Dixie says you are, it won't matter."

If my praise surprised Tony, he didn't let on, but that was normal for him.

Mike and Josh shook hands with him. Judy looked up from her novel, blew a bubble with her gum, and waved. Ariana wasn't in sight. Neither was Heather, but since her car was gone I assumed she had left. She had mentioned having to take a plate of fish, green beans, and hush puppies from Charlie's restaurant over to her grandma that evening, because her grandma had a "hankering" for Charlie's Monday special. I had to admit Charlie had the best hush puppies within a hundred miles. I could go for a plate myself.

"Why don't you play something for us?" Vince asked Tony. "Your choice."

"Nah, man. I'd rather y'all start something, and I'll pick up and join in."

Vince swung his guitar over his shoulder and strapped it in place. "All right. Key of G." He looked around. "Where's Ariana?"

Judy sighed and set her book on the bench. "Bathroom."

"Figures. Well, I'll do vocals this round." He cued Mike and Josh and started playing. I sighed with relief. It was a song I'd heard Tony play many times. Tony waited a few measures, his head tilted to one side as he picked up their rhythm and slowly added chords until Ariana traipsed down the steps from the laundry room into full view. One glance at her made Tony plunge into the song as if someone had just hit the Go button. Vince turned to face him, and they began playing off one another as if they'd been doing it for years. When they finished, they were both laughing.

Vince held out his hand. "Fantastic."

Tony slapped it with his own. "Yeah, man. We rocked."

"So are you in?"

"Definitely. At least I want to try. I'm still not sure about performing in public, but let's see how it goes."

Vince nodded.

I settled against the wall, leaned my head back, closed my eyes, and listened to the rest of their practice. Tony was really good. His ability complemented Vince's and made them both sound better. I think Vince knew it too.

Halfway through, I went outside to get a bottle of water out of the car. When I turned around, there was a guy dressed in all black staring at me — black shirt open over a black tee, and black jeans with holes in the knees and frayed bottoms where he'd walked on them. Despite the cold January breeze, he was wearing flip-flops that exposed long, ugly toes with toenails that were a good month late being clipped, all yellow, chipped, and curling on the edges. Creepy looking. He looked like he hadn't had a bath in a couple days. His hair was oily, and his face was scruffy and blotchy. He just about scared the pee out of me, walking up right behind me and squinting at me with his beady, bloodshot eyes.

"Wuz up? I ain't seen you hanging here before," he said.

I had enough sense not to talk to a creep like him; no telling what he was up to. I slammed the car door and ran back to the garage, planning to tell them all about him, but they were in the middle of a song, so I huddled in my seat hoping he would go away. He couldn't possibly be a friend of Vince's. Vince was so suave, cool, mature. Why would he associate with someone like that?

I kept waiting for a break so I could tell someone, but the one time they paused long enough, I lost my nerve. Maybe the guy had left anyway, I thought.

When practice ended, I glanced out but couldn't see beyond the huge red-tip bush by the door. While Tony placed his guitar back in its case, Vince approached me and trapped me against the wall, his hands on either side so that his arms caged me in. "I guess I owe you a kiss, babe. Tony is great."

I could have asked him about the weird guy right then, but

really, like I was going to break a comment like that from Vince to question him about some creep in the driveway? Not hardly. Let him concentrate on me and Tony. "I told you he was."

His eyes sparkled as he looked at me and leaned closer.

I was filled with this new sense of power. I put my hand on his mouth. "Not yet."

I felt his lips beneath my fingers, kissing me, before he pulled my hand away. "Not yet. *Hmm.* I hear a promise in there, so I'll wait."

He turned away and grabbed his stuff. "Everybody here at five thirty tomorrow."

"I gotta work till seven, man," Tony said.

"Call in sick. It'll be worth it, I promise. This gig is a big deal."

Tony nodded. "I'll see what I can do."

By the time Tony and I got outside, the guy was gone. So was Vince.

Heather met me at my locker the next morning. "So how did Tony work out? Did Vince like him?"

I could feel my face glowing. "Did he ever. They played like they'd been at it together for years. It was fantastic."

Tammy walked up and pulled out her compact to check her hair, then dug in her pocketbook to find a long thin tube of lip gloss that shaded her lips lightly with a deep tone that complemented her perfect complexion.

She smacked her lips together. "What was fantastic?"

Heather took Tammy's compact and checked her own hair. "Band practice."

Tammy shoved the lip gloss in a side compartment of her pocketbook. "Not that again."

"Tony played with them last night," I said. "First time playing with a group. That's what I was saying—he did a great job. I'm so proud of him."

Tammy looked me in the face. "Sure, those rosy cheeks are pride in Tony. I'm guessing it has more to do with Vince. I have to admit he's good-looking, and at least he's not a high school boy. Too bad he's not rich, or I'd give it a run myself."

It was my turn with the compact. My blonde hair fell straight no matter what I did to it, but at least it was silky and shiny, thanks to all of Tammy's beauty advice. I used the best products on the market to keep it irresistibly glossy. "He hasn't even noticed me."

"I bet," Tammy replied, taking the compact from me. "I know better than that." She snapped it closed and stashed it away.

The two of them headed down the hall together, leaving me to fish out my physics book and head to class, wondering if anyone else would notice the bounce Vince had brought to my step, or if only Tammy knew me well enough to see it.

I slipped into my seat beside Maggie, whose head was bent close to Webb's as they whispered together. Clarissa, one of Maggie's friends, was texting someone on her cell phone. Clarissa used to be really plain looking, but she'd come to life over the past year, even adding highlights to her mousy brown hair. On my other side, Asby Jones was asleep on his desk. Jeanine, a quiet girl who occasionally hung out with Maggie and Clarissa, sat at the desk in front of me with her nose in her binder, reviewing the previous day's notes. Behind me, Sam Taylor, who we called Silent Sam, leaned back in his desk, viewing the comings and goings. He rarely spoke to anyone, just watched. Even though he'd been in many of my classes in the last few years, I didn't know much about him except that he had a sister named Sophie in tenth grade. She was the complete opposite of Sam: She chattered nonstop.

At any rate, no one around me had anything to say about the flush of love-at-first-sight brushing my cheeks. It was just another morning of boring physics.

At least it was until Ellie pranced in. "Hello, classmates," she gushed. Ellie had starred in more theater productions than she could fit on a résumé and tended to live as if life were a stage. Over the years she had taken on the attributes of the characters in her plays. "Isn't it an absolutely beautiful day! The sun is shining and—oh, my, look how *radiant* you are this morning, Miss Dixie. I believe someone must have shared his Eggo with you this morning or something. You simply have to tell—what *is* your secret?"

I felt the blush deepen from my neck to my forehead. I wasn't about to publicly announce that I had a crush on a rock star, at least not until we'd been on a date. I shrugged as nonchalantly as possible. "Just a happy day, Ellie. I'd say you look rather radiant yourself."

Ellie always looked radiant. I don't think there was a girl in school who loved life more than she did. She actually curtsied in her little plaid skirt, not caring a bit that it was totally *not* in fashion. "Thank you. I do feel rather giddy today."

Mr. McCallister entered and slammed a stack of textbooks on his desk with a loud thump, ending all conversation.

Missing work was easier than we expected, at least the first day. I skipped yearbook after school and took Tony to Mickey D's. It took the last of the babysitting money I'd saved up, but I treated him to a cheeseburger and Dr Pepper.

"Don't you think I ought to call in sick or something?" he asked.

I thought about it a moment. "No. Let's just say you forgot you were scheduled today. That way you're not caught saying you were sick when you weren't."

He nodded. "Sounds good to me. Question is what we're going to do about tomorrow. They'll fire me if I miss two days in a row."

"You're going to make lots more playing for the band."

His crooked frown said he doubted that. "I don't want to lose my job."

"Let's just see how today goes."

That pacified him. He munched on his cheeseburger while I watched people come and go.

Asby Jones's mama, a thin lady whose face was aged with worry, came in with his tubby little sister and waved at me. Asby, the fake-ID-creation expert, wasn't exactly a friend, but I'd been going to school with him my whole life, so of course I knew his mama. I should have thought of how many familiar people

I'd see at a place like McDonald's, but it was too late to change gears, so I waved and acted like everything was normal. That was a mistake. His mama approached our table, all conversational.

"I bet you're on your way to meet your group about that history project y'all have due next week," she said.

I had no idea what she was talking about, but I owed Asby a favor; he hadn't charged me for my fake ID. We did have some history homework, and if I did it at band practice, I could twist it into saying it was a study group and not feel like I was lying straight out. I thought it, but I could feel the eyes of God scorning me for twisting it into a lie as I replied. "Yes, ma'am. How'd you know?"

"Well, I haven't seen Asby all week. He's been at it every afternoon. You're not in his group, are you?"

I wasn't about to go that far. I could see the uncertainty in her eyes no matter what her fixed smile was trying to portray, and I wasn't about to get tangled any further into Asby's story than I had to. With as much trouble as Asby stayed in with drugs and drinking, his mama was constantly on the lookout for holes in what he told her, and here I was patching up one of them. But that was as far as I was going. "No ma'am. I don't know whose group he's in."

She nodded, glanced at Tony, then headed off to the counter to place her order.

A flock of elderly people had flooded into the seats on our right, grandparents of my friends, many of their faces familiar from church dinners. I'd forgotten it was their Mickey D's meeting day; from four till five they sipped coffee and chatted. I watched the old folks with fascination, their cautious steps, their jerky movements, nothing done without conscious effort as they helped one another in and out of cars and into seats at the tables. It made me think of my father in the final days before his death, when he was weak from chemo. My muscles stiffened up as I watched and imagined my youth sucked from my body, making me unable to stand on my own. I watched one lady, eighty-five easy, help a feeble woman through the door, and I wondered what made her so full of vitality while my father died young. Did God control what happened to each of us? Or did our freewill choices change our path through life? How much did the choices I made every day affect the outcome of my life?

Tony interrupted my thoughts with the loud gulping of his drink. He never used a straw. He liked to take in big mouthfuls of soda with hunks of ice. I don't know how he even swallowed it without choking. He emptied the cup and wiped his mouth with his sleeve. "We forgot about my guitar. How am I supposed to get back into the house to get it?"

I was way ahead of him. "It's already in the car. I put it in this morning."

"My Gibson?"

"The brownish one and the red and white one."

"What'd you bring the Fender for?"

"If that's the red one, because it's pretty, and I thought you'd like to play something different today."

He shook his head. "You don't know nothin' about guitars."

He was right. I knew how to read music because I'd taken piano lessons forever, but I didn't know anything about guitars. That was okay, though, because I intended to learn with a private tutor — Vince.

With that settled and his stomach full, Tony reached into his book bag and pulled out his homework.

"What are you doing?"

"We still have an hour," he said, "and I'm not about to get in trouble for skipping work *and* not having my homework done."

I leaned back with a sigh. It amazed me how obedient people were. Not that I didn't do what I was told, but Tony's fear of getting in trouble seemed like the cornerstone of everything around me: people standing calmly in line, no one demanding to go before anyone else, people gathering their trays and dumping their trash into the trash bins and leaving their trays on top. What made people do what they were supposed to do? Was it fear of punishment or desire to be good? It seemed like I had been good my entire life until recently. I'd slowly stepped off that path, becoming more and more daring in breaking the limits and rules around me, and now I had convinced Tony to skip work and join the band. Was I going to be held accountable? I shivered. I hadn't really done anything bad, or at least not anything that a ton of other kids hadn't done before me.

As he worked math problems, I thought over my choices. I could still take him to work. He would be late, but we could say he had forgotten his schedule. I could quit thinking about Vince and head home to study with Maggie. I could concentrate on making straight As instead of settling for Bs. I knew if I really worked at it, I could do like Maggie and apply for the Palmetto Fellows Scholarship. It was up to me. I was making a conscious choice. It made me think of a Robert Frost poem that I memorized for an eighth grade presentation: *Two roads diverged in a wood, and I—I took the one less traveled by.* Except I wasn't taking the harder path, the one less traveled. I was doing what I wanted instead of what I ought to do. Looking at it objectively made it seem worse, more deliberate than just high school folly, but I knew what I was doing and still intended to follow through; I was running down a path, hoping it would lead to Vince.

I convinced myself it wasn't a major decision. It wasn't that big a deal that I was skipping yearbook. Everybody was absent at some time or other. And I could do my homework late that night. I had till Friday to cram for my world cultures test, and I could churn out an essay for English in an hour. Math I could do during lunch, and I was sure I could convince one of the guys to share their physics answers if I got to school early. I had it all figured out. High school wasn't about education, really, or all that future stuff adults harped on. High school was for fun times and memories you laughed about till you were forty.

Annie Smith wandered in about that time. She was a middle-aged woman, pear-shaped, with shaggy, shoulder-length, half-blonde hair badly in need of a new dye job. She had a loud voice and a penchant for talking to every single person she passed; I put my head down so as to keep from being one of her targets. She bought herself a Coke then sat at the center table where she could catch every person walking in and hail them with her megaphone voice. "How do ya, Mable? Hey there, Bobby. Why Mister Willis, where have you been?" On and on. Whenever she had someone close enough to her, she mentioned that she needed a couple bucks to buy supper and asked if they would spare her a few. Finally, some charitable red-headed lady handed her a five. No sooner had Annie sat down with a sandwich than she started talking to the lady at the next table about some fancy perfume she'd seen in Belk's for forty-five dollars that she planned to buy just as soon as she could save that much.

That got me thinking. Perfume versus food. Why would anyone make such a dumb choice?

I watched Tony scribble out math problems for a few more minutes, then took a piece of paper from his notebook and started scrawling notes: an analytical thesis on *Moby Dick*. I figured it wouldn't hurt to make use of empty time.

A page of notes later, my phone buzzed with a text message from Heather:

WhereRU

Wrapped up in seeing Vince again, I'd forgotten I was supposed to go to Heather's house after the yearbook meeting. I would call her after practice. I pressed Ignore, folded my paper in four, stuck it in my pocketbook, and pushed Tony's book closed. "Come on. Time to go."

Tony grumbled about being in the middle of a problem, but shoved the book into his bag and followed me out to the car.

We were the first ones to arrive at Mike's house. I thought it might make me seem anxious or something, but when Vince arrived, he concentrated totally on Tony and their music. I felt like an unnoticed shadow until they took a break an hour into practice.

"So what do you think?" Vince asked as he dropped to the floor beside me.

"Sounds great." How lame an answer was that? I tried a quick recovery. "You and Tony really complement each other. You have different styles, but they work fantastic together."

He nodded. "That's what I think too."

He slipped his arm behind my back, but with his hand on the floor, not my shoulder. "I'm thinking I owe you for getting him to come back."

"Well, I got him here today, but tomorrow might be a challenge. He's nervous about missing work two days in a row."

"I'll make it worth his while, I promise. Saturday's gig is going to open some doors. I've got some people coming to listen."

I should have seen that for what it was—one of the many false hopes of an entertainer—but I grasped it like a golden straw. "I'll work it out somehow. He'll be here."

Vince smiled, his straight white teeth gleaming at me, his eyes flowing over me so that if I'd been standing up, I would have swooned like some nineteenth-century Victorian in one of those classics I read in tenth grade. There was no way I'd let Tony miss the next practice.

Chapter Five

I HAD TO concentrate in physics the next day, because Mr. McCallister was reviewing for a test, but by English class, my thoughts centered on how I was going to convince Tony to go to band practice again instead of work. No way could I jeopardize a chance with Vince for the sake of Piggly Wiggly. By the time I reached my world cultures class, the only class I shared with Tammy and Heather, my mind was totally wrapped up in thoughts of Vince.

Heather slid into the seat next to me. "You're thinking about him, aren't you?"

I jerked out of my daydream and turned to see if Maggie had heard her. Maggie had no idea I had my sights set on someone. Thank goodness she had her head down. She was writing something in her notebook. I scowled at Heather. "No. Just thinking."

She laughed. "Right."

Tammy twisted around in her seat in front Heather. "Not that singer again."

Heather nodded. "Oh, girl, you know she's hung up on him."

She made me sound pathetic and juvenile. "Just interested."

Tammy pulled her cell phone out of her pocketbook and typed something into it. Heather's phone vibrated. She opened it and giggled, slapping Tammy's shoulder while Tammy grinned.

Text message secrets, obviously about me.

About that time, a quarter clanked to the floor two seats back, and Heather jumped to her feet. "Webb! I need that quarter for my collection."

Webb cast a smirk at Maggie before leaning his long body forward and stretching out an arm to retrieve the coin from the floor. "I bet you do."

Heather went into dramatic flirt mode. Webb had been Maggie's boyfriend since tenth grade, but before that he was one of the most sought-after guys at school. After all, he stood about six-foot-two, had black hair, a muscular build, and a smile that could melt any girl's heart. Before Maggie, he wasn't wild, but he wasn't all into school and work like he was now. Back then he spent his afternoons playing video games with Tony, and at school he hung out with the more popular kids and dated Sue, who had been the head cheerleader and Heather's best friend until she moved away. I never have figured out how Maggie got her hooks into him immediately after Sue was out of the picture, but he'd become as tame as a pussycat and unwavering in his devotion. That didn't stop Heather from making a play at him whenever the opportunity arose, though, and this was one of those moments. She batted her eyelashes. "Seriously, Webb. I'm taking up a collection. It's for something really important."

"What? More makeup?"

She bit her lip. "Don't be silly. I can't say; it's a secret."

Asby fished in his pocket and pulled out a handful of change. "Hey, I'll give to that."

Sean Black, an artsy boy with a ready smile, looked up from whatever it was he was sketching in his notebook. "You'll give her money for a secret?"

"Heck, yes. I love secrets," Asby said. "In fact, I've got a whole jar of pennies at home I'll bring for ya."

In the back row, Silent Sam shook his head and laughed quietly. He was kinda strange in an admirable way, never showing off like the other guys. I wondered if he guessed, as I did, that Asby was buying a future favor. Heather held a lot of the teachers in the palm of her hand, and Asby was always needing help getting out of some scrape or other; who better to help him than Miss Popularity herself? Of course, Heather and Tammy and I were already in his debt over the fake IDs, which reminded me I needed to let him know about his mama asking about that history project.

Sean watched Asby drop the change into Heather's hand, then dug in his pocket and pulled out a five dollar bill. Boys were such copycats, all of them doing what one did. At least Sean questioned Heather a bit more. "Nothing illegal or immoral is it?" he asked, looking at her earnestly.

Heather cocked her hips to one side. "Why Sean, what kind of girl do you take me for? It's something to help mankind. A good deed kind of thing. That's why I can't say till I get more money together. Then I'll tell y'all. It's an interesting story; you'll see." She looked around. "Come on, y'all. Anybody else got some money for me?"

Heather had a lot of power over her classmates, which is why I'd hung out with her for the past two years. Everyone wanted to be her friend, even if it meant emptying their pockets for her. Sam handed her two nickels, and three girls pooled together a handful of dimes and pennies.

"Thanks, y'all. I promise I'll tell y'all what it's for after a while. I'll just keep on collecting donations every day, so keep that in mind. Especially after lunch. Y'all can just give me your change on the way out of the lunchroom." With that she took her seat and dumped all the money into a pouch in her pocketbook.

I leaned over and hissed at her. "What's the big secret?"

She shook her head. "Can't tell you." When she saw the disappointment on my face, she leaned closer and whispered in my ear. "But I can tell you Tammy went out on Saturday with that new guy at the bank, the skinny guy with brown hair. He's like thirty or something."

She sat back and looked at me with raised eyebrows.

I know disbelief must have registered. How could Tammy really be interested in a guy who was thirty?

Tammy sensed something was up. "You told *her* your secret and not me?"

Heather rolled her eyes. "'Course not."

Mr. Baire finished whatever he'd been messing with on his computer and told everyone to pass up their homework and clear their desks for a quiz. Heather immediately went into stall tactic, jumped from her seat again and started regaling the class with some silly story about a cat stuck on her roof and having to call the fire department to get it down. I stared out the window wondering what game Heather played between the three of us with our secrets. How far could she be trusted with something that *really* mattered?

After school, I slid into the backseat beside Tony and whispered, "We're going tonight, right?" I hoped it was low enough that Maggie wouldn't hear.

"I gotta work."

"Come on, Tony. This is your big chance. You know how many guys would kill for a spot in such a great band? And you wanna turn that down for Piggly Wiggly?"

"But I'm scheduled, and if I miss twice, they'll can me."

"You'll make more with the band. You know you will."

I was making headway. I could see the indecision playing across his face. I pulled a candy bar out of my book bag and handed it to him. "Wasn't it great yesterday, jamming with the other guys?"

He ripped the wrapper open and took a bite. "Sure, but . . ."

"Okay, how about this. We let Mags drop you off, and you work till five; then you get sick, and I'll pick you up."

"How am I supposed to get sick at five?"

I laughed. "Like you did last month to get out of that Spanish test you hadn't studied for."

He had chocolate all over his teeth. "Did not."

"Did too."

He shoved the last of it in his mouth. "Okay, but not till six. I need to put some hours in or I won't earn anything this week."

That would put him an hour late for practice, but at least I would get to see Vince again with my prize guitar player at my side. "Okay, deal. Six. I'll even bring you some supper." Six was better anyway. I would tell Mama I was stopping to give Tony supper on the way to youth group. Mama hated for anyone to go hungry. She wouldn't suspect a thing.

I hadn't noticed that Maggie and Webb had fallen silent.

Maggie's eyes were on us in the rearview mirror. I made a quick change of topic. "What's for supper, Mags? Tony just finished off my candy bar, and I'm afraid he's going to start chewing on my math book."

Maggie was a hard person to read. She had a knack for keeping her thoughts buried too deep to reach her facial expressions. "Spaghetti. In fact, you can cook tonight. I have to babysit next door for Mrs. Graham."

Maggie nearly always cooked. She'd acted as mama to her brothers for thirteen years before my mama married her daddy. Sometimes Mama took over, but most nights they shared kitchen duty. I just lucked out by staying out of the way. Cooking was not my thing—but I could handle spaghetti, especially if it got me in everyone's good graces so they wouldn't suspect what I was up to with Tony. "Sure. I don't have much homework. I can do it."

That answer creased Maggie's forehead. Maybe I'd given in a bit too easily and made her suspicious, but it was too late to backpedal.

We dropped Tony off at the grocery store and headed home, then after a couple hours of studying, cooking, and making quick work of cleaning the kitchen, I dashed upstairs, fixed my hair and makeup, and told Mama I had finished my homework. I said nothing about youth group, and she didn't ask.

At the store, I could see Tony through the big glass windows talking to the manager. I watched intently, trying to gauge the manager's reaction, but I didn't have to wait long. Tony disappeared into the office, presumably to clock out, then appeared at the door, peering into the dusk to locate the car.

I pulled up to the entrance. "Thank goodness he let you off. It looked touch and go there for a minute."

Tony didn't look too happy about it. "I think he knows I was faking. Made me feel bad about lying to him."

"Well, that will pass." I had my own twinges of guilt for being the one to lead him astray, but I ignored the niggling voice in my head. "Just think about being up on stage."

"I guess," he said, but didn't look convinced.

I pointed to a covered dish in the backseat. "There's your supper," I said, and he spent the rest of the ride stuffing his face with spaghetti.

The important thing was Vince's expression when we arrived, like I was an angel bringing some great proclamation. He looked at me with those sexy, sparkling eyes. "You're here," he said, then turned his attention to Tony. "Let's get to it."

I sat against the wall, tapping my foot to the rhythm and texting Heather about how good Vince looked, while my heart beat crazily with expectation. She sent me back smiley faces.

I wanted to stick around after practice, to see what would happen, to see if Vince would make another advance. But Mama called asking me to pick Tony up from work, which reminded me that the rest of the family still thought he was there and that I was supposed to be leaving youth group around then, so we had to show up at the house at the scheduled time—eight-thirty.

When I hung up and told Tony we had to leave, Vince just nodded. The practice had gone well. But I was sure I saw a look on his face that was intended to have special meaning for me: We had something waiting in our future, when the time was right.

I called in sick for Tony the next day. I imitated Mama and told the assistant manager that Tony was still sick and couldn't possibly work. Tony grumbled about getting in trouble, but went along with it and embellished the story when Maggie asked why he wasn't being dropped off at the store.

"Don't have to work today," he said.

"Yes you do. It's on the calendar."

He pulled a bag of chips from his book bag. "Got a project I got to do."

Maggie looked doubtful but dropped the subject. She used to control everything in Tony's life but had made an effort to quit mothering him like she had when he was a kid. Now she let him make his own decisions . . . and mistakes.

I sank down in my seat and stared out the window, telling myself Vince was worth it. It's not like Tony was ruining a career or anything. It was just a grocery store job. Besides, the band could really turn into something big for him.

I told myself that over and over again until it opened a hole in my gut that let the bad feelings leak out and puddle at my feet. It was getting easier and easier to lie.

When practice was over, I practically held my breath, waiting for Vince to make his move, but he packed up his guitar like he was in a mad rush. "I'm on my bike, so I'm leaving the guitar here for the night, Mike. Make sure it gets put in for the gig."

"No problem," Mike replied.

I tried to pretend I was waiting impatiently for Tony, tapping my foot, heaving a good sigh or two as I watched him go over a couple notes with Ariana before getting his guitar case from the back corner of the garage.

Vince gave him a slap on the back. "Thanks for coming, man.

We're gonna rock this weekend."

As he headed to the door, I steeled myself, first looking at my feet, but couldn't resist looking into his face to see if he still had that spark of interest in there for me.

He stopped beside me and placed a palm to my cheek. "'Bye, beautiful. We still have that kiss coming, don't we?"

I smiled like I held a sweet secret. "Maybe."

He touched my lips with one finger. "A promise of ecstasy to come," he said, and left me there in a daze.

A promise of ecstasy to come. That was enough to buoy me through what was waiting ahead.

Chapter Six

TONY WASN'T SCHEDULED to work on Friday, but the band didn't have practice either. They had an agreement that if they had a paid performance, they would play, but if not, they would take Friday to unwind and visit with friends. So Tony was free to do what he wanted, and I was left moping, wondering if anything was ever going to come of my obsession with Vince.

Frank, my stepfather, had just walked through the door when the phone rang. He paused a moment and glanced my way. Even though he was dressed in a suit and tie, his tall, lanky figure had a friendly, disheveled look that Tony had inherited, along with the same bright smile. He surveyed the room in a flat second, noting I was the only one there, other than Whizzer sleeping at my feet. Maggie was studying in our room, and we'd reached the point that if I even breathed too loud when Maggie was studying, she would sigh or moan or something, so I had opted to stretch out in Frank's recliner while I waited for Heather to call with some Friday night diversion. Even on vibrate, my cell phone would get Maggie riled.

Anyway, I was only a step away from the house phone, but Frank reached it before I could get my feet to the floor. I figured it wasn't Heather, anyway—she would call my cell phone—but Frank's expression caught my attention. His forehead creased with concentration. His mouth drew to a tight line. It looked like trouble.

He murmured agreement to whoever was on the phone and hung up, then walked to the bottom of the stairs. "Tony!" he yelled.

Whizzer raised his head and whined.

That puddle of bad feelings rose from around my feet and filled my stomach. I knew what was coming.

Tony knew too. He clomped down the steps and stood at the bottom, his face as pale as the white walls around him. "Yes, sir?"

Tony knew manners, but he wasn't in the habit of using "sir" on a regular basis.

The holler drew Mama from the kitchen. She stood to one side with a quizzical expression crinkling her pixie face. She could pass for a teenager if she wanted to, with her perky haircut and innocent blue eyes, but right then she looked full-force like a mama in charge. Flour dusted her hands and even one cheek, but the seriousness that crossed her face erased any sense of comic appearance.

Frank's face turned red as he spoke. "I hear you've been sick the last couple of days, son."

"Uh . . ." Tony didn't have a comeback ready, dumb kid.

Mama hurried to his side and pressed a hand to his forehead, flour and all. "You didn't tell me you were sick. Where does it hurt? Your stomach? Head? What?"

Maggie had come down from our bedroom and stood behind him, listening. Cindy and Billy would have joined in too, I suppose, but they were off at friends' houses till supper. Cindy no doubt had carried a case of Polly Pockets up the road to Rachel's house. Billy, Maggie and Tony's fourteen-year-old brother, was probably out doing skateboard stunts with Jasper and would arrive home just in time for supper, his flaming red hair plastered to his head and his face flushed with sweat. He was heavier set, even muscular, next to his dad and brother, taking his looks from Maggie's mama's family with their red hair, but he had a more jovial attitude, easygoing, like Frank.

Or Frank's usually easygoing attitude. I knew from the looks of things I was about to see a new side of my stepfather.

He continued. "Mr. Phillips says you came home sick on Wednesday and were still too sick yesterday to go in, but you weren't here. What gives?"

You couldn't not look at Frank when he caught you at something—looking at the floor was a sure sign of guilt and conviction—but I could tell Tony was struggling to keep his eyes on his daddy's face. "I, uh, had something I really had to do. . . ."

Mama was astonished. "Tony!"

Frank stood his ground. "What could be so important that you would lie to your boss and yet not tell us?"

He looked over his dad's shoulder at me, and I knew the game was up, even though I pleaded for him not to tell with every bit of expression I could conjure. I had my heart set on Vince, and I knew I needed Tony in that band to get to him.

Tony looked at his feet. "I've been playing guitar with a band."

Maggie sank to the steps and dropped her head into her hands as if she'd failed at motherhood.

Mama went from astonished to incredulous. "You what?"

"A band. A rock band. Dixie fixed it up for me. They needed a guitar player, so I joined them. We're really good, and they have paying gigs coming up. I'll make a ton of money."

Frank crossed his arms over his chest. "You can't give up a regular, good-paying job in hopes of making money in a band."

Tony hunched over as if the confession had deflated him. It wasn't like Tony to question his father's opinion. "Why not? It's better money."

"Maybe this week, but what about next week and the week after that?" Frank asked.

"Vince has gigs lined up for a month."

Mama rolled her eyes and applied her most sarcastic drawl. "Wow. A whole month."

Maggie raised her head as if to speak, but held her tongue. She rarely voiced an opinion without considering all sides of an argument, whereas I tended to blurt out the first thing that came to mind, which is exactly what I did. "He's a kid. Why does he have to have a steady job? I don't."

"Something we're all aware of," Mama said.

"You told me you didn't want me working, that it was more important to keep my grades up."

"True," she said with a sigh. "I think babysitting is enough for you to handle."

I nodded, though it wasn't true. School was a breeze. I could have easily held a job. I just didn't want one. I liked hanging out with my friends. Maggie and Tony were different, though. Maggie had worked at First Street Pharmacy during the summer because that's where Webb worked, but during the school year she only babysat to earn money. She spent her evenings studying and doing volunteer work, most recently at the retirement center where she read poetry to old ladies and wheeled them to the cafeteria and stuff. Tony had his sights set on owning his own car, so he'd opted for a real job. Besides, I'd heard him tell Webb he thought the grocery store was a great place to meet girls—like his life ambition was finding a cashier at the Piggly Wiggly or meeting some girl coming through the line with her mother—as if there might be someone in town he didn't already know. But that was Tony. I think our parents expected him to hold a job just because he was a guy, which made no sense to me, at least not at his age.

"It's not fair," I continued, not stopping to think of how I was going to be hung for my part in the crime. I was still intent on going out with Vince at all costs. "This is his chance to use his talent."

"He can play his guitar at church if he wants to perform in public," Frank said, "but he's always insisted he doesn't want to do that."

I tried to imagine what kind of choir they must have for it to sound right with an electric guitar accompaniment. I didn't go to Maggie and Tony's church. I'd been a few times with Maggie when we were growing up, and my mother had switched over to their church back when she and Frank started dating, but I was involved in my youth group and didn't want to leave it. This year I was the youth leader, but hearing a choir suited to an electric guitar was a strong temptation to visit their church again.

"The teen service is lame," Tony said, "and I prefer electric guitar nowadays."

Well, that solved that riddle. Frank meant his old acoustic guitar. I could envision that. Still, I couldn't see Tony playing at church. He wasn't what you'd call a religious teen. He went because his dad made him go.

Maggie finally spoke up. "You aren't scheduled to work tomorrow, are you?"

"No," Tony replied.

She nodded. "Then I suggest you let him perform," she said to Frank. "They are relying on him to be there; it's not their fault he skipped work to go to practice."

Actually it *was* due to Vince's coercion, and a tad of my own, but I wasn't about to spill those beans.

Maggie continued. "I'd like to hear them anyway. It'll be a treat to see Tony perform after all these years of tolerating that noise coming from his bedroom."

"The band is not going to override his job. His first obligation is to Piggly Wiggly," Frank said, not at all upset by Maggie's input. She had acted as mother to Billy and Tony for so many years that she had equal standing in almost everything their father decided about them. "For now we're dealing with today's schedule, and the manager has asked if he can come in to cover for another boy who has somehow come down with Tony's fake illness. Go get ready. I'm dropping you off myself."

Maggie looked at Tony and shrugged. She had tried to help.

Tony stomped up the stairs to get ready.

I flopped back in the recliner and sighed. It was left up to me to go break the news to Vince. Unless I could convince Tony to show up Saturday despite Frank's declaration.

My phone buzzed. Heather. I carried it outside and spent the next hour telling her what was up.

I crept into Tony's room after everyone had gone to bed and shook him till he moaned and rolled over to gaze at me with dream-clouded eyes. "I didn't kill him," he muttered.

"I hope not," I replied, knowing his mind was lost in la-la land. I glanced at Billy, but he was still sound asleep. "Snap out of it. We've got to talk."

He moaned again as he came awake and pulled the covers up over his chest. "What now?"

"*Shhh.* You'll wake up Billy," I hissed. "Look, you've still got to play tomorrow."

"Are you crazy?" he mumbled. "I would be grounded forever if Dad found out."

"How's he going to know?"

"He'll know."

"Your dad isn't the snooping type. He's never checked behind your back, ever."

"After this episode he might."

"So? You aren't scheduled to work. If you're not skipping work, what rule is it breaking if you play with the band?"

He stared at the ceiling a minute. "I guess you're right. He didn't say I couldn't play. He just said I couldn't skip work."

"All right. It's settled then. We have to be at the festival by five to set up."

"Good," came a voice from the doorway. It was Maggie, leaning against the doorjamb. "I was hoping I'd get to see you perform. We'll all ride together."

Maggie was going behind her father's back—that was a surprise—but I wasn't about to question it. Thankfully, this show wasn't in a bar. Luck was running with me. Or that's what I thought anyway.

Chapter Seven

THE SHOW WAS at a street festival in the next town, which normally wouldn't pay anything, but Vince had convinced one of the local businesses to sponsor them in exchange for a little advertising on the bandstand.

I left it up to Maggie to get us out of the house, and she did it superbly. Frank never questioned her actions.

"Jessie," she said to Mama, "we're all heading out to the festival over in Camden. The Civinettes have a booth, and I want to check it out to get ideas for the summer festival downtown, so we'll eat there if that's okay."

Mama was sewing a button back on a blouse and nodded absentmindedly. "What's Civinettes?"

"A group that raises money for charities like soup kitchens and such. I'm trying to start one at our school."

I sighed. Maggie's good works seemed unending.

"Great," Mama said as she tied a knot and bit off the thread. "Your father and I are going out to dinner anyway."

I was screaming *Yippee for Maggie* inside my head for getting us a green light, but walked over and sedately gave Mama a kiss on the cheek. "See you later, then."

We were halfway to the door before our luck changed. Mama stowed her sewing things in her basket then looked up. "Oh, what about Cindy? Can you take her with you?"

Cindy was a major blabbermouth, the last thing I needed along on a trip to see Vince.

"Sure," Maggie replied without even consulting me. "She'll love it."

Mama left the room to get her, and I lit into Maggie. "Are you crazy? She'll tell them about Tony."

"You already determined there's nothing wrong with Tony performing. What are you worried about?"

I sighed. Maggie was as thick as Tony sometimes. They were two innocents with no teenage conniving built into their psyches. I couldn't understand it. "You're asking for trouble taking her along."

"Nonsense. We'll buy her a hotdog and some cotton candy, and she'll be putty in our hands."

I had to laugh at that. Maybe Maggie was a bit more manipulative than I thought.

As it turned out, Heather wasn't coming to this show. We'd gone to a party together the night before (a pretty lame excuse for a party at some freshman's house, as it turned out) while Tammy went off on a clandestine meeting with the banker. So Heather had gone along with her on a shopping spree in Columbia to get all the juicy details, but I wasn't about to pass up a chance to see Vince for the sake of hearing about Tammy's date with some middle-aged banker.

Anyway, the point was that I would have been walking around the festival all by myself like some pathetic loser if it weren't for

Maggie and Webb. It was kind of weird doing something with them as a couple. Before they started dating, Maggie and I were inseparable, but then I started hanging out with Heather and Tammy, so it had been ages since I'd been anywhere with Maggie. Webb had been around Maggie's family as Tony's friend long before he and Maggie became an item, so it wasn't having Webb along that felt any different; it was having Webb and Maggie as a couple at my side that seemed weird, even with Cindy tagging along. They were a lot more affectionate without our parents there. Webb had his arm draped over her shoulders as we walked through the crowd; they talked to each other in hushed tones and exchanged an occasional kiss. It felt strange watching them act like that, and me walking along with my arms hanging at my side, no boyfriend or anything. They acted so in love, and I had nobody.

While the band waited its turn to set up, Webb, Maggie, and I took Cindy around to the various booths. Webb would toss hoops or throw balls to win some cheesy stuffed animal then kiss Maggie, and Maggie would hand the toy to Cindy. Cindy was grinning from ear to ear. It was a bit too mushy for me. After all, this was straightlaced Maggie and lazy-slacker-gone-good Webb.

We lucked out with the weather. It was beautiful for a Saturday in February—sixty-five, even with dark settling on us—and Cindy was in her prime, enjoying all the attention she was getting. After drizzling ketchup down her shirt from a hot dog, chocolate ice cream from her cone, and getting pink cotton candy stuck in her hair, I figured she would be happy enough to do whatever I asked of her. I was wrong.

"I'm tired," she said. "I'm ready to go home."

"We can't go home yet," I explained. "We have a surprise,

but we have to walk to the other end to show you." We were surrounded by the tinkling canned music from so many booths and fair rides that we couldn't even hear the music from the band-stand where we were, other than the thump of the bass. I had to get closer before Vince started playing.

Maggie took Cindy's sticky hand. "Why don't you go ahead? We'll meet you up there in a bit, near the candy-apple stand under the streetlight, across from the bandstand."

I daresay Maggie, planner that she was, had staked out the meeting place when we first entered, but the truth was Maggie had a candy apple fetish and probably couldn't wait to buy one.

"Not a candy apple," Webb said. "Last time you got it in your hair."

Maggie swatted him. "So what? I love them."

I left them to their teasing and headed toward the band, relieved that I would have a chance to talk to Vince without Maggie watching me.

I was so hung up on him that I swerved between people and strode toward the bandstand like a woman on a mission.

I got there just in time. The other band was finishing up, saying their thank-yous and announcing their Web site and the CDs they had for sale. I circled around to the back and found Vince talking to Tony.

He turned and smiled at me, standing with his feet planted apart and one thumb hooked in the back pocket of his jeans. "So you came to listen again?"

"Of course."

"It's good to know we have one devoted fan. I guess I have Tony to thank for that."

I wasn't brave enough to contradict him, but Tony did it for me. He laughed. "You've got to be kidding. Dixie coming to hear me? I wouldn't be in the band if she weren't hung up on you."

I blushed from my hairline to my toes. Tony had the finesse of a one-eyed monkey. I had to save myself before Vince thought I was desperate, standing there all alone like some loser. "Actually, I'm here with Tony's sister, his best friend, and my little sister. They'll be along in while. They're browsing the booths right now. Everyone in the family wanted to hear him perform."

"Yeah, right. Maggie, maybe."

Vince had lost interest in the bickering. The other band was exiting the stage, and he was gathering equipment to take up. "We have ten minutes to set up, so let's get to it."

I made myself useful carrying the lighter pieces and plugging in cords. I knew the routine from observing at practices. Vince watched me for a second but said nothing and went back to work. When everything was done, I carefully descended the stage steps. Vince followed close behind and called out my name. "Dixie, wait up."

I turned, expecting him to scowl at me for having done something wrong, but he smiled. "Do you think you could hand out business cards for us? You know, they have our website and phone number on them. Helps us to line up more gigs."

His eyes were so dreamy I almost lost track of what he was saying but managed to croak out, "Sure. No problem."

"Thanks, babe." He touched my cheek then reached into Mike's SUV and retrieved a thick stack of black cards with *Blind Reality* printed in bold yellow letters across the center. "Here. Just hand them out to everyone who comes by."

He rushed back to the stage, and I moved through the crowd handing out cards as I made my way to the candy-apple cart.

It was actually a great vantage point directly across from the bandstand.

As Vince stepped up to the microphone, chills ran over my skin. Everything about him excited me.

"Tonight I'm dedicating this first song to our number one fan," he said.

I almost fainted. I probably wouldn't have a Valentine from him to flash around at school the next week, but he'd dedicated a song to me in front of an entire community. How cool was that? He flashed a smile at me that lit up my whole body. He still hadn't made a serious move, but now I knew he had really noticed me.

I kept an eye out for Maggie. I wanted her to hear them play, not just for Tony's sake, but so she would hear Vince too. I wanted her to be impressed.

As I glanced around, I didn't see Maggie, but I saw that freak who had shown up at one of the practices. Fortunately, he was looking at the ground and didn't see me.

Further back in the crowd, I finally saw Maggie's red head bobbing alongside Webb, the rest of them eventually coming into view with Cindy. Maggie grinned at seeing Tony on stage and came to stand beside me. They sounded good; she had to know. A crowd was gathering to listen. They were that awesome.

Webb whistled and clapped when they finished. I felt warm with pride as I finished handing out the business cards, as if I'd had something to do with how good they were.

They played five numbers during their time slot, with quips from Vince and Ariana between each one—including a plug for their sponsor, which Vince made with the glow of dollar signs alive in his eyes. He knew how to work the crowd, which grew and grew throughout their performance. When they finished, it was as if people woke up to where they were and dispersed back into the mayhem of the festival.

I wanted to stay behind to hang out with Vince. I thought maybe he would buy me some ice cream or win me a teddy bear like Webb had done for Maggie, but Maggie tapped my shoulder. "Ready to go? Cindy is really tired."

I couldn't say no. I couldn't say I wanted to stay behind with Vince. I wasn't ready to let Maggie in on my secret just yet. Besides, if I didn't return with the rest of them, there would be questions about where I was, followed by twenty questions about Vince. My mother could be ridiculous about having to know everything there was to know about a guy—his family, where he lived, what church he attended, his school, his grades—you name it. It hadn't ever bothered me before because generally she knew the boys I dated, but I sensed her reaction to Vince would be different, partially because he was older, yet something more than that too, that I couldn't put my finger on. There was a sense of mystery around Vince because he was a stranger and not some-one from school or church.

So I talked with Ariana a few minutes, helped them stow the equipment in Mike's SUV, told Vince the show was great, and walked away with Tony to our car. I could feel Vince's eyes on my back, or maybe a bit lower, and grinned. Maybe playing a little hard to get would pay off. For sure the hook was dangling in front of him. I just had to wait for that first real bite, for him to claim that kiss.

We were barely in the door when Cindy destroyed my entire future. She ran straight to where Mama and Frank were sitting together on the sofa reading the paper and jumped into their laps. "Guess what? Guess what?"

I expected her to tell them about the blue bear Webb won for her, or the cotton candy or something, but no, she couldn't be that normal.

"Tony played his guitar up on a stage. It was so cool. Everybody was clapping for him. It was awesome."

The newspaper crumpled in Frank's lap as his attention switched to Tony. "You did what?"

Tony didn't respond quite the way I expected. He beamed with pride and excitement as if still hearing applause. "I played with the group at the festival."

"We discussed that and decided you weren't playing with the band."

"All you said was that I couldn't quit my job."

"You're stretching it, Tony, and you know it."

I couldn't stand it. Tony was going to collapse under the pressure again. I could see the exhilaration draining away from his face. I hung up my coat and took a seat on the hearth. "Come on, Frank. You didn't say anything about not playing with the band. You just said he couldn't skip work anymore."

Mama cast me a quelling glare. "He was speaking to Tony, not you."

Maggie stepped up, her coat unzipped but still on. "Really, in all fairness, Dad, they're right. You didn't say he couldn't play, and he was fantastic. After all these years of practice and lessons, it was great to hear him play for a crowd. You should have heard the applause. People went crazy over them."

Frank's frown softened a bit. He always listened to what Maggie had to say. It was strange seeing a teenager act as an equal to her father, but it had always been that way between them. I could see him really considering what she had said. He nodded slowly and turned back to Tony. "Okay, you're right, I didn't forbid you to play. I just said work had to come first, and you haven't violated that tonight. But it had better stay that way, and you'd better keep us informed from here on out, or it'll be the end of the band for you."

Mama sighed as if she'd been holding her breath. She really didn't like discord between family members. She always preferred laughter to tears and happiness over anger. At Frank's consent, she instantly became her usual, more diplomatic self. "He was good? I knew he would be." She turned to Frank. "Why don't we go listen? I'd love to see him perform."

Frank's stern expression dissolved into to the lopsided grin that my mother loved. "So would I." He concentrated a serious glare at Tony. "But you won't play again without my permission. Is that understood? Or next time there will be serious repercussions."

Right, like Frank would actually punish Tony. Fat chance. Our parents were such marshmallows I should have known we could win them over, especially with Maggie as an ally.

Then it hit me. The best way to get them to approve of Vince was to get Maggie to like him.

But first I had to get *him* to like *me*.

Chapter Eight

TONY AND HIS boss worked out a compromise. Apparently the man had been at the festival and heard Tony play. Turned out he'd been in a high school band too and understood what it was like battling against parents and schedules. So he agreed to only schedule Tony till six o'clock on practice days and on Saturday mornings so it wouldn't conflict with the band. Vince said he could live with Tony showing up at six-thirty. What it meant was a lot more shuffling around for me. If I wanted the car while he was at work, I had to take him and pick him up, then take him to band practice. Obviously, I didn't complain. It was all to my benefit anyway.

After all my scheming and work, I didn't get to go to a practice again until Thursday. The art club put on a display at the library on Monday, which I couldn't miss since I was club president. Mrs. Newell threatened to kick me off the yearbook staff if I skipped another meeting, and I had to go to youth group on Wednesday because . . . well, because it kept it all real. But Thursday's practice was worth the wait.

The rest of the band had been there awhile, so they stopped for a break when Tony and I arrived. Vince gripped his guitar by the neck and surveyed me standing there, making me glad I'd taken extra time with my appearance: precisely an hour and a half of showering and hair drying, and then, even though my hair tends to hang poker straight on its own, I flat-ironed it and sprayed it with ultrasheen so not a hair was out of place. I followed up with makeup, the best stuff I had. I looked *sweet*. My hair shone like satin, my skin glowed, and my eyes stood out with the merest eyeliner traced around the rims.

The look Vince gave me made me wish we were meeting somewhere else, like a luxurious club or hotel lobby or some high-class restaurant, instead of Mike's dusty garage with the smell of gas and oil hanging in the air and Mike, Josh, Judy, Ariana, and Tony looking on.

"Glad you made it today," he said. His voice was a little slurred, but I shrugged it away at the time as him being tired. "I've missed my number one fan."

"Really?" I said, casually taking a seat in the lawn chair so I wouldn't pass out from heart failure. "I didn't think you ever noticed me here."

Playing coy was obviously the way to go with him. He cocked one eyebrow, as if unsure how to take my lack of excitement at his special greeting. "Of course I've noticed you."

I played it cool, leaning back in the chair and looking past him to where Tony was tuning up, plucking strings while Judy played selected notes for him.

"Come on, Vince," Mike said. "Let's get it together. I've got other stuff to do."

Vince wheeled around, his guitar swinging with him and just barely tapping my chair, which made him jump and snatch up the guitar to examine for any sign of a scratch. I'd definitely rattled him.

Throughout practice he kept tabs on me: a glance, a grin, a nod. I tried not to react much, even though my veins pulsed with expectation.

When the band finally finished, I remained seated. I was in no hurry to leave. I wanted to give him a chance to approach me if he was going to, but Tony packed up quickly and rousted me from my seat. "Let's go. I have homework to finish."

Schoolwork. It interfered with everything.

Vince dropped the cord he'd been untangling and intervened. "I can take you home later if you want. Let Tony go ahead."

I knew this was it, the moment I'd been waiting for.

Everyone sensed what was going on, including Tony. He looked from Vince back to me, worry crossing his face momentarily. But then he shrugged. "Whatever. See ya."

Ariana took one look at Vince and rolled her eyes. "Oh, get over yourselves. You look like sick lovebirds."

"My parents will be home in the next ten minutes," Mike said, as if he were afraid we were planning to make out in his garage.

Vince grabbed his guitar and jacket and gave me a sideways nod. "Come on."

I gave Ariana a backward glance. I really liked her. She seemed so sophisticated, and she was looking at me like I was a dumb little kid. It made me pause a second, but I couldn't figure out what the look was for, so I turned and followed Vince.

That same weird guy was standing around outside again, still dressed in the same clothes—a black shirt over a black tee—looking as if he hadn't washed or slept since the last time I'd seen him. Vince motioned for me to stay put by the door and took him around the corner, out of earshot. When they came back, the guy climbed into the passenger seat of a banged up 280Z and took off. I couldn't see the driver.

I shivered. Whoever the guy was, he gave me the creeps.

Vince waited till the car was out of sight, then waved me toward an old delivery van stuffed full of boxes and sundry things. "Got my uncle's van today. Next time I'll bring my motorcycle," he said. I think it embarrassed him to be driving such an old wreck, but the car I shared with Tony and Maggie wasn't much better, just cleaner and sportier.

He had modified the stereo with a CD player, into which he slid a gold disc with something scrawled across the top in black marker. "Made this in the fall, before Ariana joined us. Had to cut that singer. She kept skipping practices."

The music flared, filling the cavity of the van with pounding notes that kept us from talking anymore.

"I love Ariana," I said. "She has such a clear, beautiful voice."

He nodded and turned the music louder.

After a few minutes, I realized I had no idea where he was taking me. In fact, I didn't know anything about him except his name and that he was the brains behind the band, which wasn't a lot to go on. I thought about his creepy friend and wondered if there would be more like him wherever it was we were going, which made me tense up so much I couldn't even absorb the music blaring in my ears. I knew what could happen to a girl with a guy she didn't know. Maggie was an expert on that and preached rape-awareness classes all over the place. But I shut off that cautionary voice in my head to give in to the other, more persistent voice — the teenage heart that throbbed at the sight of a really good-looking guy who's flattered her. After all, Vince was a star in the making. He was head of a band, older than any guy

I'd ever dated, and not sophisticated, exactly, but more worldly, more experienced, more impressive. I saw him becoming famous, hitting the tabloids at the grocery store checkout, and there I would be, pictured with him, hanging on his arm, smiling at the camera, *me*.

Turned out he was taking me to his trailer. He had a single-wide in a trailer park just outside Columbia. He obviously wasn't rich yet. From the look of it, I assumed he'd bought the trailer used from a long line of owners. The dirty white aluminum was dented here and there at angles and spots that suggested bodies had been thrown against it at some point. A few trailers in the park were new, but most were in about the same condition as his, and the shouts and hollers escaping from the thin walls suggested the neighbors were none too genteel. I guessed they were probably at least adults and not nasty-looking teens like the guy in the black shirt. There wasn't anything wrong with living in a trailer park, but the creepy feeling crawling up my spine wasn't going away. I was a long way from home—we'd driven at least twenty minutes from Mike's house, and that was a good ten or fifteen minutes from home already.

I shoved the misgivings away as we were greeted by the neighborhood mutts, two yellow Lab mixes that barked like crazy but wagged their tails as they rushed toward us, and one dark shepherdlike dog that bared its teeth and growled.

Vince stomped the gravel driveway. "Get on, Devil."

I rushed up the wooden steps to the small deck as he shooed the dogs away. Then he tromped up after me and let me into his home.

My first impression was the similarity between it and my stepbrothers' room. He had clothes tossed on a chair, mismatched furniture (a blue sofa that had seen better days and a tan recliner that sagged on one side), and nothing but cruddy old blinds on the windows, which were completely closed to shut out the view from inside and out. A white plastic plate and a glass sat on a makeshift coffee table that consisted of two metal milk crates and a board painted with red and blue stripes. A stack of newspapers and magazines lay in one corner beside an old tarnished brass standing lamp.

The room wasn't exactly messy (especially by my standards), just not clean. I ignored the dust and dirt and followed him to the worn sofa under the double-hung window, which faced a huge television and stereo system, the only new things in the whole place, both of which were perched on a scratched-up oak dresser with fat, heavy pulls that put its age somewhere in the middle of last century.

Our bottoms barely settled into the seat before he turned on the television with a click of the remote and watched it for a minute before turning to me.

"It's great you came to the practice tonight. I really like it when you're there listening to us."

"Sure. You have a good band."

"Did you get how me and Tony worked out the harmony in that last number?"

I nodded. I really didn't know guitars well enough to have much of a conversation about them, so I turned the attention on him. "Have you been playing a long time?"

"Since I was a kid. All I ever wanted to do was sing and play guitar."

"Do your parents ever come listen?"

"Nah." He kept glancing at the television.

I knew I wasn't holding his attention. I needed something better to talk about. I'd long gotten over my shyness from earlier years, but I still wasn't great at small talk. Most of the guys I went out with had known me for years, so it was easy to discuss school or families or whatever. But I didn't know enough about Vince to even know where to start, and he didn't seem very interested in helping me.

I tried changing topics. "Have you lived here long?"

"'Bout a year."

"Really? It's so cool that you have your own place."

He shrugged and looked back at the television. "There, finally. It's on. Can't miss my show."

It was some sitcom I hadn't ever watched before, but that wasn't surprising. I wasn't big on television. When I wasn't doing schoolwork, I was at the mall or out with Heather and Tammy somewhere. I thought of television shows as watching other people's lives instead of living my own, which didn't make much sense to me. Maybe it would have if I was old, like fifty or something, and didn't have any living left to do.

It didn't matter to me, though, because I was there beside him, at his place, watching television with his arm slung behind me, across the back of the sofa. By the end of the show I was leaning into him as he caressed my shoulder and touched my hair, and then he was kissing me, and I was in heaven.

Maggie knew something was up when I got home. I slipped in the front door, hung up my coat and keys, and flew up the stairs to my bedroom before Mama could even step out of the kitchen, where the murmuring of her voice and Frank's rose and fell together. I hoped maybe she was too distracted to hear my arrival or notice it was after ten o'clock.

Maggie wouldn't let me slide that easily. She sat up in bed and dropped her physics textbook to the floor. "Where have you been?"

There was a time I would have told her everything, and even that year I'd come rushing in with stories of various dates, taking us past our struggles over my piles of clothes and shoes and books interfering with her neat-freak cleanliness. But something about Vince made me hold back, made me feel like I shouldn't divulge the truth. It's like I knew deep down there was something that just wasn't right about him and that I shouldn't be seeing him — as if I had myself on the edge of something dangerous by going to his trailer. If I admitted it to Maggie, somehow she would know right away that it was wrong, and she would stop me from going again. So I shrugged. "Just out."

Under the blankets, her knees came up in a lump, and she hugged them to her chest as she watched me intently. I knew she was astute enough to see the flush on my cheeks, but I hoped she would attribute it to the chill outside.

We'd been undressing in front of each other since we were five, so it was easy to act like I didn't notice her steady gaze as I peeled out of my clothes — shoes first, socks, jeans, shirt, then, because she was watching me, I put the shoes in my closet and the clothes into the hamper she'd installed in the corner since I was so bad about getting them down the stairs into the laundry room.

"What's he like?"

Her question threw me. "Who?" I responded, as I fished through a dresser drawer for pajamas. I had a stack of my father's old shirts that I'd worn to bed since the day he died, and somewhere in the stack was my favorite, an old T-shirt with a huge fish jumping from the water at the end of a hook. My daddy and I had loved fishing together, and I needed that shirt on so I could feel close to him, as if it would somehow give me his approval of Vince and how things might go between us.

Maggie pressed on. "Come on. You know. The singer. The guy from the band."

I tossed my bra into the hamper, pulled the fish T-shirt over my head, slipped on a pair of striped PJ bottoms, and shoved the drawer closed without once looking her direction. "Oh, you mean Vince."

That was as far as I let it go before I made my escape. I padded down the hall past Tony and Billy's closed bedroom door, past Cindy asleep in her room under the soft blue glow of the aquarium Mama had bought to replace the pet parakeets that had died a few months earlier. In the sanctuary of the bathroom, I could give myself time to think while I brushed my teeth and washed up. Maggie wasn't likely to give up her quest for information, and I had to concoct an evasive answer good enough to satisfy her without letting her know how hung up on him I was. Maggie would be full of cautionary platitudes, and I wasn't about to let her dampen my high spirits or feed those suspicions that were curling around in the pit of my stomach.

By the time I returned to the bedroom, she had her nose back in her physics book, and I remembered with a pang that we had a test on chapter ten the next morning, first period, which didn't leave any quick study time like I could manage for classes later in the day. I hauled my book out of my bag, which I had dropped at the foot of my bed that afternoon, and crawled under the covers to review the info, thinking not only could I get my studying done, but it might keep Maggie from asking any more questions. That sounds weird, considering we had been best friends forever and used to share every secret in the world with each other, but our romantic relationships had been different. Maggie had only dated one other guy besides Webb and had been reluctant to share what happened with him — but she'd been going through some hard times then, so I never held it against her. Then she started dating Webb, and everything was so aboveboard and morally perfect that there wasn't anything for her to tell . . . so I began to withhold more and more from her about my dates. We still talked about our parents and other stuff we didn't share with anyone else, but Maggie had strict morals when it came to dating. Even though I hadn't ever done anything morally wrong, I felt like I couldn't live up to her expectations, so it was best to avoid such a discussion — unless whatever happened was humorous, and I'd put a guy off on an attempt to even kiss me.

So I didn't really want to discuss Vince with her.

No such luck. She looked up from her textbook and started in on me again. "Where did he take you?"

Inside I grumbled; Tony must have told her we had left together. I got the feeling Tony was okay with playing in the band, but he didn't want me dating Vince. He probably said so to Maggie too. I pretended total absorption in the words swimming on the page, as if I hadn't heard her question. "Huh?"

"Victor? Vince? What's his name? Where did he take you?"

"Oh, Vince. Nowhere special. We went to his house and watched television. No big deal."

I hoped she wouldn't suspect he didn't live with his parents. Maggie could be tenacious about details, but keeping my eyes on the text worked. She let it slide. She didn't even ask where he lived. "Do you think you like him?"

I made a face. "Oh, you know, hard to tell yet, but maybe. He's cute. Don't you think so?"

"Sure, I guess. Kind of rough looking."

That gave me pause. Older, slightly mysterious, maybe more worldly than me—but rough? I hadn't thought of him like that.

I plumped up my pillows and changed tactics. "Let's go over the review questions together."

That did it. She flipped pages and leaned back. "Okay, you first." And she proceeded to read question one.

I was totally the opposite with Heather the next morning. I couldn't wait to tell her because I knew she thought Vince was something special. I waved her toward me. "Guess what?"

She arrived at my side as I pulled my locker open, and a small envelope fell to the floor at Heather's feet from where it had been wedged into one of the air-vent slits at the top of the locker door. She snatched it up and tore it open.

She laughed. "Oh my gosh, you won't believe it. It's a Valentine from Sam."

Sure enough, it was a corny Valentine like a kid would pass out in grade school. Silent Sam's signature was scrawled across the bottom.

"How cute," Heather said. "I knew he had a thing for you."

"Oh, please," I said. Sam was a nice guy and fairly good-looking, but he was nothing next to Vince. He lacked the excitement and mystery that Vince had. I grabbed the card from her and shoved it back in my locker. "Give me a break. What would I want with Sam when I have Vince?"

"Vince? This sounds interesting! What's happened?"

"I went out with him last night."

"With Vince?"

"Yes. Can you believe it?"

Her eyes sprang open wide. "Get out of here. You didn't."

The shock on her face made me think of Tony that morning, passing me as I came out of the bathroom. He shook his head and told me I was nuts and that I'd better watch what I was getting into. At the time, I was flying too high to care much what he thought of Vince. Looking at Heather's round eyes made me reconsider his words, but only for an instant. Dating Vince was what I wanted more than anything in the world right then. I grinned at her. "Did too."

"Tell me more! Where did he take you?"

A smile crept across my face as I let a pause build before answering. "His place. Can you believe it? He has his own place."

"What? An apartment?"

"Nah. Just a trailer, but how much cooler is that than one of these high school boys borrowing his daddy's car?"

Tammy sauntered up, in no hurry to join the daily school rush, but not about to miss any good gossip. She knew I had something juicy to tell as soon as she caught sight of me. "Someone is psyched about something. What's up?"

Heather gripped her arm. "She went out with Vince last night. Can you believe it?"

Tammy gave me a quizzical once-over. "The guy from that band?"

I nodded. "He is *so* good-looking."

"How did you run into him?"

I told her about Tony and the band practices, but only briefly. The bell was about to ring, and my classroom was down the hall, so I promised more details at lunch and hurried away to face Silent Sam in physics.

Sam blushed when I stopped at his desk. "Thanks for the Valentine, Sam." His whole face turned red, but he didn't say a word, which is what I expected. As I stood there looking at him, I realized he really was a good-looking guy. It was a pity he wouldn't talk to anyone; he could have been really popular if he tried.

I took my seat and immediately forgot about Sam. I couldn't wait to get through my morning classes so I could get to lunch to talk to Heather about Vince.

Tammy didn't give me a chance, though. She wasn't interested in hearing more about Vince at lunch. She had her own story to tell about a new dentist her mother had taken her to see. A dentist was more in her realm of prospective dates, not some guy in a band living in a trailer and much better than a guy working as a bank teller.

I didn't get a chance to talk to Heather again until world cultures. I was already at my desk when Heather came dashing into class three minutes late and stood inside the door making huge motions with her arms. "Mr. Baire, Mr. Baire, I just know you won't give me a tardy when you hear what happened to me. It was absolutely horrible, Mr. Baire. You see, I was leaving the lunch-room right on time like I always do, Mr. Baire, when that little freckle-faced boy in the ninth grade, you know, Macky Jackson? He's just as cute as he can be, for a ninth grader that is, except he's short as a fence post. You ever notice that? Well anyway, I was going past his table. He sits right there by the door with Jack and Tim, those skinny twins? Wouldn't you know he knocked over his Coca-Cola just as I was walking by. Well, Mr. Baire, he got soda all over the hem of my jeans. I was simply in a panic thinking someone might actually see me that way, but luckily everyone that actually mattered had filed out in front of me, so I grabbed some clean clothes from my locker and changed just as quick as I could, and here I am," she twirled around for effect, "good as new."

Mr. Baire's face was as blank as a sheet of paper. "You keep a change of clothes in your locker?"

"Why, don't be silly, Mr. Baire. I keep *three* outfits in there."

His eyes registered the barest bit of interest. "I know I'm going to regret asking you this, but why?"

"For emergencies. Why, what if Tammy showed up in an orange shirt, and I was wearing red? We would clash! Can you imagine?"

I knew that would never happen because we coordinated our color scheme every day. The three of us didn't look good just by chance. If Tammy wore red, Heather would wear black with a touch of red, and I would wear white with red and black accessories. We were photo-perfect every day.

Mr. Baire looked from Heather to Tammy and back again. I could tell from the expression creeping over his face that he had never realized it before, but it was slowly dawning on him. We always looked good beside one another.

Tammy wrinkled up her nose. "Orange? I would never wear orange."

"Everyone knows that, silly," Heather said with a tinkling laugh. "It was just an illustration."

Asby jumped to his feet and paraded around the room, fluffing his hair like a girl. "Yeah, we know that. Only girls like me can wear orange."

Heather frowned and flipped a lock of hair back over her shoulder with an exaggerated air. "We have to be prepared for fashion emergencies."

"Sure," said Mr. Baire, "or civilization as we know it might have come to an end."

Heather smiled her sweetest smile. "Well, I wouldn't know about that, Mr. Baire." She headed to her seat, confident that by now he had totally forgotten she was supposed to be given a tardy and detention. "All that stuff about civilization is what you're supposed to be teaching us, Mr. Baire. And we sure are obliged."

She slid into her seat and batted her eyelashes at him.

He sighed and turned back to the board.

I shook my head at her. She could put on a show faster than anyone I knew, and it was definitely a show. She liked to act like she was brainless. That was okay, though. That's just how Heather was.

She leaned over to my desk and whispered, "You still have to tell me what happened with Vince."

"I know. After class," I whispered back.

Heather slipped from her seat and picked up a dime she spotted under Jeanine's desk, then slid back into her seat again and deposited it into the mystery money pouch in her pocketbook with all the other money she'd been collecting. Every day kids gave her more money. I couldn't understand it. She held this unbelievable power over everyone so that they wanted to do whatever she asked, including giving her their money. She still wouldn't tell me what the money was for, but I had a feeling Tammy knew; she turned around and whispered something to Heather that made her laugh. It made me grit my teeth.

But not for long. Soon after I got home, a florist delivered a dozen red roses with a simple card saying *Love, Vince*. I danced around with excitement. I didn't have Vince's phone number, and Maggie had gone out for a special Valentine supper with Webb, so I called Heather. I stretched out on my bed and rejoiced in having a bit of privacy, thinking how great it had been having my own room back before Mama had married Frank. I could talk to Heather about boyfriends and stuff without anyone listening in.

I had Heather's full attention. "Vince kept flirting with me throughout the entire practice," I said, and proceeded to give her all the details, embellished just enough to keep it interesting. She hung on every word, as if it somehow elevated her to a new status with the band too.

Maggie came into the bedroom and stood staring at me. I figured she wanted to do homework and was mad that I was on the phone, but I ignored her. After all, it was my room too, and I had just as much right to it. She couldn't expect to go for some fancy dinner with perfect Webb and get all dreamy about their perfect love, and then come back and expect me to vacate the room just because she was back home. I told Heather to hold on a second and glared at her. "What do you want?"

She assessed me for a moment as she twirled the ring on her finger, then shrugged. "Never mind," she said, and walked out, closing the door behind her. I guess she could tell I didn't want to be interrupted. Maybe she even guessed from my tone that I was mad about her always claiming rights to the room.

I sighed. *Let her sulk,* I thought, and went back to my phone call. I still had misgivings about the creep, and Vince's connection to him. Maybe that's part of why I was so ill toward Maggie. I guess I wanted to be secure with Vince, like she was with Webb, and not have some weirdo messing up that dream. "Have you ever seen some other guy hanging around with Vince's band?" I asked Heather. "Dressed all in black. Kinda creepy?"

"Some creepy guy with the band? Why, I sure hope not."

I wished I hadn't asked her. I didn't want her thinking ill of Vince or she would join forces with Tammy in thinking I shouldn't date him. And then who would I talk to about him? Or worse, she might ask Vince or Ariana about the guy. Word would get back to Vince that it came from me and . . . well, I wasn't sure what I was afraid might happen, but something about that guy still didn't sit right.

"I guess it was just a fan hanging out, listening to them."

"Probably," she said, and I could tell she dismissed it without a thought as she changed topics to our next shopping trip—she needed a new pair of earrings—and then on to Tammy's excitement over Dr. Wright, the dentist. She talked with such enthusiasm that I wondered if she had some news of her own—maybe something about that money bag—that she hadn't shared.

Maybe I should have withheld a bit of my own story, but there really hadn't been all that much to divulge. Yet.

Chapter Nine

NOTHING COULD MAKE me miss band practice after that.

Vince and I hung out together after practice several times during the next couple weeks, mostly to grab something to eat or to just drive around and park somewhere. Sure, we made out, but we didn't go too far. I hadn't ever let any guy take advantage of me. He wanted me to go back to his place both Wednesdays to watch television and hang out, but I passed. First off, I had to go to youth group. After all, I was the teen leader and I really enjoyed our group. We went on lots of trips together, some recreational, some missionary, and had some pretty deep discussions, which was cool. Second, getting home late on a weeknight was really pushing it, and I didn't want to chance messing up having a real date on the weekend. Unfortunately, the band's performances ran late both weekends, so we didn't have any time together then, either, and some afternoons he would be in a rush to get somewhere.

One evening, though, his eyes lit up when I entered the garage, and he smiled that special smile with a twinkle in his eye. When practice was over, he stowed his gear then took my hand and led me to his car. "We have until ten o'clock, right?"

I nodded, wondering what he expected of me.

At the car, he stood that way he had with one thumb hooked in his back pocket and gazed at me, slowly taking in every detail from my hair caught up in a knot at the back of my head with tendrils falling loose around my face to the cleavage of my pink sweater to the brown fabric of the hip huggers swelling over my hips to my suede clogs. I was dressed warmly against the night air, still cold for spring, but, judging from his expression, you'd have thought I was a pinup girl. "You look great tonight."

"Thanks," I replied, and slid into the car.

From the look in his eye, I thought he was taking me back to his trailer, but a short time later we arrived at a posh restaurant. He led me in, opening the door and everything. I knew he'd made reservations ahead of time because he gave the hostess his name, and she escorted us to a table nestled in the back corner and secluded by hanging pots of huge ferns and a fancy screen made of silky fabric. I gazed around in disbelief. Dim lights, red carpets, candlelit tables, and formal waiters dressed in stiff white shirts. Who'd have thought Vince would even know of such a place?

He took the seat beside me instead of the one across from me and opened a menu for the two of us to share.

"What's the occasion?" I asked.

He reached over and touched my cheek, the gentleness of his spirit shining in his face. "Every day is a special occasion with you, babe. You deserve the best."

We shared a wonderful meal. He ordered fried mushrooms, which he dipped into a spicy white sauce and fed to me one by one, followed by an entrée of steak and asparagus, with dinner rolls that melted in my mouth.

We talked a lot. Mostly about the band and their future. A little about me. I mentioned prom, thinking it could be much like this night, but he only smiled and changed the subject, so I let it drop, thinking it made me sound juvenile when he was treating me like a woman. How important was prom anyway?

He held my hand and talked in whispers, and after supper he led me back out to the car and carried me home, dropping me off in the driveway. When he drove away, he carried my heart with him. I was totally in love.

The last Friday in February the band didn't have a gig, so I knew Vince would plan something for us to do. When I said I couldn't go home with him on Wednesday, he stood for a moment, thumb in his back pocket as usual, then reached for my hand and rubbed my arm. "Okay. Friday. I'll pick you up at eight."

I nodded, my whole body on edge, waiting for his lips to touch mine with a kiss that said he couldn't wait for Friday night. I wondered what spectacular evening he would plan this time.

I hadn't counted on him arriving at the house on his motorcycle.

Mama heard him in the driveway. "What on earth is that?"

I already had my shoes and jacket on, ready for flight. "My ride. See ya, Mama."

I dashed out the door before she could react, knowing there would be grief to pay later.

We zipped through the streets, bending around corners,

roaring up hills, and coasting down slopes, the cold February air cutting through my coat and freezing my ears. We didn't have helmets on, which would have infuriated my mother, but in South Carolina they weren't required for motorcyclists over twenty-one, so few guys bothered with them. I wished Vince had one for me, if for no other reason than to keep my face warm. I ducked behind him, my arms wrapped around his waist, and held on, praying we'd get to our destination soon.

I should have known he would take me to his place.

The dogs went crazy barking until we got inside. I felt like a popsicle, and stood rubbing my arms and legs trying to get warm again, not caring at that point if I looked nerdy doing it.

He had on a leather jacket, which apparently kept him warm. He laughed at me. "I should have warned you to wear something heavier."

I didn't think it was funny. "Have you got any hot chocolate, coffee, tea, or something hot?"

He led the way to the kitchen and opened the refrigerator. "How about a little wine to warm the bones?"

I wasn't into wine. I'd had a taste at a party once and didn't really like it, but my whole body was shaking, and I had to have something, so I nodded.

Wine in hand, we moved back to the family room, and I sank into the sagging sofa. He left the room and came back with a ratty blanket that he draped around me as I rubbed the shivers away. We'd become so close in just a few weeks. I had no doubts about how he felt about me. He was the real thing, the kind of guy I thought only existed in movies, a guy a girl couldn't help but love.

From the far wall, he picked up a five-string guitar and took a seat beside me, strumming, tuning, and humming softly, as the wine took effect. I leaned back and closed my eyes as he played softly.

Finally, when the sound seemed to satisfy him, he spoke. "I wrote this for you."

Music flowed from his fingertips, soothing and soft, nothing like the rock he sang on stage. The melodious notes floated from the guitar, joined by his voice, softened to suit the mood.

When I look into your eyes, I see where I want to go.
When I smell your hair, all the roses fade away to nothing.
When I hold your hand, I become who I'm meant to be.
When I kiss your lips, forever has new meaning.
Look at me, my lover, and give me my future.
Surround me with the essence of all we'll be.
Give me your hand, and don't let go.
Kiss me, and say forever belongs to you and me.

I was speechless. How could he feel all that for me? I was filled with a soul-deep ache that only he could fill up.

He set the guitar aside and pulled me into his arms. I ran my fingers through his hair and down his back. The essence of him enveloped me, the sweat of his T-shirt, the muskiness of his after-shave, the taste of his mouth joining mine.

I sank into him and drank him in, knowing this was leading to all or nothing, and I wasn't walking away. I was caught in his web, too tangled up in him to know how to escape. Only once did I shudder with apprehension, with the thought of stopping the clock, of turning back with all the conviction Maggie had taught me. I knew what I was about to do was morally wrong, against everything I'd ever been taught, and that Jesus was crying as He watched me move step by step away from Him . . . but my heart screamed against my conscience, my emotions raged and filled my head with excuses as to why it was all right, why I would be the exception, why Jesus should somehow approve of it this one time. We were in love!

I fell into Vince's arms, his forever. Or so I thought.

Chapter Ten

MAMA WAS WAITING for me when I got home at midnight. "Where have you been?"

I couldn't understand what she was so riled about. I had to be home by ten on weeknights, but she'd never given me a weekend curfew. I pretty much came and went when I wanted. She always said she trusted me to do the right thing.

As I pulled off my jacket, Mama stared at the sweatshirt I'd borrowed from Vince to add an extra layer against the cold, along with an old ski cap that I had pulled off and stuck halfway into my coat pocket before I got in the door.

"Where did that come from?"

"I borrowed it. I was cold."

"From who? Who were you with?"

Normally my mama is sweet as sugar. She has these sparkling eyes that dance when she's excited, and she's usually fairly even-keeled, but her eyes had turned to steel gray stones, and she wasn't smiling.

"A guy from the band. Vince."

"And what do you know about him? Anything?"

The churning in my stomach started up at her words, but I

ignored it. Vince and I had made love! We were bound to each other. I was his girlfriend.

I shoved my coat in the front closet. "Is this about the motorcycle, Mama? Because I didn't know he was coming on his motorcycle, or I would have talked to you about that. I didn't know."

She had moved to within a few feet of me. Frank watched from his recliner, letting her have full play. "Which proves my point. You know nothing about him, do you? We don't know his family or his background. And you're dumb enough to ride off without a helmet, even, like your head isn't going to crack open and spill out that pea brain if it hits the ground."

"I'm not a pea brain, Mama. You know that."

"Well you could have fooled me tonight. I don't want you seeing him again. He's bad news."

"You don't even know him! How can you say that?"

"If he was a respectable boy, he would come in and meet us, not take off with you without a word to anyone. And you would have sat and told me everything about him before going out with him, the way you've always done."

That was true—before Mama married Frank. We used to sit up at night in the kitchen and share snacks and cups of hot tea as I told her about the boys I liked or problems at school or funny stories about Maggie, Heather, or Tammy, but we'd slowly lost that intimacy as she spent more and more time with Frank. And when we moved in after the wedding, those times ended completely. I guess she hadn't noticed. "When would I have told you, Mama? You're always with Frank." Or Maggie, I could have added, but I was getting too emotional to go down that path. Tears welled in my eyes, and my throat felt clogged with unspoken jealousy. "We haven't talked in ages."

That shifted her attention off Vince and onto us. She got angry when she was afraid of losing control, but she'd never faced the prospect of losing the close relationship we'd always shared. We'd been everything to each other since Daddy died.

I could see the realization of what we'd lost cross her face. "We haven't, have we? Not since . . ."

"Since we moved in here."

"I don't want to lose what we had. You know that, don't you? I still want us to be as close as ever. I want to know what's going on in your life, even after you graduate. I want to know who you're dating and where you're going. I'm your mother."

There was nothing left to do but give in. The anger had gone out of both of us. "I'm sorry, Mama. I wanted to tell you. Maybe it was stupid of me to ride his motorcycle. I won't do it again without your permission."

She recovered a bit of severity. "You won't ride it again, period."

I sighed, then stepped forward and hugged her so we wouldn't get into it again. "I love you, Mama, especially when you worry about me."

How else could she react to that but to hug me back? Then she swept the hair out of my eyes and kissed my cheek. "Stay away from that boy. He's going to lead you to do something stupid, I just know it. You've got too much going for you to waste time on some motorcycle guy with stars in his eyes."

She didn't understand how good Vince was and that he was going to be famous, but I knew there was no use trying to say so to her. She would just get mad again.

"Promise me you won't do anything stupid."

"I won't, Mama."

I rushed up the stairs before she realized she still didn't know where I'd been or what I'd been doing.

The lights were off in the bedroom. I assumed Maggie was asleep, so I moved about as quietly as I could, dropping my clothes and shoes beside the bed and pulling my pajama pants and shirt out from under my pillow, then sliding between the sheets.

I closed my eyes, ready to relish the memory of what I'd shared with Vince by reliving it in my dreams all night.

Maggie whispered, breaking the image in my head, "Tony says you were out with the guy from the band again."

"That's right."

"You had them in a tizzy about the motorcycle, you know."

"So I found out."

"And you didn't answer your cell phone."

I'd left it in my pocketbook in the family room. Vince and I had been in the bedroom. I never heard it ring. But I wasn't about to say that to Maggie. She had been dating Webb for two years without sleeping with him. They were waiting for marriage. I could never tell her what I'd done. "I had it on vibrate."

"Oh."

I should have let it drop there, but I was on cloud nine and had to share at least part of my feelings. After all, this was Maggie, my bosom buddy. My forever friend. I hadn't wanted to tell her anything before, but now — now things seemed permanent between Vince and me. It was time to tell her how I felt. She would have to get to know him. I mean, at that point, in my mind I had us married. How could I not tell Maggie about him? "He's so wonderful, Mags. We're so in love."

"What's he like?"

I hugged Vince's image to my heart: the flowers he'd sent, the meals we'd shared. The way he looked at me. "Kind. Generous. Treats me like I'm special."

Silence stretched through the dark for a minute, and I wondered if she'd fallen asleep, but then she spoke again. "You haven't done anything you'll regret, have you?"

Maggie had been mother to Tony and Billy for so long she never could get out of that role even with Mama in the house, so her question didn't surprise me. I knew what she was asking. I answered it honestly. "No, Mags, nothing I'll regret." How could I ever regret committing myself to Vince?

When she spoke again, her voice was so quiet I could barely hear her. "Tony says he's bad news."

What could Tony know about Vince that I didn't know? "That's silly. I know him better than Tony. He's everything I want in a guy." I thought of his smile and the way he stuck his thumb in his back pocket when he was talking to people. I thought of his mussed hair and his steady gaze, so like my daddy's, and my heart did a flip just thinking of how things were between us. "I love him, Mags. And he loves me."

I fell asleep dreaming about how things would be with us. I had us married and living in a beautiful house with him famous and me his silent partner, his number one fan, his support system. I woke up floating on air. I was sure Vince was my future, and I put myself totally in his hands, willing to follow him wherever life took us. He loved me!

I'm not sure what kept me from telling Heather about sleeping with Vince, other than I now felt totally filled by him and didn't need a girl confidante as much anymore. I didn't want to lose her as a friend, though, so I convinced her to join me at the performance that night, a big to-do being sponsored by a radio station, held in a Columbia high school. Heather and I stood among the crowd, mesmerized. Vince's voice pierced the air and sent shivers down my spine. Ariana sang and he backed her up. He was so into his music, so absorbed in the sounds coming together, I could tell he was living through it, giving it life and taking life from it. His whole body lived the music. He vibrated with it. It shone in his eyes and poured from the depths of his soul. The audience could see it, and they were blown away. His eyes traveled across their faces, making contact with as many as possible even though there were lights glaring in his face, and he really couldn't see them at all. They thought he saw each one of them. They thought he was singing to them.

There was a break between each band, and after Blind Reality's performance, girls flocked to the stage to fawn over him. He stood there in his glory, puffing up like a peacock. He was such a hunk! And so composed. He touched an arm here, a hand there, and talked to them like each one was his best friend—and they believed it. They thought he connected with them. He looked bigger than life up there.

I waited off to the side and watched, even when Heather joined the crowd on the stage as she went in search of Ariana and then left with her. I had told her I had a date with Vince, though we hadn't actually planned anything. Yet I also knew instinctively that if I made an appearance while the fans were crowding around, it would annoy him. A rock star without a girlfriend holds much more appeal for the girls. Blood rushed through my veins and pounded in my chest. He was mine! I worried that all the attention would diminish my place to nothing. How could I compete with all the beauties thronging around him?

Finally, they started leaving, one by one departing the stage and fading away. There was only one girl left, a tall, thin blonde with flawless skin the color of peaches and cream and eyes as green as emeralds. She had held back, waiting until the crowd had cleared before she stepped forward. She laid her hand lightly on his arm and smiled sweetly at him. She wasn't overly flirtatious, but had a touch of naiveté blended with just a glint of vixen that promised she'd be fun if not promiscuous.

Vince leaned into her, listening intently, and nodded with his hand over hers. My heart did three flips, wondering what they were saying to one another, how much deeper it went than the expressions passing between them. I may not lose him to a crowd, but I could lose him to one determined girl.

She traipsed off the stage, his gaze following her until she reached the steps. Even Mike was watching her.

I glanced at Judy, but she was oblivious. I was convinced she tuned out the rest of the world; her reality was held in some dreamland of her own making.

I strode onto the stage with the intention of making Vince kiss me. At that point I didn't care what the rest of them thought; I hoped that girl would see me before she got out the door.

I stood over him as he pulled the plugs from a speaker. "Great show," I said, imitating the girl's smile.

He looked up but didn't quit working. "Thanks. The fans seemed to agree. Wasn't that cool? Quite a crowd tonight."

I wanted so much to ask him if he knew the girl, but I bit the words back. He didn't even stand up to talk to me, so I could hardly force a kiss on him unless I pulled him to his feet. Would I ever feel that comfortable with him? Maggie certainly did with Webb; she would smack him on the head for something and then say, "Come here and kiss me, you fool." She had practically grown up with Webb, so maybe it was different, but she told me she used to be nervous around him, afraid to say what was on her mind. It wasn't until they had some real heart-to-heart talks about personal beliefs and values, about the meaning of life or something like that, that they really started to see each other as more than acquaintances.

I couldn't imagine such a discussion with Vince. Not yet. We were with each other, and yet I realized at that moment we knew very little about each other. I couldn't even imagine having a deep life discussion with him.

So I backed up and let him work. Mike and Judy had packed up most of the gear. Tony had collected his own share of fans around him, but he was too shy to say much to them. He'd turned his attention to unplugging cords and such, only answering when they asked him specific questions, so they didn't stick around for long. Most of his stuff was ready before Vince's crowd even left.

I didn't help with the gear. I felt above that now. I wasn't a groupie. I was Vince's girl, someone to be admired by those other girls who had walked away empty-handed. I wasn't about to let them see me unplugging cords.

Even with everything stowed in Josh's van, Vince remained somewhat aloof. I made myself believe it was part of his image.

He waved good-bye to the other guys with a flip of his hand. "Take tomorrow off. See y'all on Monday at Mike's."

He hadn't needed to say it. Everyone knew the schedule. But he said it every Saturday night.

Of course Tony and I had ridden together, but Vince had been dropped off at Mike's in the same blue Z that had carried away that creepy boy in black. I had to ditch Tony so I could offer Vince a ride. "Can you get Mike to give you a ride home?" I asked Tony.

Mike knew what was up. All of them did. They weren't blind. Mike nodded at Tony. "No problem. Come on."

Tony pulled me aside. "You sure you know what you're doing?"

I had to admit I questioned why Vince had arrived in that freak's car, but I felt sure he had some explanation. "He's great, Tony, really."

"You better be careful," he said. "I've heard stuff about him."

"What?"

He shrugged. "I don't know. Just junk."

I rolled my eyes. "People probably talk about you and me, too, Tony. You know they do."

He frowned. "It's your life."

Yes, it was my life, and I knew what I wanted.

Tony grabbed his guitar. He and Mike got on well together. They often talked during breaks, something he did less and less with Vince, I'd noticed, but I figured it was just a difference in personalities. "Wanna get something to eat on the way?" he asked Mike. "I'm starved."

"Definitely."

Their voices disappeared into Mike's SUV, and they left.

I turned to Vince. "Okay, let's go."

He looked up, startled. "Oh, okay. Hang on." He turned away

and called someone on his cell phone, then gathered his stuff.

Once we were alone in the car, the rock star Vince slid away, and he became my Vince. We stopped to get a bite to eat at some out-of-the-way diner and headed to his trailer. He put his guitar away in the corner, then turned and pulled me into his arms, and I was assured once more that here in private—away from the pubic eye where he had to be everyone's guy—I was his girl, his one and only girl.

A couple weeks later, things went a bit differently. The usual throng had gathered to hear the group sing, this time at the Springfield Frog Jump festival, but not many people lingered afterward—there were too many other attractions to pull them away. I hoped the guys would pack up the stuff quickly and we could all spend time on some rides together.

I hadn't figured on that girl showing up again.

She stood at the side of the bandstand and waved at Vince. He couldn't quit clearing the equipment away; another band was waiting for their turn. Instead, he waved back, hurriedly finished up, then stepped around to the back and motioned to her.

That was more than I could take. The anxiety building inside me overpowered any bashfulness I had about being too forward. I crept up to Vince and looped my arm through his. "Who's your friend?"

Vince raised his head, startled a moment, but smiled quickly. "This is Pamela. Says she's my number one fan."

I looked her straight in the eyes. "Too bad that spot is already taken by me. You're welcome to be a groupie, though."

My announcement didn't faze her. She kept on as if I hadn't spoken. "I brought the demo CD for you."

"Thanks," he said, taking it and flipping it around to look at her photo on the front cover. It was a close-up of her perfect face, with her hair blown slightly back, as if she were on the beach or something. I'm not sure why, but it was alluring, almost sexual, the way she looked into the camera. "Nice pic," Vince said, his eyes gleaming a bit too much for me to stand.

"Daddy took it. He's great with a camera."

The way she said it, you'd think it was something special to have a photo taken by a father. Or maybe it just hurt me because my daddy had died four years earlier and would never be able to take my picture again. But I know one thing: *My* daddy wouldn't have taken a picture like *that* of me and put it on a CD for everyone to see, not unless he was trying to sell me. Maybe that was her father's intent. Maybe he wanted Pamela to succeed no matter what, and her objective was obviously to get into the band. Why else would she be giving Vince a demo CD? I knew right then she was sneaky; I was going to have to watch out for her. No telling what she would do to get what she wanted.

Vince tapped the case against his hand. "I'll listen to it tonight, okay?"

"Sure," she said. "My friends are waiting. I'll talk to you later."

As she wove her way between people, I tried to get Vince's attention back. "How'd she know you were playing here today?"

"She's a fan; I told you. She checked out the Web site."

"Ah." I hadn't imagined anyone actually going to the Web

site to find out when they could see Vince play again. It gave me a new perspective on all the hot bodies clinging around him after the shows. I had to remind him that I was his girl. "Well, how about a little fun? Want to try out the Ferris wheel?"

He leaned in and kissed me. "I know what I'd like to ride."

I smiled. Others could flirt with him, but I was his girlfriend.

"Oh, come on," he said. "We'll try out a couple rides first. How about that one that spins you upside down?"

"In the metal cage?"

He laughed. "Yep."

"I might lose my supper."

"In that case I won't bother feeding you until after the ride."

He slung his arm over my shoulder as we joined Mike and Tony and headed into the crowd.

Tony glanced at us, frowned, and rolled his eyes, but didn't say anything. For a stepbrother he was all right.

Chapter Eleven

EVEN THOUGH MAMA and Frank had mentioned attending one of the performances, it had been so long ago that I was lulled into complacency, thinking they wouldn't ever take time out to see Tony onstage. Big mistake.

Friday night, the group was performing at a party being held in what had once been a restaurant; our town had bought the building for civic functions and often rented it out for private parties, wedding receptions, and such. This event was a charity fund-raiser for updating our town's park, to turn it from a patch of dirt with a single jungle gym to a play area with swings, slides, a clubhouse on stilts with a slide-down pole, and some of those little horses that bob back and forth on huge springs. People of all ages had turned out for the event. Of course, since it was for charity, the band wasn't getting paid, but Vince had agreed to fill an hour slot to build the band's fan base.

I should have known my parents would show up. It was the first time Blind Reality had played in our little town, and the park renovation was something Mama and Frank both shared enthusiasm toward. Maybe if I'd been home more, or at least more involved in family happenings, I would have known to expect them there, but that week I had two yearbook meetings and youth group, as well as essays due in world cultures and English class that kept me shut in my room glued to the computer as soon as band practice was over. I was oblivious to what the rest of the family was doing and didn't bother to ask. I'd begun to live in my own bubble, just trying to get through everything I had to do so nothing would keep me from going off with Vince on the weekend.

Anyway, I had no idea they planned to attend.

I was sitting off by myself, watching from an obscure point, so they didn't spot me either. As far as Mama knew, I was out with Heather, which wasn't a lie; Heather and I had ridden there together. Heather had been psyched about the fund-raiser all week. She had helped decorate the hall and tacked up posters about it all over town. Heather had this thing about kids. She loved them. She went on all the time about wishing she belonged to a big family with a bunch of brothers and sisters, like in the movie *Cheaper by the Dozen*. She swore she'd been switched in the hospital. She liked to imagine that her real mama had ended up with some quiet kid by mistake, a girl who sat in a corner wondering what she was doing in a house full of crazy people. Heather hated how quiet her house was. So to make up for it, she was always doing fund-raisers for some kiddy event or other, and she'd been telling everyone at school about this one all week.

When the band finished, I rushed forward as they cleared their gear away, and caught Vince around the waist. "You were great tonight. The crowd loved it."

My move startled him. I'd remained rather reticent about showing affection in public, especially where they were performing, but I couldn't help but show off just a bit in front of Heather to prove to her that we were a couple.

I guess he was in pretty good spirits, too. He turned around and laid a kiss on me that left no doubts as to what we were about.

When we came up for air, Mama was staring at me from ten feet away.

I stumbled backward, out of Vince's arms. "Mama! Wow! I didn't know you were coming tonight."

"So I see." She walked past me to Tony with Frank a few steps behind. "Tony, you were wonderful. It was great to see you perform. We're so proud of you."

He snapped his guitar case closed. "Thanks, Jessie. I felt funny playing in front of so many people who know me."

Frank slapped him on the back. "Believe me, everyone was impressed. A dozen people came up and told me how much they enjoyed it. Glad you kept it toned down to some softer rock than what you've told me you usually play."

I stood off to the side trying to come up with something to pacify Mama, because I knew she wasn't done with me.

Tony pointed toward Vince. "Vince is good at laying out the right songs for an audience, but I had a little input this time."

"Well, good job," Jessie said. "We'll see you at home in a while."

"Sure," he replied. "Can I hang out with my buddy Mike here and buy a dinner plate?"

"Sure," Frank said just as Mama turned back to me, and Maggie and Webb approached from the opposite direction. I was trapped.

Maggie smiled at me, oblivious to what Mama had seen. "Webb and I are getting in line to get some food. Want to join us?"

I think she was referring to both me and Vince, maybe as a way of getting to know Vince one-on-one, but Mama didn't give me a chance to find out. "That's very gracious of you, Maggie, but Dixie is coming home with me and Frank. Do you think you could bring us a couple of take-out plates, if you're not out too late?"

"Oh, we'll be along shortly," Maggie said as she tried to sum up what was happening between us. "We'll bring you something home."

"Thank you," Mama replied. She nodded to Frank, and he pulled out a twenty and pressed it into Maggie's hand. Then Mama grabbed my hand and pulled me from the building. I only had time to toss Vince a backward glance. He shrugged and turned away to talk to Heather, who was staring at me with an open mouth.

So much for impressing anyone.

I tried to reason with Mama when we got home, but all she could think about was the kiss. "There you were, eating face in public."

Eating face. Definitely slang from her high school days.

"It was just a kiss, Mama."

She wouldn't be put off. "If you kiss like that in public, I have to wonder what you're up to in private. How old is he, anyway? I thought I told you I didn't want you dating him."

I wasn't sure if I was meant to answer all or any of the questions, so I stood there in the kitchen, leaning against the counter, saying nothing.

"Talk to me," she demanded.

I guess she did want answers. "You said not to ride his motorcycle again, and I haven't. But you didn't say I couldn't date him.

He's wonderful, Mama. He treats me so special. And he could have anyone. Can't you see that? He's such a fantastic singer and so good-looking."

"I did tell you not to date him, and you've gone against me. You are grounded."

"Grounded? For how long?"

"Maybe from now till graduation, but for sure for the rest of the weekend."

"No way. I'm going shopping for prom dresses with Heather tomorrow. You know that!"

"Too bad. You're not going now."

"That is so unfair! You can't control who I date the rest of my life."

"I will if you continue to gauge your relationships on looks!"

"Oh, Mama." I was so frustrated, I felt like sulking in a chair, but I didn't. I had to act like an adult, or she wouldn't respect my position. "I remember a time when you giggled over good-looking boys alongside of me. What's different now?"

"Back then, that was all it was. Just ogling. You're to the age now that you're thinking and acting more seriously about relationships, and you have to think smart. I thought I taught you that. You can't give in to a guy just because you think he's cute."

"I'm not *giving in*, Mama." I was sure I wasn't. Vince hadn't demanded anything. Our lovemaking had been by mutual consent. But Mama wouldn't understand that. Neither would Maggie. They didn't understand how we felt about each other. "We're in love."

Mama started unloading the dishwasher, slamming dishes into the cabinets. "What can you possibly know about love? You've known him for what? A month?"

"Over *two* months, Mama."

"Exactly. Not nearly long enough to base a real relationship on."

"Frank and Maggie's mama only dated a couple months before they got married, and they were happy, weren't they? They had three kids."

Mama shoved a stack of plates into place on an upper shelf and wheeled around to face me. "You don't know the half of it, or you wouldn't be using that as an argument."

Ah, a way to sidetrack her, and to finally solve the mystery of what really happened between Mama, Frank, and Maggie's mama, Mallory. Maggie and I had often speculated about what their relationship had been, ever since Mama told us that she had dated Frank once, long ago, before he hooked up with Maggie's mama. "So tell me, Mama. Tell me what happened that's such a secret."

Mama slumped into a kitchen chair and dropped her head into her hands. "It doesn't really matter. It was all so long ago."

"So tell me," I said, joining her at the table.

"I don't think I should. I don't want you to misinterpret what happened. It's all so much more complex than how it will sound."

"Oh, come on, Mama. Tell me."

She shook her head, but I knew the words were building in her. I could see it in the way her hands began twisting a napkin. So I waited patiently, hoping the spell wouldn't be broken.

"I knew both your daddy and Frank in high school. They were friends. Did you know that?"

I knew that much, so I nodded for her to continue.

"They both played on the basketball team with Nate, the guy

I was dating at the time. Really good-looking guy, but a bit full of himself. Anyway, the more I sat in the bleachers and watched them practice, the more I was drawn to the two of them, Frank and your daddy, I mean. They flirted with me constantly despite threats from Nate. They were both such great guys, but in the end, I broke up with Nate and started dating Frank instead of your daddy mostly because your daddy was too shy to ask me out. Richard Chambers, the shyest boy in school, even though he ranked as one of the best-looking. It wasn't just that he was shy, I guess. He tended to be silly, too, always joking and cutting up, which I didn't like in high school because I thought it was immature of him. I came to appreciate it later on. He always kept me laughing."

Her eyes had taken on that faraway look, and she was back there again, flirting with them both.

"Frank, on the other hand, was serious. He had everything planned out all the time."

"Like Maggie," I said.

She flattened the napkin out, pressing at the wrinkles she'd made, and nodded. "Yes. Maggie is very much like Frank, both of them practical. He had a schedule worked out for every phase of our lives." She smiled whimsically. "From the day I started college till I graduated, and then how long we would wait to get married, and when we would buy our first house. Everything was planned out."

"That's Maggie, all right. Do you think she knows her daddy was like that?"

"Probably not. It just comes naturally to them both. It will probably work for her and Webb, though, because they're going to the same college, and Webb shares in her plans. But with me and Frank, that's what came between us in the end. He wouldn't be flexible about anything. At least not with me."

Distress crossed her features, and I wondered if that comment had something to do with him being different with Maggie's mama.

Mama continued. "He knew my parents wanted me to go to college, and he insisted I follow through with their plans, so off I went. He stayed here and went to work with his father. We kept dating for a while, but I couldn't come home as often as I wanted to because the courses were tough and I had to study hard to keep up. So we rarely saw each other. You can imagine how hard it was with him here in town and me so far away. We talked on the phone and saw each other on occasional weekends and during the first summer, but it was like we lived in two different worlds. College is so different from high school. I was swept up in everything happening on campus, while he was grounded in his few technical courses and getting established in a job. It's like I was still playing, and he was getting on with life. So we grew apart even though we still loved each other." She sniffed. "Meanwhile, I saw Richard—your daddy—all the time, because he lived in the dorm beside mine. We started out going places together just because we knew each other, but as time passed and I saw Frank less and less, we let it go further than that. Frank called me less, and I hardly ever went home. Richard and I were together all the time. After a while we started talking marriage even though I had no intention of that happening until after I graduated; I was too focused on my degree. Finally, Christmas of my last year, your father made it official and gave me a ring."

She bit her lip a moment as if bracing herself to admit the last bit aloud. "I should have told Frank myself, but I didn't, and when

I saw him during Christmas break, he turned and walked away without speaking. It was so unfair of me. I tried to make it up to him, but he put up a wall. We finally became friends again, but we never got past that."

I sensed more was coming. "Did you want it to be more, Mama? Didn't you want to marry Daddy?"

She wouldn't answer. She just fiddled with the napkin.

I knew that wasn't the end because she still hadn't mentioned Maggie's mama and what that did to the mix. But she dabbed at her eyes with the napkin, then wadded it up and blinked at me, her eyes red and still full of tears.

"But Mama, what about Mallory and Frank?"

"What about them?"

The door had closed. She wasn't going to say anything else. But I knew there was more she hadn't admitted to me.

More importantly, she'd dropped her persecution of me and Vince.

Chapter Twelve

I COULDN'T WAIT to share Mama's story with Maggie, after all the nights we'd discussed what we thought may have happened between Mama and Frank. Maybe between the two of us we could figure out what Mama had left out.

When she got home, she delivered our dinner plates to the kitchen and immediately headed up to the bedroom. By the time I finished eating, she had settled on her bed, lying on her stomach with a binder and textbook spread out in front of her, her feet playing a slow beat against the wall above her pillows, as if it helped her to think.

I burst in and closed the door behind me. "Guess what?"

She looked up from her notes with one of those sideways expressions that meant I was irritating her. "I'm studying, Dixie. Can it wait?"

I bounced onto her bed and slammed the book closed. "No, it can't wait. You're always studying, and this is something you don't want to miss."

She sighed. "What? You finagled some dumb lie to keep your mother from punishing you? I heard about the kiss."

I frowned.

She continued. "Or is it something really important like Heather has a new hairdo? Tammy got her nails done?"

Okay, sometimes those would be realistic guesses, but I wasn't about to let her dampen my spirits because I knew this was something she really was going to care about. I crossed my legs and settled in to tell her what I knew. "Mama told me about her and Frank. You know, way back in high school."

That got her attention. She sat up and slid the books to the floor. "Seriously?"

"Yes, just now. She didn't mean to spill it, but she got caught up in lecturing me about Vince, and it led to telling me all about it. You won't believe it."

She snatched up her old monkey beanie pillow and held it to her stomach like a security blanket. It was as if she wanted to shield herself against what she was about to hear. "So tell me," she said.

"Well, it started back when our parents were juniors, and Mama was dating this other guy on the basketball team. Nate, I think she said his name was. Anyway, she said he was really good-looking."

Maggie was enthralled now. She leaned forward as I told her the rest of the story. When I finished, her face relaxed as she leaned back into her pillows. "I wish she had told you about my mother."

"Me too. But we'll get it out of her now that I got her started. We just have to get her talking again."

"What do you suppose she was thinking?"

"Mama?" I asked.

"No. My mother. I wish I knew that end of the story. If Daddy was still in love with your mother, how did he end up getting my mother pregnant so soon after that? I was born the same year you said your parents were married. That's what I keep thinking over."

"Why?"

"Because I'm sure my mother didn't know my daddy very long. Besides commitment and all the rest, didn't she worry about venereal diseases? Didn't she even stop to think of who else he may have been with? Was she that clueless?"

"That's your daddy you're talking about."

"Duh. I know that. But if he slept with her . . ."

"You mean you think your daddy slept around?"

"I don't know. I'm sure not going to ask him. That's not the point."

"Then what is?"

"That she must not have considered his past or the consequences before they did it. I mean, would they have gotten married if she hadn't gotten pregnant? What would have happened if I hadn't come along? What if he had been with a bunch of other girls and she'd gotten some horrible disease?"

I know it sounds like Maggie had some serious hang-ups about sex, but she also had a point of truth. The giddiness of having the scoop on the story passed away and fell to a knot in my stomach. I hadn't even considered that possibility. What if Vince had some disease? Like, do most girls ask? I'd been so caught up in the moment, I hadn't thought about it. I hadn't even considered that he'd probably been with other girls. For some reason I had assumed I was his one and only girl—but what if I was wrong?

I hated that Maggie had taken all the good feelings I had about me and Vince, and Mama and Frank, and turned my stomach sour. "You think too much."

She groaned. "Come off it. You have to think of that stuff."

"You don't understand. I mean, she was probably just caught up in the moment. Not everyone walks around thinking all the time like you."

"What? You think Webb and I haven't wanted to? We've been dating two years. We're not angels, you know."

"So, like, has Webb been with other girls and you're afraid of catching something from him?"

She sighed. "Not hardly. We just know we want to wait. It's what God expects of us, and we're both dedicated to following our faith because in the long run it makes our commitment stronger and, eventually, our marriage stronger."

"The girl with the plan. That's you, Mags."

"You have to have a plan or life gets away from you."

"What?"

"Like my mother. She didn't have a plan. She lived life as it came at her, and look how she ended up. Pregnant with me at sixteen and dead at twenty."

At that moment, I understood Maggie better than I ever had before. Maybe I should have put it together before then, but I guess I was too self-absorbed to see it: Maggie had to have a plan because her mother hadn't. She saw her mother as a foolish child with no thought to the future, and she blamed Mallory for leaving her to act as mother to her brothers. She didn't want to make the same mistakes her mother had made.

And Maggie had deep faith in God. I was head of my church youth group and believed in God too. Why didn't I apply all I had learned the way she did? Was it a difference in our churches? Or was it something different in us, in the way we saw the world and kept our faith? Nothing swayed her from following the commandments and applying her faith to everyday life. Why did I find it so hard to do that?

She was, I don't know, more real about what she believed, had it all in her heart, and not just in her head and spouting out of her mouth. None of it was for show. It was for real.

I wondered what God thought. Was I too far offtrack to get back to what was preached at those youth groups I cherished so much? Could I say no to Vince the next time he made an advance, or was it too late now? Did it even matter if I stepped back and tried to start over, or was my soul stained forever?

Go, and sin no more. That's what Jesus said to the adulteress He saved from being stoned. I could be washed clean and start over. The idea filled me with hope and the will to think through everything with more clarity and more devotion to becoming the girl I was meant to be.

Maggie plucked at her monkey pillow. "I wonder if she even thought about getting pregnant when she slept with Daddy."

I shook my head. "Probably not." I sure hadn't. I was too carried away with emotions and . . . well, you know. All those feelings pouring through me. But I wouldn't say that to Maggie.

"She should have. How can a girl not think about that?"

I shrugged as if I didn't care, but my insides were churning. I had been as clueless as her mother. I was so wrapped up in Vince and me having some kind of relationship that I hadn't thought about any of those things—not diseases or pregnancy or God. Well, I had thought about God, but I figured I was the exception. As long as we were in love and were committed to each other, God would forgive us, wouldn't He? He would know it was as good as making a vow of marriage. And that's what it was to me. But now I wasn't so sure that God would see things my way. It was something to think about.

Maggie's deep thoughts had worn me down. I didn't want to talk about any of it anymore. I slipped off the bed and headed to the bathroom for a shower.

Nevertheless, as the water poured over me, everything Mama and Maggie had said came back to me. I kept thinking about how Mama and Frank had lost touch while she was away at college, and she'd ended up marrying my daddy instead. That couldn't happen to me and Vince, could it? Maggie and I had both been accepted to Clemson; we'd applied together back in the fall when Mama and I first moved in, and we'd celebrated our acceptance together. We had even talked of sharing a dorm room. But how would Vince fit into those plans? There was nothing in life I wanted more than him.

Maggie's warnings kept running through my mind and made me ponder the whole sex thing more objectively—without Vince there, without Maggie staring me in the face. Could I have some horrible disease I'd have to live with the rest of my life? I tried to remember the symptoms they'd taught us in health class.

But pregnant? That one didn't worry me a bit. We'd only done it a couple times. Nothing to worry about.

Mama kept me at her side all weekend, but it didn't make me any happier to see the end of it. I dreaded Mondays. I guess, given my standing in school—being popular, making good grades, running the art club, and helping with the yearbook—I should have been one of those kids who loved school. Sometimes I did, but mostly on Fridays. I hated getting up, rushing to get ready, and sitting through all those classes. The good thing was there were only eight Mondays left in school, and that particular Monday was cap-and-gown-picture day, which put us one step closer to graduation.

I kept thinking of Mama fussing about Vince kissing me in public. I was ready to get away from high school so I would be treated like an adult and not like a little kid incapable of making my own decisions. College would be different. I would be on my own. I could do what I wanted to with whomever I wanted. And I could choose my classes and the hours. If I didn't attend class, no one was going to send me to the principal's office.

I was tempted to stay home. I'd eaten a ton of cookies and junk all weekend since I was trapped at home and felt sick as a dog, but I figured Mama would say I was lying because of getting in trouble with Vince. It was easier to go and sleep through class than go through another round with her.

I groaned when I saw Heather headed my way full of smiles that morning. She loved school every day. She floated down the hall toward me like she was on a modeling runway, her hand raised in greeting. "Dixie!" she yelled, then she stopped suddenly about ten feet away, stooped down to pick up a quarter, and slid it into her money pouch. She'd been collecting money from people for months now, at school, at the mall, at games—anywhere she saw someone jingling change. I wondered how much she'd collected. She still hadn't told me what it was for.

She rushed forward and gave me a hug. "Dixie, I got your voice mail; why on earth were you grounded? I've been dying to talk to you."

That subject added to my Monday morning attitude. "Mama

went berserk over Vince's kissing me."

Heather might have been sincere in saying she wanted to talk, but I wasn't so sure she really cared why I was grounded. She pulled out her compact while I was talking and touched up her makeup.

"I wondered if that was it. Like your mama didn't know you and Vince kissed? How lame is that?" She pulled at a stray hair and tried to force it into place. "Wouldn't you know I would have a bad hair day when we're getting pictures made?"

I didn't bother replying. She looked perfect and knew it. And she really didn't care why I was grounded other than the fact that it had messed up our plans to shop for prom dresses. Not that I had an official date to the prom. I hadn't mentioned it to Vince again; I wasn't going to push the issue. I didn't want him thinking of me as some pouting little high school girl.

I opened my locker and fished out my physics textbook and binder. "So what did you want to tell me? You found a dress?"

"No. No dress." She snapped the compact closed, and her face came to life. "But wait till you hear! It's so fab! Ariana talked to her talent agent about me, and I'm going to see him on Wednesday. I am so psyched."

Heather shone with excitement. She saw herself walking down runways and making it into movies. She definitely had the face and body for it, but it seemed like an impossible dream to me, though I didn't say so. I was just glad Ariana was helping her. It confirmed my feelings about Ariana being a caring person and trustworthy friend. "That's cool, Heather. Sounds like you're on your way."

I had to dash off to class, but when I joined her and Tammy at lunch, she was still talking about it. Tammy was just as enthused.

"You will *so* make it. You'll be in a movie by this time next year."

Heather ran her fingers through her hair. "I can't wait." She pushed her lunch away and grabbed my arm before I could sit down. "Come with me to the restroom."

Tammy harrumphed. "You're going to leave me here alone?"

"Amber is coming," Heather replied, pointing to a new girl who'd been trying to work her way into our little group bit by bit. I'd noticed her talking with Tammy in the hall a few times between classes and was surprised Tammy tolerated her. She didn't usually allow anyone else to hang out with us, but I had to admit that Amber fit in. She walked with the grace of a ballerina, lithe and poised, her auburn hair often coiled into some fancy hairdo. She held herself just so, even when she stopped to chat. It's like she had natural airs that the three of us had to work at to achieve. Who else *would* she hang around with at school but us?

I left my lunch sitting on the table and followed Heather. I had no appetite anyway, and I had to pee too.

A couple minutes later, I heard Heather cussing in her stall.

"What's wrong?"

"I started. Darn. Three days early and right before my big interview with the talent guy. How miserable is that?"

I stifled a laugh. "I don't think he'll notice if you don't tell him."

"But what if he wants me to model a bathing suit or something?"

"Heather, you are such a crack-up. Like you've never worn a bathing suit during your period?"

She came out frowning. "You know. It's just . . . icky. What rotten luck."

I thought about my discussion with Maggie and pulled out

my little pocket calendar. At first I just glanced at it, thinking about having to plan around my own period, but as I counted the days, my heart began pounding, and I almost lost it right there in the bathroom. I was three days late.

How could that be? I couldn't be pregnant. I just couldn't be!

Chapter Thirteen

AFTER SCHOOL I dropped Maggie, Webb, Tony, and Billy off at home, then headed to the drug store. I couldn't possibly be pregnant, but I had to know for sure. I pulled into First Street Pharmacy's parking lot, then realized I was bound to see someone I knew inside, especially since Webb worked there, so I drove almost to Vince's trailer on the outskirts of Columbia before I stopped to buy a pregnancy test—where no one would recognize me.

I thought about taking it to Vince's house to do but changed my mind. It's hard to explain why. A part of me didn't want to take a pregnancy test right there in Vince's trailer. I didn't want him to catch me doing it, in case it was negative and there was nothing to worry about. It seemed silly to get him all worked up for nothing. There was another reason though. Something about being at home made me feel safe. Nothing bad could happen to me there. I felt protected from the world.

I decided I couldn't do the test during the day. Someone was bound to come banging on the bathroom door. So I called Vince on my cell phone and told him I wouldn't be at the practice that evening. I just knew I couldn't sit there with this hanging on my mind. I'd go crazy.

Vince didn't seem too bothered when I told him. "That's cool, babe," he said. "I got stuff to do tonight anyway."

I wished he'd said he couldn't go a night without seeing me and that I absolutely had to go by his trailer for at least a while, but I guess that would have been expecting too much.

I felt funny walking into the house knowing I had a pregnancy test stashed in my pocketbook. I walked in and said hello as if nothing was out of the ordinary, as if Mama hadn't been screaming at me over Vince just two nights earlier. Now I was waiting to see if I was having his baby.

Mama was stretched out on the sofa reading a magazine. "Where have you been? Everyone else was home an hour ago."

Obviously she hadn't gotten over the need to watch my every move. I could have thrown it in her face that I wasn't grounded anymore, but that would have caused more ill feelings. Instead, I smiled sweetly so she wouldn't suspect anything. "Heather wanted me to see her prom dress." I knew she would swallow that since we were supposed to have shopped together.

Mama started to say something in response but stopped. I guess she felt guilty for not letting me shop. Instead she just turned back to her magazine and said, "There are some cookies on the counter if you're hungry."

The smell of the cookies wafted through the air, enticing me to have at least a few, even if my waistline didn't need them. I dropped my big floppy pocketbook down on the floor, the pregnancy test hidden in its depths, and grabbed three cookies and a glass of milk. I sat down on the sofa beside Mama with my feet kicked up on the old chest that served as a coffee table, a remnant of Andrea, the woman Frank was dating before he married Mama. Maggie and I couldn't stand that lady, and we'd used Mama as a decoy to get rid of her, never suspecting the two of them would end up getting married. If I'd been Mama, I would have tossed the chest out, but she laughed when I told her so. She said she liked its rustic charm and didn't have any worries about it creating any lingering memories about Andrea in Frank's mind, at least none that would be a threat to her.

Mama reached out and laid her hand on my leg for a moment, a light squeeze and pat, then went back to reading with a quizzical smile playing across her face. I'm sure I had her wondering why I was hanging out with her, but she didn't ask and I didn't say.

I sat there with her for about half an hour. It was nice just being beside her, thinking of how we used to sit up at night watching spooky movies together, or having our deep mother/daughter talks over hot cups of tea and doughnuts at the kitchen table in our old house. I missed those days. She and I were best buddies back then. I was more than her daughter; I was her confidante. Now she had Frank to talk to. And Maggie. The two of them had become increasingly close as I became more distant. It didn't seem fair.

After a while, I headed up the stairs to see if Maggie was in the bedroom.

Maggie had her head in her physics book, as usual, but came to at the sight of me. "You're home!"

"So?"

"Still grounded?"

"No."

"Did you have a fight with Vince or something?"

"No. I just wanted to be home tonight. Is that okay?"

"Fine by me," she said and went back to her book, then glanced up once more. "If you need to talk, say so."

"No problem," I replied and flopped on my bed with a magazine. I could have joined her in studying physics, but in light of what I was facing, physics didn't seem all that important anymore.

Maggie made big sighing noises, like I was making too much noise turning the pages of my magazine, but I ignored her. It was my room too, and I was sick of her acting like she was queen of my world.

I tried to think of unimportant stuff—like the prom dresses on the glossy pages and the Hollywood gossip about teen stars—but Maggie's picture of Jesus on the wall kept staring at me, and I forgot about the article I was reading and prayed instead. Something felt oddly wrong about praying to not be pregnant, but I did it anyway—like if there was some chance I was pregnant, maybe God could give the baby to somebody else out there that was praying to have a child. Weren't there, like, millions of couples wanting babies? If God is capable of anything, I figured He could zap a few cells from my body into somebody else's. I really didn't care how He did it; I just prayed that the test would come out negative.

I was determined to wait until the wee hours, until I was sure everyone was asleep, before doing the pregnancy test.

I must have dozed off for a while, but wild dreams woke me at two. The room was dark except for the streak of light coming from the streetlight. No moon, no stars. Menacing clouds hung heavily across the sky with the promise of a bad storm brewing. How appropriate.

Maggie was making guttural noises, almost a snore, but not quite. She'd been like that since she was a kid. I hardly noticed it anymore, but if I listened closely and heard that wheezing, I knew she was out cold.

I slipped from my bed and headed for the dresser, to my floppy pocketbook. I'd taken the pregnancy test out of the crackly plastic bag so I wouldn't have to worry about making noise. The box slid out from between my wallet and a handful of tissues with barely a whisper of the cardboard against material. I slid it up under my nightshirt, then after a glance at Maggie, tiptoed to the bathroom and closed the door before feeling around in the dark for the light switch. I wasn't taking a chance of even a small beam of light waking someone up.

I sat on the toilet and pulled the plastic stick out of the box and stared at it, the magic genie ready to tell my fortune. I didn't really have to read the instructions—it was pretty common sense—but I read them anyway because I didn't want to do something wrong and mess up the results. It wasn't rocket science, though. I held it down in front of me and peed on it for the required five seconds, then waited for the results.

It could have taken longer. It could have dragged the results out slowly so I could have gotten used to it as the lines came up in the screen, but it didn't. It changed so fast, my first thought was that it was negative, just like I knew it would be, but I did a double take and looked again. Positive. Positive! I was pregnant. I was pregnant. I was *pregnant*! I stared at the stick and felt like I was going to vomit. What was I going to do? How could this have happened to me? Things like this didn't happen in my life. I was a good person, a good student, a good daughter. I attended church, and I helped little old ladies cross the road. I was going to graduate from high school and go to college. I couldn't be pregnant!

I wrapped the test stick in toilet tissue about twenty times, then shoved it down the side of the trash where no one would see, and washed my hands for ten straight minutes before slumping back across the hall to bed.

I didn't sleep much that night. All I could think about was how I was going to tell Vince and what changes it was going to bring to my life. I couldn't really go as far as envisioning a baby. It didn't really mean a baby to me right then; it just meant bad news, being pregnant, walking around with this huge belly and everyone looking at me, and having to tell my mother and my friends.

I had bags under my eyes by morning. My face stared back at me from the mirror like some ghostly waif in a horror movie, like I had been running from demons all night.

Maggie noticed. "What's wrong? You don't look well."

"I don't feel so hot."

Her face took on that motherly look that folded her eyebrows together. "Did you take something last night?"

"Huh?"

"You got up in the middle of the night, and when you came back to bed you were as restless as a caged cat."

I flopped on the bed. "No I didn't take anything. I just had nightmares that wouldn't go away."

Maggie nodded. She understood nightmares. She'd had a lot of them in the past, bad things that had happened to her and wouldn't leave her head, and the dreams wore her into the ground. Maybe this was going to be the same for me, but it wasn't something I could just get over, like what happened to her.

She stood by the dresser watching me, concern written all over her, as if she knew how bad things could get and how it could eat up your brain from the inside. Maybe she hadn't gotten over all she'd been through. Still, it wasn't the same as being pregnant and knowing an entire life was going off course.

I stayed in a daze most of the day. I made a C on the physics quiz because I couldn't concentrate . . . and hadn't studied. Heather kept poking me during lunch because I wasn't responding to her inane questions about her hair and makeup. How had either seemed important last week? And Maggie kept looking at me with that *something's wrong* squint of her eyes during English class. I was relieved to see Webb hurrying her down the hall after class so she wouldn't start with the twenty questions again.

Meanwhile, I was desperately trying to formulate the right words to tell Vince, and to imagine his reaction.

I had every intention of telling him that night. I figured after the band had finished practicing, we'd go back to his place for a while, and when things heated up, I'd slip him the news, like a whisper of what our love had created. It would be romantic, something to remember. Unfortunately, things didn't go as planned.

Tony and I arrived at Mike's garage to a heated argument between Ariana and Vince. You wouldn't know it to look at the rest of the band. Judy had her nose in a book the same as usual, and Mike was busying himself with equipment, but Ariana was right in Vince's face, spitting words at him. "This is the first time I've asked for a blasted weekend off for a photo shoot, and you think you can replace me?"

"Pamela is good. She fits our sound."

"She's going to fit the end of my fist if I see her on my way out," Ariana screamed.

I followed her outside. Her eyes were throwing such heated sparks they could have melted steel. "He listens to some girl's CD and decides she's a *better fit* than me? I can't believe it. Who does he think he is? I've gotten gigs for this band in some of the best clubs around here. Let's see her do that."

"Pamela?"

"You know her? I have a photo shoot in Atlanta, one I've already agreed to do, and Vince thinks I should give it up for this freebie gig. I'm not about to give up a good-paying modeling job for that."

Pamela? He was going to replace Ariana with that wannabe? Her face swam before me and made me feel sick. "When did he decide to replace you with her?"

"Just now. But you know what? I think he's been waiting for an excuse. He was just too quick on the draw."

I wish I had listened to her demo with Vince. I couldn't imagine anyone better suited to the group than Ariana. She was beautiful *and* talented. She drew guys to the stands without even trying. "That's unbelievable!"

I still didn't know Ariana very well, but I knew her well enough to know she wouldn't cool down any time soon; if Vince didn't change his mind pretty quick, he'd never get her back.

"Look at what he's got," she continued. "Judy, who is half dead. Mike, who is about as personable as a stuffed scarecrow, Josh, who is stiff as a statue, and Tony, who . . ." she bit back whatever comment she had planned for Tony. "Well, at least Tony is a nice guy, even if he is a bit shy."

I didn't want Ariana to leave the band. She wasn't exactly a bosom buddy or anything, but I liked her. I liked being around her. She had a certain air of authority and purposefulness that I admired — somewhat like Maggie had, but different. Maggie had the ability to get things organized and done. Ariana was more of a commander; she expected things to be done and people just did them. She had charisma, not in the sense of being popular like Heather and Tammy, but of being self-assured, confident, and ready to face life. I guess that's what I lacked. I hadn't even been able to choose a college without Maggie's input. I ended up applying to the same one as her because I figured she knew best. Same thing. I could follow Ariana. She didn't seem like she had any big game plan worked out, yet she knew where she was going.

"So what are you going to do?" I asked.

"Leave him to his fate. Pamela is hopeless. No talent."

"The band will be lost without you. You have to stay and make him see that."

"Why don't you talk to him?" She eyed me up and down. "You're the one with the leverage."

Leverage — that's how she summed up my relationship with Vince.

She added, "At least for right now."

"What do you mean by that?"

She rolled her eyes. "Guys like him don't stick with anyone for long."

Guys like him? She didn't know Vince like I did. How could she say such a thing? He was kind and caring. He was deeply committed to our relationship. "He'll stick with me. Just watch."

She laughed. "Sure. Go test a bit of that commitment by asking him to keep me in the band and see what he says."

Pride swelled up in me till it threatened to strangle my lungs. "I will."

I strode back into the garage where the guys were still tuning instruments. Vince and Tony were standing close together, muttering something between them, but that only made me hesitate a second. I was sure enough of my position at Vince's side that I could interrupt and speak my mind to him. I sidled up between them with my back to Tony. "Hon, you need to think twice about letting Ariana go. She's fantastic. She draws a great crowd."

He concentrated on the string he was tuning. "I already struck a deal with Pamela. Move. You're in the light."

I stepped to the side. "If Ariana leaves, she won't come back."

"And that's a problem?"

"Yes!"

He looked up, his expression saying volumes more than his words. "It's my band."

I took a step backward and bumped into Tony.

"Oh snap! Watch what you're doing, Dixie."

I turned, ran back outside, and slumped against the side of the house where the sun warmed the bricks and bounced off the sidewalk in a reassuring glare of brightness.

Ariana watched with one hand to her hip. "That's what I thought." She climbed into her car and spun wheels as she sped out of Mike's driveway.

I closed my eyes and breathed slowly.

Everything would be all right. It had to be.

Chapter Fourteen

I LISTENED TO the band practice, to Vince's voice echo in the garage as the guitars and drums rattled the shovels and rakes. I wondered when Pamela would show up for practice. She never did.

When they finished, one by one strolling out to their cars and pulling out of the driveway, I was tempted to climb in with Tony and return home with him, but I had to face Vince and tell him the news, even if it meant getting home late and getting another lecture from Mama. I couldn't go home with the news of my pregnancy weighing me down and spend the night thinking about Vince's obvious annoyance when I interfered about Ariana. I had to reconnect to him, to reassure myself that we were as united as I thought.

He was the last one out. He paused in the driveway and glanced around looking for me.

I waved an arm. "Here I am. Ready to go?"

"Yep." He pulled me to my feet and laid a kiss on me. My ill feelings melted away under his touch. It was his band. I had no right to interfere. What he did with the band had nothing to do with our relationship. I leaned into his chest, returning the kiss with vigor.

His eyes twinkled as he stepped toward the car. "Missed you last night."

That's what I wanted to hear. I knew exactly what he wanted, and all my thoughts of stepping back, of rethinking my commitment to God and the commandment, disappeared. After all, I was already pregnant. If we were going to get married and have a baby, wasn't that a bond between us whether or not we'd taken a vow of marriage in a church?

Back at the trailer, we lay side by side in the quiet, his breath running even with mine. A dozen emotions tugged at my heart: love for Vince, fear of the future, indecision. . . .

I knew the time was right to tell him. Everything was so right and peaceful between us, like a good omen for how things could be. I formulated the words in my head, words I had arranged and rearranged during school that day, built up with romance and cut down to bare bones, and rewritten with all the sensitivity and uncertainty I felt. I lay there counting the little pinprick holes in the tile ceiling, thinking it shouldn't be this hard, that I ought to just blurt it out. But I didn't want to disturb the moment or shift the mood between us.

Still, it had to be done.

I took a deep breath and opened my mouth to tell him — the words were there ready to pour out — but a wave of nausea raced over me and sent me flying to the bathroom. Morning sickness at nine at night.

I rushed from the bed to the bathroom with my hand over my mouth and slammed the door behind me just in time to vomit into the toilet.

"Are you okay?" Vince hollered.

I was still gagging and spitting, but I cleared my mouth out and wiped it off with tissue. "I guess," I moaned.

"Are you sick?"

I wasn't about to tell him right then, not with my head in the toilet and vomit on my tongue. Maybe it would have been easier, more realistic to face it right then, but I couldn't do it. I wanted everything perfect when I told him. So I lied. "It's probably food poisoning from the pizza at school today," I hollered from behind the closed door.

His voice was faint from the bed, but loud enough to distinguish his concern for himself. "That's good. I don't need to wind up with some bug right now. We've got too many gigs lined up."

I rinsed my mouth and brushed my teeth with a washcloth, but my stomach still felt queasy, like I would barf again any minute. I stared at my pale face in the mirror. "Crackers," I muttered. "They always talk about crackers for morning sickness."

Vince was sitting on the edge of the bed putting on his shoes.

"Where are you going?" I asked.

"Out. I have a meeting."

I should have known right then something was up. "A meeting at nine o'clock at night? Who has a meeting that late?"

"I do."

I didn't believe him. I thought he was grossed out by my vomit. "You didn't have one five minutes ago."

"I didn't realize what time it was."

I ambled out to the kitchen and searched his lone food cabinet for some crackers.

"Are you staying?" he asked.

That made my mouth drop open. He wanted me to leave. Didn't he trust me there without him? But then I thought maybe he wanted me with him. "Do you want me to come?"

"No. I just figured you'd be leaving when I did."

I looked suspiciously at the single graham cracker in the open cellophane on the shelf. What were the chances a mouse or roach had taken a turn at it? I fondled the wrapper in my hand and stared at Vince's calm expression. I couldn't read what he was thinking. "I have to get dressed. Go on if you're in a rush."

He nodded. "Okay. Well, I'll see you later."

"When will that be?"

He shrugged. "Tomorrow? I have no idea." Then as an afterthought he added, "You don't look so good anyway."

I really needed that kind of confirmation. "I don't feel so hot either."

He didn't kiss me, not that I blamed him. I'm sure hearing someone puke is a real turnoff, but he could have kissed me on the cheek or something.

The trailer was quiet after he left. I crackled the cellophane in my fingers and thought about eating the cracker, but it just wasn't what I wanted, so I slipped on my jeans and shoes, pulled my hair into a ponytail, and headed home. I'd already stayed out too late for a weeknight, and Mama would be full of questions again. I didn't care. The important thing was Mama would have food, and that was all I could think of at the moment.

Chapter Fifteen

I REALLY DIDN'T want to go to school the next day. I'd spent the night tossing and turning, thinking about being pregnant, about how I was going to tell Vince, and what we were going to do. The few times I did fall asleep, I dreamed about Pamela pushing Ariana off the stage so she could sing in the band. Ariana landed on her bottom, cussing up a storm, but Pamela didn't care a bit. She grinned and bellowed into the microphone. I woke up wanting to punch Pamela.

To make things worse, the first pair of jeans I put on almost cut me in two, like some proof that I was definitely pregnant. I felt miserable. Then I remembered that I often got bloated just before my period, so in my head I kept telling myself it was all a false alarm and I would start while I was at school.

Mama had fixed chocolate chip muffins for breakfast. I could smell them all the way upstairs. I ran a brush through my hair and dashed down the stairs in my nightgown before Tony and Billy devoured them all. Mama had already served Cindy the first of the muffins. She sat there primly peeling back the paper and taking tiny nibbles at it. I snatched up two and stood at the counter to wolf them down before the boys showed up—Billy fully dressed and ready to go, Tony dressed but looking like he'd picked his clothes out in his sleep the way his buttons were done up all crooked and mismatched. His hair was plastered to his head, and his eyes were barely open.

I left them eating and went back upstairs where my stomach heaved and threw up everything I'd eaten. Thank goodness Tony and Billy were still in the kitchen and Maggie had already left with Webb for some early morning club meeting, so no one heard me gagging into the toilet.

With a heavy heart, I brushed my teeth, got dressed, and trudged down the steps to slump by the front door and stare into space, wondering what I was going to do.

Billy and Tony finally showed up, ready to leave for school, but I didn't move till Billy shoved me with the toe of his tennis shoe. "Come on. We gotta go."

Tony pulled me to my feet, and off we went, none of us too exuberant. Even in my self-absorbed mood, I could tell something was eating at Tony too. I just hoped it didn't have anything to do with me. I had enough on my plate.

Halfway to school, I asked him. "So what's up? Something bothering you?"

He pulled his book bag into his lap and searched for something. "No, nothing."

I could have pushed a bit harder and probably got something out of him, but I let it drop. At least I had asked.

I met up with Tammy and Heather in the parking lot, where they were talking to Amber. Tammy had on this coconut lip gloss that I thought was going to make me puke again. It was like I could suddenly smell a hundred times better than usual. I noticed the exhaust in the air, the smell of cigarettes just outside the school doors, and the horrible odor of boys' tennis shoes in the hallway. Everything made me feel queasy.

I forced myself to put on a smile and act all bouncy. The last thing I wanted was Heather and Tammy prying into what was wrong with me. Not yet, anyway. Maybe that was strange. Maybe they were the first ones I should have cried to, but even though they were my best friends, they weren't kindred spirits like I used to be with Maggie. We never talked about anything of importance. I'd learned that whatever I shared with them was likely to leak out to someone else by the end of the day. They couldn't keep a secret for anything.

Tammy didn't quite buy my perkiness. "What are all the smiles for?" she asked.

I kept the smile plastered to my face. "Graduation isn't far off. The prom is in a few weeks, and it's a beautiful day. Finally getting warm. I guess I just have spring fever."

Heather, so easily distracted, took the bait. "Oh, you're so right. I have spring fever, too. We ought to skip school and go to the park."

I would have agreed with her except I'd already been slack lately, and my grades were starting to suffer. The last thing I needed was to fail something on top of everything else I had to deal with.

Tammy saved me from playing the bad guy. "Don't you even think about it, Heather. We are weeks from graduation. Weeks! You want to risk getting suspended?"

"Don't be silly, Tammy. Graduation is still two whole months away. That's like forever. And since we're seniors, we're like *obligated* to play hooky and stuff. We could go to the mall, y'all, and spend the entire day shopping. I heard about this sale from Miss Willis—"

I cut her off. "Let's wait to skip when it's bathing-suit weather and we can get a tan." I shoved away the thought of how I'd look in a bikini with a pregnant stomach.

"I can't tan anymore, you silly," Heather whined. "Sun can age a person's skin. You see, I was watching this show on TV the other night, and this man, I can't rightly remember his name, but he showed these pictures of the effect of the sun on skin cells, and, well, I don't think I can *ever* lay out in the sun again without thinking about what it's doing to me."

You couldn't ever count on Heather's being consistent. Just last year she had lived for sunbathing.

Tammy stopped in her tracks. "Prom dresses . . . oh, I almost forgot . . . we're voting for prom queen today!"

That was enough to make them both rush through the school doors.

Mama seemed to have a sixth sense that told her I was still seeing Vince. I shouldn't have gotten home so late on a school night the night before. It had her wary, keeping a close eye on me, and I was afraid if I lied and said I was going to Heather's house that she would catch me. Besides, I had youth group on Wednesdays and so much homework to do, including a research paper I'd been putting off, that I really needed to stay home. I told myself that was the reason, but really, I was sick to my stomach over having to tell Vince the news. I kept hoping my period would start so there wouldn't be anything wrong, nothing to worry about. So as much as I wanted to see Vince, to get him alone and tell him, I didn't get to that night, or Thursday.

On Friday I had to babysit the Johnson twins, something I'd promised to do weeks earlier and couldn't get out of; besides, I was flat broke and really needed the money, so I put off telling Vince one more night.

The two five-year-old Johnson boys would have tried the patience of someone like Maggie who liked things quiet and in control, but they were great fun to me. I kept them playing the wildest games I could imagine, which kept them from coming up with something worse on their own, like they had the first few times I sat with them — typical boy things like frogs in my coat pocket, batteries out of the remote, hiding out till I got in a panic, or pretending to be injured . . . you name it. No one else would take care of them, and because of that and the fact that the boys actually liked me, I got paid dearly. Mrs. Johnson relished her nights out alone with her husband. In fact, thanks to me and those nights alone, they actually had another baby on the way, which created an even stronger desire to hire me so they could go out as often as possible before child number three made her appearance.

The twins weren't identical, or they probably would have come up with even more mischievous acts. Daniel was thin to the point of being bony, with a sharp chin and beady eyes. If he'd had dark hair instead of his light sandy mop, he would have looked evil. His twin, Marshall, had his father's round face and pug nose, but was saved by his mother's big blue eyes, which often caused me to believe him when he was knee-deep in a fat lie.

After a game of pirates, in which I was tied up and had to escape, followed by supper, half of which landed on the floor during a food fight, I resorted to plugging in a video game of Tony's I'd snuck from his room. Instant silence.

I stretched out on the sofa where I could keep an eye on them and called Heather on her cell phone. I could tell from the background noise that she and Tammy were at some party. They hadn't even mentioned it to me.

"You've been with Vince every Friday lately, so we assumed you would be with him tonight," she said.

"Well, I'm not. I'm babysitting. I told you I was."

I could hear the impatience in her voice. "Either way you couldn't come with us, so what's the big deal?"

"It's not," I replied, "except I was thinking I could meet y'all after I get off here. The Johnsons won't be out very late. Mrs. Johnson gets tired around ten-thirty. She only stays out long enough for me to have the boys fed and in bed so she doesn't have to deal with it."

"So come join us."

By us, she didn't mean just her and Tammy. I could hear Amber in the background. They were probably celebrating Tammy's getting prom queen. Not that they knew for sure. It wouldn't be announced until the prom. But the word in the school halls had been that Tammy had won by a long stretch. I wondered whether Tammy would have been able to handle losing if Heather had won. She didn't like to be less than number one, but Heather didn't seem to have a problem bowing down to Tammy. And now Amber had joined the clique. I wondered where she fit in. Maybe she would take my place. Maybe they didn't care much about having me around anymore. Truth was I really didn't care about joining them. I just wanted to gab on the phone to waste time. What I intended was to go straight to Vince's trailer when I got off. Normally a performance might run till one in the morning, but tonight's gig was a class reunion, and they were contracted until eleven—which sounded awfully lame to me, but all the better. It meant he wouldn't be worn out and we could have some time together. I wasn't about to tell Heather my plans, though, or I would aggravate her even more. "Sure, maybe I'll get over there. Give me the address."

As she rattled it off, I wrote it in the air, never to be used.

Mr. and Mrs. Johnson didn't get home until almost twelve. I'd tucked the boys into bed hours earlier and put them to sleep with a story I made up about a dinosaur coming through a time machine and landing in their closet. With threats of letting him out to get at them, they stayed in bed and gradually fell asleep to the drone of the story unwinding. As I watched their sleeping figures, I thought about what it might be like to have a son, a mischievous little boy like one of the twins, full of pranks and precious moments. Maybe he would look like a small version of Vince with sandy hair, a bony little kid full of energy. He might stand in front of me in a tiny pair of blue jeans, his feet spread apart, and his thumb hooked in his back pocket just like his daddy.

I shook the thought away. I didn't want to go there yet. I didn't want to think about really having a baby. There were still too many confusing thoughts in my head.

Tony had dropped me off on his way to the performance, so Mr. Johnson took me home in his car. Our Nissan was back in the driveway, and the house was silent. Apparently Tony had gotten home and gone straight to bed along with everyone else. The only light on was the reading lamp in the corner of the family room.

I grabbed the keys off the hook in the kitchen and headed

back out the door hoping Mama didn't hear me getting dropped off or the door opening and closing. I eased out of the driveway, letting the car roll down the slight slope, then puttered off into the night.

Normally I would have gone from whatever show the band was doing or from Mike's house to Vince's trailer. This was the first time I'd driven straight from home without Vince taking me, and in the dark of night with the roads empty and the streetlights shining dim circles here and there, the way seemed much farther. I passed very few cars, and those I did seemed more ominous in the dark, filled with strangers that might seek to harm me. Every light had me tapping the wheel impatiently until I turned on the radio to ward off the silence. I hadn't ever really considered that he lived on the far side of Columbia, which is why no one in town knew who he was. Despite the apprehension, I drove onward, slowing as I reached his trailer park, searching in the dark for where the entrance met the road, and carefully turned in. As the wheels crunched on the gravel, the three dogs leapt to their feet and let out warning barks, the two Lab mutts tied to posts for the night and the black mutt Vince had called Devil growling in the dark. He looked more suited to guarding a junkyard than being a family pet. His short hair rose across his back in warning at the mere sight of an intruder during the day, let alone one arriving at night. He knew Vince, but not me.

I pulled in beside Vince's trailer and stepped out of my car, keeping one eye on the dog as I sidled up the steps to the porch. There was only one light on inside, but I wasn't about to wait for Vince to let me in. I pulled the spare key out of hiding and slipped in the door. The main room was dark except for the light shining from the clock on the microwave, but I knew the layout well enough that I skirted around the dark shadows of furniture to the bedroom beyond, my heart still beating with terror, and my head filled with the idea of telling Vince I'd risked death to see him.

As usual, the bathroom light was on; Vince never turned it off, and it filled the bedroom with a yellow glow, not enough to startle the eyes, but enough to see faces and bodies, and limbs entwined as we loved each other.

I turned to the bed.

At first I didn't trust my eyes. What I was seeing couldn't be true. Vince was sprawled across one side of the bed with his arm cast over the bare shoulders of a thin blonde. Pamela!

I was in such shock, I don't know if I screamed or stood there in silence, but somehow in the long minute that followed, the two of them came awake, Vince sitting up and her pulling the sheet over her naked breasts as she rolled over and blinked into wakefulness.

Vince squinted in the dim light. "What are you doing here?" His voice sneered with accusation, as if I were the one doing something wrong.

"Since when do I need an invitation?"

"You said you had to babysit."

"So that gives you the right to let some whore into your bed?"

Pamela gasped. "Who are you calling a whore?"

"He's my boyfriend. I told you that, you slut."

Vince pulled on a pair of boxers and took a step toward me. "Come on, Dixie . . ."

"Come on, what? Join the two of you in bed? Get a life."

I turned away and headed to the door.

"But Dixie . . ."

I didn't want to hear what he had to say. I stormed out of the house, stunned. As the dog approached again, baring his teeth, I cussed at him and kept going; all fear had been replaced with anger so strong I felt like I could have shot them both and the dog as well.

Halfway home tears set in, pouring down my face with such force I had to pull over because I couldn't see.

Chapter Sixteen

I COULDN'T QUIT thinking of Vince all the next day. Tony was elated because they didn't have a Saturday performance. He said there was something going on at church that he had to attend, which really surprised me since Tony wasn't big on church that I knew of. I pretty much figured Frank forced him to go most Sundays. But whatever. I wasn't into knowing what Tony was doing. And I didn't care one way or the other about the band's practices or performances anymore. I had no intention of seeking out Vince. I figured it was his place to make a move, to come begging forgiveness about being with Pamela.

But at the same time, I was in knots over what to do. I had to tell him about being pregnant.

I couldn't sit in my bedroom thinking about it anymore. I called Heather and headed to Columbia to buy a prom dress. Whether or not I would have an escort was yet to be seen.

On Sunday, everyone in the family headed out to church, Mama and Cindy with the rest of the family. I would have left for our old church, but I didn't want to go because I couldn't stand up without feeling like I was going to vomit. And I was so incredibly tired I felt like I could stay in bed all day. I'm sure a large part of it was depression over Vince and worry about what on earth I was going to do, but either way I didn't have to fake being sick. Anyone could look at me and know I wasn't up to par, so Mama didn't say much when I moaned and rolled over. She felt my head, which wasn't feverish, of course, because pregnancy doesn't cause a fever. Nevertheless, she brought me a bucket in case I really did get sick. I've always thought there was nothing to speed up the chances of actually vomiting like looking into a bucket or toilet. It's like an invitation for your stomach to hurl. So I pushed it under the bed and asked if she could please bring me a piece of toast, which she did, and which I ate, and then fell back to sleep.

I woke up with Maggie's picture of Jesus staring at me. *Yes, Lord, I need you now more than ever before, and I didn't go to church. Are you mad at me? You're probably more mad over all the things I've done wrong, like sleeping with Vince, which is why I'm pregnant. I guess missing church doesn't seem that big a deal compared to having sex with somebody.* I closed my eyes and thought back over the previous months, of how I'd gone down the wrong path step-by-step, knowing it all the time and doing it anyway—and knowing God was watching the whole time, waiting for me to stop and think and make the right decision. *So what's the right decision now, God? Getting married? I would love to marry Vince. Can You arrange that? I think You might have to do something about Pamela first.*

God didn't answer out loud or anything, but there was a stirring in my heart that I needed to read Scripture, that maybe that would help, so I turned to Psalms, which has lots of comforting words if you know where to look. Like Psalm 25:6-7: *Remember that your compassion, O Lord, and your kindness are from of old. The sins of my youth and my frailties remember not; in your kindness remember me, because of your goodness, O Lord.*

I closed my eyes and imagined being at the gates of heaven, imagined Jesus greeting me. I didn't want to be bad. I wanted to make the right decisions in life, but it was so hard when life put this great thing like Vince out there. He couldn't really be a wrong decision. If he was, how could I feel so strongly about him? How could my entire life seem to revolve around him?

My mind wasn't at rest on Monday, either. I didn't hear a thing my teachers said because my head was filled with that image of *her* in Vince's arms. How could he do such a thing? What was I going to do? What was going to become of me?

Heather had found the perfect prom dress during our shopping spree that weekend and couldn't quit talking about it, except to ask what was eating at me. But I was less than thrilled about prom at that point, and I couldn't tell her why. If I told her Vince had slept with Pamela, she would never let it go. She was like that. She loved to get dirt on somebody and hold it over them forever. She'd bring it up again every time the person was mentioned, and if I decided to work things out with Vince, I didn't want her reminding me of what he had done.

I couldn't tell Tammy, either. She would have just shrugged and said there were more fish in the sea. Even the banker hadn't been up to her expectations, and she dropped him after the second date, her sights set on the dentist. I doubted he would ever ask her out. He probably thought of her as a kid and not old enough to even consider dating, but I didn't say so to her. I pictured her married to some guy about twenty years older than her, in a mansion, no doubt, with maids and a chauffeur to boot.

I wanted to talk to Maggie, to have a heart-to-heart talk like the good old days before we were sisters, when spending the night together was great fun, full of whispered secrets and giggles. Not that I would be giggling over any of this, but Maggie would have words of wisdom to share.

I couldn't confide in her, though. She would be so shocked at knowing Vince had cheated on me, she would never get beyond that, and that would lead to me telling her about being pregnant, which obviously would mean she would know I had slept with him, and, well, I just couldn't go there. I was upset enough already without hearing one of her lectures or seeing that disapproving look in her eyes.

So I stayed miserable all day.

My mood didn't escape the notice of Silent Sam. He followed me around like he was my shadow, and even though I knew he liked me (even more so since the Valentine), he never had the nerve to say anything to me. He was all right looking: very tall and thin, big brown eyes, and a beautiful smile—but quiet. Too quiet. Even in class when the other boys were cutting up, he would smile almost to himself, like he was sitting in an audience watching other kids act out the school day. I couldn't imagine any girl actually dating him. They wouldn't have ten words pass between them. So it surprised me when he caught up to me in the hall after the dismissal bell and spoke. "You need cheering up."

I was so startled by his deep voice, I stopped in my tracks. "Me?"

"I've seen depressed before, but you look like you're trying to swim in quicksand."

Heather and Tammy had disappeared down the hall with Amber, jabbering away, leaving me alone at the lockers, so it was kind of nice having someone to talk to. I let him fall into step beside me. "That obvious, huh?"

"Yep. So I'm taking you out to the Ice Cream Palace for a milk shake."

"That's the cure?"

"Always works for my mom."

It didn't matter that the day was chilly enough that I had a hoodie over my favorite blue shirt; I constantly craved ice cream, so I wasn't about to turn him down. After all, he'd actually dragged up the nerve to not only speak to me but to ask me out. That earned some respect. "All right. Let's go."

It was his turn to be shocked. "Really?"

"If you're paying."

He grinned like a possum. "Sure!"

Tony did a double take in the parking lot where he, Billy, Maggie, and Webb were waiting for me by the car.

"Go on without me," I hollered and left them wondering what on earth I was doing with Silent Sam. I didn't quite know the answer to that, myself. *Rebound* came to mind, but in my heart, dumb as it sounded, I still wanted Vince. I wanted him to come crawling back to me, begging forgiveness.

Rejection was hard to swallow, and Silent Sam's attention was like a balm to my ego. He looked at me like I was prize to covet.

Sam's little sister, Sophie, was waiting at his car, talking with Courtney Downy. She paused when we approached. "I thought I'd better remind you that Mama said I can ride home with

Courtney," she said. "I didn't want you out here waiting on me."

"Thanks," he said as he unlocked the door, took her book bag and put it in the back seat with mine and his, "but I remembered. Have fun."

"You're Dixie," she said, looking at me with wide eyes.

I smiled at her. "And you're Sophie."

I could tell she was tickled that I knew her name. She went off with a grin, telling Courtney something with secretive whispers. I imagined it was about me and Sam.

The Ice Cream Palace was located on the outskirts of town where the interstate brushed by us. It wasn't much of a place—as old and worn down as the town and just large enough to serve the travelers that straggled in—but there was no argument about the quality of the homemade ice cream churned out by Mrs. Peebles. It was fantastic. She should have marketed it nationally, but she said she didn't want to become some corporate conglomerate with any more headaches than she already had raising five boys and running the shop. At least two of her boys were there at a time, one in back helping make ice cream, and one at the counter waiting on customers or cleaning up tables during slack periods, which he did to about the same standard Tony would have had—a quick swipe with a wet cloth.

Sam never once asked what was making me so depressed. He told me a couple locker-room jokes that were just stupid enough to make me laugh. "That's better. You're like a light being turned on when you smile."

That was so corny it made me smile even more. "Thanks for the ice cream, Sam. It did make me feel better."

He drove me home after that, filling the time with funny reenactments of dumb things that people said at school. He was especially good as Heather, imitating her voice with an exaggerated high-pitched southern drawl and one hand let loose from the steering wheel to flail around in the air like Heather's did in history class, as he reenacted her most recent story. "Mr. Baire, Mr. Baire! You won't believe what happened to my homework. I had it sitting on the kitchen table where I'd been working . . . you know my mama makes me work where she can see me, and she was making a casserole last night to carry over to Mrs. Yost on account of that surgery she had. Such a sweet lady, Mrs. Yost. She bought me a dolly when I broke my arm in third grade, that year we had a bit of snow and I borrowed a sled from Karey Wittmore, that strange Yankee girl that lived in that big house in town for a year before Runney Smith ran the whole family off. That sled wouldn't steer right and I ran into a tree, so I really think a lot of Mrs. Yost, even if she does keep those pit bulls in her backyard and they look at my sweet kitty like she's a doggie treat. Anyhow, Mama was fixing her this casserole, see, and I left my papers sitting on the counter so Mama could see how hard I'd been working, and somehow they got on the stove. You know, we got one of them gas stoves with the little flame? Scares me half to death, which is why I don't cook none, but Mama says real cooks prefer that kind on account of how it heats the food more exactly and all. Anyway, Mama, she turned on a burner for something in the casserole, and somehow my papers scooted over to the edge of it, and *poof*! My homework just went up in flames!"

He did such a perfect parody, I laughed till tears ran down my face. "That sounded just like her."

He grinned. "If she used as much creativity in her homework as she does with her stories, she'd have all As."

"It's all just a decoy to get out of tests or as some excuse why she doesn't have her work done, you know, and she gets away with it, every time. The teachers just roll their eyes at her."

"No, she doesn't. They still take points off her grade. I'm guessing she just likes to be the center of attention, and they've learned it's easier to let her string out her little explanations than to keep telling her to sit down and be quiet. Besides, it would be like skipping morning announcements, wouldn't it?"

I had never suspected that Silent Sam absorbed so much of what went on in class. He never commented on any of it at school. It made me wonder what he had been observing about me.

I worried he was going to take our ice cream outing as a sign that he should ask me out again, but he didn't. He dropped me off at home as if we'd been best friends for ages and left with, "See ya at school tomorrow."

Billy rode up on his bicycle. "Who was that?"

"Nobody," I replied. I wasn't about to explain my love life to my stepbrother.

Billy was used to being put off. He changed topics. "You missed your ride. Tony already left for band practice. He said you had lost your mind."

"Doesn't matter. I have homework anyway."

Only Billy would miss the fact that a few weeks ago I would never have put homework ahead of going to practice to see Vince.

Luckily neither Mama nor Maggie was home. Mama was still at work, and Maggie was with Webb, probably at the library or something. I lay on my bed and stared at the ceiling, unmotivated to do anything but think about Vince and how the whole thing with Pamela must have been a mistake. She must have thrown herself at him or something. That's what I wanted to believe, anyway. I couldn't decide if I should call him. I kept hoping he would make the first move, but I was beginning to doubt that was going to happen.

Sam played it cool on Tuesday. He stopped by my locker once to ask if I was feeling better, then strolled on. I breathed a sigh of relief; he wasn't after anything. He was just a really nice guy, and I'd never acknowledged it before.

Tony was trying to gauge what was going on without asking me directly. At four-thirty, he got his guitar and stood in my bedroom doorway. "Are you ready?"

"You go ahead. I've got too much homework."

Like Tony would believe that after all I'd done to convince him to skip work and homework to join the band. Maybe if I'd been heading out to babysit, he wouldn't have suspected anything, but it was obvious I was only doing homework. "Does this have something to do with Sam Taylor?"

I wrinkled up my nose. "Nobody dates Sam. He's just a nice guy. I had a bad day and he bought me some ice cream."

"Sure. What is it about nice guys? Why don't girls like them?"

I knew he'd forgotten about me and was talking about himself and some girl he must have his sights set on—which reminded me that he'd been pretty depressed lately himself. "That's silly," I said. "Lots of girls like nice guys. Look at Maggie and Webb."

He shook his head. "Webb wasn't so nice before they started dating."

Well, I couldn't argue with that. Webb had been a lazy good-for-nothing; I still couldn't understand what had made her pick him out of the pack, but whatever. "It's whether a guy pays a girl the right amount of attention and makes her feel special." As I said it, I wondered at my own words. Was that what made me so attracted to Vince? Was it because he made me feel special? Or because he made me feel more important than I felt on my own? Maybe that was the same thing, but it triggered something in me and made me consider it more deeply. If Vince weren't in a rock band getting all that attention from fans, would I still be so flipped out over him? I would have to really think about that.

But then there was Sam who had been really kind, yet I didn't have a flare of emotion toward him. He was just a friend, nothing like how I felt toward Vince.

I could see wheels spinning in Tony's head too. "So who's the girl?" I asked.

He shrugged. "Nobody. See ya," he replied, and headed out.

On Thursday, Mr. Baire announced a quiz, which immediately threw Heather into her usual storytelling delay tactics. "Mr. Baire," she said in her sweetest southern drawl, "I do wish you'd do me the favor of explaining a bit about Chinese culture before we take that little quiz."

Mr. Baire blinked and then stared at her kind of perplexed. "What does China have to do with our quiz? We're studying Russia."

"Well, they are neighbors, aren't they? Anyway, Mr. Baire, I read this interesting story on the Internet about a little Chinese girl. She had this problem, see, something wrong with her face called a cleft lip. Have you ever heard of that, Mr. Baire? Well, this poor little girl, her mama abandoned her because of it. She left her in a trash can. In a trash can! Well, luckily someone found her and took her to this orphanage place. Poor little thing. Can you imagine someone not wanting a little girl? It's not like her lip couldn't be fixed. All she needed was an operation. Isn't that the saddest thing you ever heard tell of, Mr. Baire? My mama says that Chinese people can't have big families like we can here in the States. They're only supposed to have one baby, two at the most. I just don't understand."

Mr. Baire glanced around the room to see how we were reacting. Truth was, we all understood Heather's game at this point, and we didn't want a quiz any more than she did. Well, none of us except Maggie. She was always ready for quizzes. The rest of us feigned interest in Heather's story, leaning forward on our desks, our eyes wide and eager for more, just to get Mr. Baire talking.

Mr. Baire looked back at Heather. "Well, China is overpopulated, so back in the seventies or eighties they started limiting families to one child to try to reduce the population. Nowadays they don't enforce the limit as strictly as they did back then, but they still encourage the one-child limit with incentives."

"But Mr. Baire, that's not fair."

"There are lots of things in life that aren't fair."

Somehow I managed to listen to the whole exchange with

detachment, never equating those Chinese babies with my own pregnancy.

"Well, I'm going to help those poor little things. You wait and see."

Asby flicked a wadded-up piece of paper at her. "Heather, Most Likely to Save the World."

That got everyone laughing.

"I will. You wait and see."

Mr. Baire held up his hand. "Quiet down, everyone. At least it's an admirable goal. Now, back to our review . . ."

Sam stopped by my locker after class. "That's the first story she's told with any merit to it, but I still think she was just trying to waste class time."

"Probably," I said.

He stood there a minute, and dread filled me. It was Thursday, the day guys made their plans for the weekend.

His mouth seemed to move in slow-motion. "I hear Tony is playing at the Cooper River Bridge Run in Columbia this weekend."

"I guess. I don't really know."

"We could go listen if you want."

I searched his features for any sign that he might know that Vince and I were an item, but he seemed oblivious. He took my pause as my trying to come up with a rejection.

"Not like a date or anything," he stammered. "Just friends. I'd like to hear Tony play, but I don't want to go alone. I figured with y'all being steps and all, maybe you would want to go."

Would I? Not to hear Tony, of course, but to spy on Vince and Pamela with a guy at my side. That was a no-brainer. "Sure."

I didn't tell Tony, but I think Sam must have said something to him because he didn't seem surprised to see us when we showed up on Saturday. I had found out their performance would be at three o'clock, so we got to the festival around two and walked around looking at the booths full of arts, crafts, and souvenirs. The sun had broken through the clouds and shone summerlike on the crowd, making people giddy with spring fever. Many were dressed in shorts and T-shirts, but I had on a pair of tight jeans with this really cute blue top that brought out the blue of my eyes and the blue in the gems of my teardrop earrings and bangle bracelet. I hoped Vince would react the same way Sam did when he saw me — with an expression that lit up his entire face.

The air rang with jingling carnival music from some of the fancier, more professional booths, the ones that made a living from joining festivals in towns all along the coast. Over the noise of their tinny music, I could hear a band in the distance playing a Christian pop song I recognized; it wasn't Blind Reality.

"Do they get paid for performing at festivals like this?" Sam asked.

"I don't think so. Mostly they do it for exposure. They hand out business cards during the performance. I used to do that for them for a while."

"That's nice of you."

I shrugged. I hadn't done it to be nice, really. I was gradually acknowledging that a lot of my motivation was fame; if Vince became famous, that somehow made me more valuable. Did that make me a bad person? I didn't think so. Fame could take you places in life like nothing else could.

But it came back to the fact that I couldn't remember the last time I'd done something just to be nice. Where had that person disappeared to, that old me?

I pushed the thought away. I had more pressing issues in my life.

Sam and I made our way up to the bandstand about twenty minutes before the show. Tony and the gang were hanging out behind it waiting for the other band to finish and clear out.

Sam walked up to Tony and slapped him on the back. "We came to check it out."

"Hey, thanks, man."

It surprised me that the two of them even knew each other let alone spoke. I hadn't known that Sam talked to anybody.

Something behind the band's van full of stuff caught Sam's eye. I turned to see that creepy guy in black leaning on the far side of the van. I'd almost forgotten about him since I hadn't seen him in a few weeks, but Sam nudged Tony, and shivers went down my spine.

"Is he with the band?" asked Sam.

A dark look passed over Tony. "Not with the band, but something to do with Vince. He's bad news."

"I know. I've seen him around."

"Who is he?" I asked, wondering if the mystery would finally be revealed.

Tony shook his head.

Sam said, "No one for you to know, that's for sure."

The guy's back was turned to me, but it was as if he heard us. He stepped away from the van and disappeared into the crowd with a circle of cigarette smoke hanging around his head and shoulders.

I stuck to Sam's side like glue and cast a sideways glance toward Vince to see if he had noticed us. He had. He was messing with speaker wire or something but paused to look up at us.

Pamela was off to the far side talking to a girl and a couple boys who looked like they probably knew her from school. I had no idea where she actually lived, but in my gut I was sure her school had to be my school's rival.

She had her hair in a ponytail that made her look sweet and innocent and way closer to sixteen than eighteen. For all I knew, she may have been twenty, considering she was at Vince's house at midnight, but she looked like a kid. She had on this skimpy little shirt like she was ready to go to the beach, and these black pants that hugged her hips and flared at the ankles, with sequins or something sparkly all over. Performance attire, I guess, but standing there on the grass just talking to people, it looked tacky.

I flipped Vince a coy smile and turned away, slipped my arm through Sam's, and so Sam wouldn't get the wrong impression, tugged on it a bit. "Hey, let's go get a drink before it starts. I'm about to die of thirst."

I felt him tense under the pressure of my hand on his arm as he turned to me with an expression that fell somewhere between a smile and surprise. "Sure. Come on."

I knew I shouldn't have done it, but I left my hand there as we walked away. I felt bad and all, because I didn't want Sam to think I'd changed my mind about just being friends, like I liked him or anything. But I could feel Vince watching, and I had to do it to get to him. I wanted him to be so jealous that it ate a hole in him and brought him running back, or at least made him call me.

I pulled Sam to a stop as we passed him. "Hi, Vince. You must have been busy all week. I haven't heard a word from you." I felt like Heather in flirt mode, so totally unlike myself, but I was desperate.

"Guess so," he said with his eyes more on Sam than me.

I smiled again, a smile I had practiced in the mirror the night before. It was intended to make me look alluring, so he wouldn't be able to think of anything but me while he was on stage. "So call me," I said and turned away, pulling Sam with me.

Sam knew something was up; he retreated into silent mode, which reminded me of his keen observation skills. No doubt he realized he was a decoy. I had to make it up to him. "I don't really want him to call me. Well, actually I do, so that I can hang up on him. What a jerk." I laughed, but Sam didn't, so I changed tactics. "Look, there's a food stand. I've just got to get something to eat. It's been forever since lunch." That wasn't a lie. All I ever wanted to do anymore was eat. It kept the nausea at bay. Besides, who could resist food at a festival, with all those smoky smells of sausage, barbeque, and burgers wafting around us, and people stuffing their faces everywhere I turned?

Sam relaxed a bit. "I'm hungry too. Let's order something and sit over there at those tables. We can see the bandstand from there."

So we settled down with a couple Cokes and a huge order of fries doused in ketchup between us.

I did all the talking. I don't even know what I talked about. Some drivel about people walking by and the people who had run the race the day before. Sam added a comment here and there but concentrated on the french fries.

Then my eyes settled on a teenage girl about my age as she walked by with a lady, presumably her mother since they looked so much alike—brown shoulder-length hair, glasses, dimpled cheeks, and narrow shoulders. You could tell looking at the girl that she was pregnant, not just fat. She had a swollen belly that started under the boobs and ballooned out, but the rest of her was pretty skinny. She was laughing and eating an ice cream cone, and waddling under the weight of the baby.

It was like looking in mirror, seeing myself in a few months. The reality of my fate, even though I'd thought about it over and over again, slapped me in the face. I was pregnant. I was going to look like her. Everyone would look at me and know I was having a baby. Would I be laughing? Would my mother be walking at my side? Would Vince be with me?

"What's wrong?" Sam asked.

I jerked back to the present. "Nothing. Just wondering where she got the ice cream."

"We passed about five places. Do you want some?"

I shrugged. He probably thought I was a complete pig. "Maybe later. Just made me think of when you took me to the Ice Cream Palace. I doubt any booth has ice cream as good as Mrs. Peebles's."

"You got that right," he replied, and pulled a couple more fries from the stack.

Vince's band was setting up their gear, which got Sam talking about Tony and how long he'd been playing and so forth. It was just easy conversation, so I thought maybe everything was all right again; maybe he wasn't upset about my talking to Vince earlier.

Finally the band spent a minute tuning up together, then they all stepped up to their microphones and Vince introduced them, warmed up the crowd, and started in on the first song, bobbing his head and swinging his arm to the beat as he took giant steps back and forth, one, two, three, four . . . striking his guitar. Mike joined in on the drums, and the music burst forth.

I didn't want to look at Pamela, but I had to. I had to compare her to Ariana. I had to admit she had a good voice — it was sweet and clear but had nothing like Ariana's range and depth. She clutched the microphone in one hand and motioned a lot with the other. I got the impression she had been performing since she was a kid, yet she didn't seem professional. It was more like she was a puppet playing a part, standing up there pretending to be a singer instead of really being one, like some of the flunkies that don't make it through *American Idol*. She had the desire and talent, but it wasn't part of her like it was Ariana. Ariana was a natural.

So was Vince. My gaze moved back to him, and I became mesmerized. My head throbbed with the need to be with him. He was so into the music, and the music flowed through him and from him and drew me into him. I wanted him to reach out to me, to be singing to me personally like he had that other time, alone in his trailer. I wanted him to dedicate another song to me out here in public to show I really was his girlfriend and the whole thing with Pamela was a mistake he regretted. I wanted his every breath to be for me.

Minutes went by before I realized Sam was staring at me. He was watching me watch Vince.

"You've got it bad for him, don't you?"

What could I say?

Chapter Seventeen

ON TUESDAY VINCE was waiting in the parking lot after school, leaning against my car like it was perfectly normal for him to be there.

I didn't see him until I was halfway there. I stopped in my tracks, dumbfounded. Sam, glued to my side for the last two days, stopped too and followed my gaze. He frowned. "Well, I guess that answers that question," he said.

I felt him leave my side as he walked off to his car without so much as a good-bye.

I caught my breath, shifted the book bag on my shoulder, and hugged my extra books to my chest a bit tighter, then stepped slowly toward him. Questions flew through my head. Was he here because he was jealous of seeing me with Sam? Why now? Why hadn't he called me?

Or had something happened between him and Pamela? Maybe he realized he loved me, not her, and it had taken him a few days to end things with her.

I wasn't sure how to act as I approached him. Confident that we were still a thing? Mad over him and Pamela? Nonchalant, as if I had a thing going with Sam?

I decided to let him take the lead. I shifted my books to my left arm and put on my social smile. "Hi."

"Hey, babe," he said, smiling just a bit too brightly, almost giddy or silly. "Can I give you a ride home?"

That didn't tell me much. I shrugged.

He took it as a yes. "Leave your books here. I'm on the motorcycle today."

I glanced around and saw it parked under a tree on the far side of the lot. I debated it a moment. Should I turn my back on him? Would that make him want me more? Or would it make him mad, make him walk away and never look back?

I could see Maggie out of the corner of my eye. She and Webb were talking, lost in their own world as they weaved between the cars. Tony wasn't far behind. Billy would be along any minute. I had to make up my mind.

I absorbed everything about him: his brooding eyes looking so sultry, his thick hair and how good it always felt when I ran my fingers through it, his muscular chest, his gorgeous smile aimed just at me. He was everything I wanted. How could I not go with him?

Maggie had noticed us. I saw the disgust on her face—and she didn't even know what all had transpired between us.

She would try to stop me if she could get to me.

I set my books on the hood of the car and swung my book bag on top of them, then held out my hand. "Let's go."

He took my hand and shivers went through my body. Despite everything, I couldn't deny that he made me feel alive. My heart fluttered as we headed toward his motorcycle.

Maggie called out my name, but I ignored her. She didn't know I was having Vince's baby. She didn't know I had to work this out. He was my future.

He got on the motorcycle first, then I swung my leg over and wrapped my arms around him, hoping every kid in the parking lot was watching us. I have to admit it made me feel cool, like I was hot stuff seated up there behind him — not just an older good-looking guy, but a rock singer revving up his motorcycle and peeling off down the road. For a split second I thought of my mother. She would have a fit, me riding his motorcycle again. If she found out, I would be grounded forever. But I was in a string of doing stupid things, so I quit worrying about it. Being cool won out.

I knew he wasn't taking me home. He headed off in the wrong direction. I didn't care. I didn't want to go home. I wanted to go where he could touch me and tell me it was all a mistake with Pamela, that he loved me and had been crazy not seeing me since the night I caught them together.

I expected him to take me to his trailer, but that's not where we ended up. He headed out of town to the interstate. Even though the April air was warm, much warmer than my last ride so many weeks earlier, the air became magnified as it swept over us, cutting through my hoodie and freezing my arms and face. My cheeks and ears stung, even when I buried them into the back of his leather jacket.

We rode a long way, me wondering what he was up to, and then shot off on an exit that looked like it went nowhere. A few businesses and houses flitted by, thinned out, and disappeared, leaving us in a no-man's-land of farms. Tractors droned in fields, churning charred plants into the spring-warmed earth, preparing the fields for planting and filling the air with the musky smell of dirt.

A few miles more, we turned down a gravel road, past an

abandoned farmhouse, to a grove of pecan trees with buds just beginning to open into leaves.

I had no idea what he was up to.

He parked the bike in the middle of the grove and held it steady while I got off.

"Quite a ride, huh?"

He was still a bit too enthusiastic—or something—not his usual suave self, but I thought maybe he was just in an overly good mood.

I rubbed my arms, trying to get feeling back into them. I was developing a permanent dislike for motorcycles. Give me a heated car any day. I didn't admit that to him though. "Sure. It was great."

He took off his coat and put it around my shoulders. "Sorry, I keep forgetting how cold you get."

I stuck my arms into the sleeves and smiled.

"I wanted to bring you somewhere special," he said as he unbuckled a saddlebag and pulled out a blanket, which he spread on the ground in a little patch of afternoon sun. Then he opened the other saddlebag and pulled out a bag with little cubes of cheese, a small dark brown bottle of wine, and two plastic glasses. He was definitely in making-up mode.

I dropped to the blanket and put on my most alluring pose, at least the best I could do with his coat gaping around me; I was still too cold to take it off. "How sweet. You came up with this all on your own?"

"I've seen a few movies," he said with a laugh, and joined me.

I picked up the wine bottle. It was a different brand than what he'd served me after our first motorcycle ride. "Is this your favorite?"

"Favorite what?"

"Wine."

He chortled. "No. I can't say I'm much of a connoisseur. It's what my parents used to drink, so I figured it couldn't be too bad."

He hadn't ever mentioned his parents before. In fact, he'd never told me anything personal about himself. I didn't even know where he grew up or if his parents lived nearby. "Tell me, what are they like?"

"My parents?"

"Yes."

He shrugged and laughed again. I wondered if maybe he'd already had a bottle of the stuff before he picked me up. He was just too cheerful to be real. "Not much to tell. They're just parents." He took the bottle, twisted off the metal cap, and poured some of the rosy liquid into the glasses.

I swirled the wine around in that cup as if it were a crystal wine glass and I knew what I was doing, but reality was I didn't. I didn't think about it being alcohol, or my being underage, or that I was pregnant and wine could hurt the baby. I didn't think about anything except how romantic it was of Vince to bring wine and cheese to share in the spring sunshine. As I held it to my lips, sipped, and swirled it in my mouth, I imagined myself being an actress in a movie or being grown and graduated, out on my own, as independent as Ariana. It tasted bitterer than I expected, but not bad. I smiled at Vince and sipped again. Life was good.

He held out the dish of cheese, and I plucked a small chunk out and popped it in my mouth with my little finger poking out with the kind of airs I'd expect Heather to use. "You are so sweet to have thought of this."

He moved closer and laid his hand on my shoulder. "I want you to know how I really feel."

Hope welled in me that he was going to say I was his true love. I took another sip of wine, letting the silence pull more words from him.

He reached into his pocket and pulled out a silver chain with a heart pendant and dangled it in front of me. "I got this for you."

I gasped. How could I doubt that he cared about me? Pamela was just a fling.

And then I made a huge mistake. I excused him. I let every bit of anger I'd stored up fall away. I told myself that all guys wandered once in a while, and I ought to forgive him and give him another chance.

He scooted closer and fastened it around my neck. "Things haven't been the same without you around."

Wow. That was an original line.

"I can't understand why you quit coming over."

I almost spit out the wine at that one, but swallowed and gawked at him. "You're kidding, right?"

He managed to maintain an innocent, provocative expression, his eyes shining, steady on me, his eyebrows slightly raised. "We're so good together. So right."

I know my mouth must have hung open while I gathered the wits to reply. "And what about Pamela? Is she right too?"

"Oh, babe, don't be desperate." He laughed. "It's not like we'd said we wouldn't date anyone else. And you've been with that other guy. What's the difference?"

"He went to the festival with me. I didn't sleep with him."

"He was with you at school when I picked you up."

"Only because you took up with Pamela. I thought we were a couple, exclusively."

"We never said that."

"I didn't know I had to say it. You said it."

He made this jump back motion with his head. "I did?"

"The song, Vince. You wrote that song for me."

He shook his head. "That's my job. I write music."

"But you made such a big deal out of it, taking me to your trailer and singing it just to me. How could you do that if you didn't mean it?"

"It was just a song, Dixie. A song." His tone seemed to change from jovial to aggravated in a split second. "I write songs every day."

"It shouldn't be just a song. It should mean something, or it's just words and you're no more than air and notes."

"That's stupid."

Stupid — that was me.

I threw the rest of the wine across the grass. "Well, I took it as more than entertainment. I guess I was crazy enough to think you meant it for me."

He scooted closer, took the cup out of my hand, and laid it on the blanket. He had this way of making his eyes look all dreamy that sucked me in even when my brain was screaming *idiot*!

"I did mean it for you," he said.

He laid one hand on the back of my head and pulled me in to a kiss, deep and passionate, filling places words couldn't go.

I was ready to scream at him. If I had been at his trailer, I would have stomped out and slammed the door behind me, but I was stuck out there in the wilderness with no escape route except him — just like my predicament with the baby. I needed

Vince. There was no future, no way to travel the road ahead of me without him. He didn't understand yet why we had to be in love forever. I had to give him another chance. This baby would be the glue that would bind us.

But I couldn't bring myself to tell him. Not until he said he loved me.

I touched the heart hanging against my chest. "Sing it to me," I said. "Sing it and mean it."

He sang out, quiet at first, a whisper between us, building, his melodious voice resonating around us, and I sank into him and absorbed it as truth. Again.

As he reached the last refrain, he leaned over and let his hands wander.

I sat up. "Uh-uh. Not here."

He spoke into my hair. "There's no one here. Just us and nature, the way it's supposed to be."

I wasn't the nature type, and as I sat up, a wind picked up and slapped a bit of reality in my face. I wasn't completely convinced that he was being one hundred percent honest. "No," I said. "Not here."

He sighed. "Well, come on then, I'll take you home."

"Why not to your trailer?"

He hesitated, but only for the briefest moment, just long enough for me to notice a shift in his glassy eyes. "My cousin crashed there this afternoon." He zipped his leather coat up on me, a sweet action I took for caring and love. "That's why I brought you out here, instead," he said. "I was desperate to be alone with you again."

Anyone looking on would have gagged, but I was seriously dumb enough to believe his story. I reached out and caressed his face. "Tomorrow. I'll come to you tomorrow after school."

A look passed over his face I couldn't quite read, but then he nodded and smiled. "Tomorrow. That will work. But wait and come after rehearsal. Meet me at the trailer at eight."

I sighed. He did want me. Just me.

Everything was going to be perfect.

Chapter Eighteen

MAGGIE, TONY, AND Billy must have kept their mouths shut about my taking off with Vince because Mama didn't say a word about it when I got home. I passed Tony in the upstairs hall and thanked him for not saying anything.

He gave me a strange look, something between anger and aggravation. "You're so stupid. I can't understand why girls can't see when a guy is using them. You'd be better off with Sam."

I nodded. "I know, but I don't love Sam."

Tony rolled his eyes, but that's how I expected him to react, especially if Pamela had been putting the moves on Vince at practice.

When I got to our room, Maggie launched into one of her morality lectures as she dusted the bedroom and scowled over my piles of dirty clothes. I felt like shoving everything off her neat little shelves and screaming that she was as dry as old toast and lacked the passion to even know what life and love were about . . . but instead I gathered up my clothes and dropped them into the hamper. I couldn't risk getting her mad enough to tell Mama I was still seeing Vince.

I played it cool all day the next day, not even letting on to Heather and Tammy that I was meeting Vince that night. I played the good girl; rode home with Mags, Webb, Tony, and Billy; and went to my room to do my homework. I even helped fix supper and cleaned up the dishes without being asked, then I grabbed the keys and told Mama I was going to youth group and then to the library, and I would be home late.

"Have you got your cell phone?" she asked, barely looking up from what she was reading.

"Yes, Mama," I replied as I slipped on a jacket. I jingled the keys in my fingers, wondering how Tony had gotten to band practice. Maybe Mike had picked him up. I shrugged the question away.

A full moon brightened the night, giving me a joyous feeling, entirely different from my last drive to Vince's place. I took it as a good omen that things were going to work out between us.

He was there waiting for me, his trailer cleaned up and smelling good. The newspapers were gone. The rug had been vacuumed and a new beige blanket lay folded neatly over the back of the sofa. He even had a candle burning on the coffee table.

I dropped the keys into my pocketbook, which I set by the sofa, and waited for him to come to me. I didn't have to wait long. He wrapped me in an embrace and kissed me like he had in the field, making my feel weak all over—as cliché as that sounds. I had it bad for him. And I just knew he felt the same about me. The emotions passing between us couldn't be faked. They went soul deep.

"Do you want something to eat?" he asked.

I shook my head. "I just had supper."

We stood looking at each other, not knowing what else to say.

I knew what he wanted. It smoldered in his eyes.

I could have sat him down right then and told him about the baby, about the future we needed to plan and what wonders we had ahead of us, but our relationship circled around to one thing.

He took my hand and led me to bed.

I didn't mean to spend the night. Sleep came over me like a warm blanket on a cold night — something I couldn't resist. I snuggled down beside Vince, intending to nap just a short while to stave off sleep on the weary ride home. Several times I heard my phone buzzing in the next room, but it was buried in the depths of my pocketbook, just a soft purr, easy to ignore while Vince had an arm slung around me, holding me as close in sleep as he had in lovemaking.

I awoke with a jerk at four-thirty, disoriented for a moment, and then coming fully awake with a pounding heart, knowing Mama would kill me for being out all night.

I pushed the worry away. I could make up some story. Or slip in while they were all still asleep. The important thing was that I was with Vince and everything was fine.

I didn't move right away. I could feel Vince's breath on my back. Is this how it would be when we got married? We would sleep curled up together. I would wake up every morning with him wrapped around me.

I lay for about another five minutes before my stomach felt like it was suddenly being worked over with a plunger. I hadn't thrown up in several days; I knew the nausea would pass if I ate something, and I kept a bag of cookies in the car now. So I eased out of bed, pulled on my clothes, and headed home, leaving Vince with his mouth hanging open and his feet tangled in blankets.

The sun was still sleeping, making it feel more like midnight than predawn. I headed down the near-empty interstate to my exit and entered town near McDonald's. Other than a few early risers passing by with cups of coffee balanced against their steering wheels, I felt like I was alone on an abandoned planet. The street lights shone down on the pavement and emphasized the quiet.

I was tempted to stop to get a biscuit but decided not to risk it. It was almost morning, and I had to slip in before anyone woke up.

I pulled into our driveway and crept to the house wondering if the sound of the car woke Maggie in the room above. She would be waiting with twenty questions. I unlocked the front door, conscious of the click of the lock, of the door swishing open and thumping back into place, of my shoes on the small square of tiles before the hushed whisper of carpet.

As I reached out to hang the keys on the row of hooks by the closet, a lamp popped on by Frank's recliner, blinding me for a moment before revealing Mama stretched out, wrapped in a blanket. Her blonde hair was mussed, sticking out from her head like some mod spiky hairdo. Her eyes, paler than usual, were rimmed in red and underlined by dark splotches.

"Where have you been?"

Her tone wasn't one to be ignored. "The library, then Heather's house. I told you that." The lie rolled off my tongue as if I'd been lying to her since early childhood, but it curdled in my stomach and felt like lead in my heart.

"How stupid do you think I am? I called Heather. I called Tammy. I even called Amber. Then Maggie tracked down Sam

Taylor, since she says you went off with him last week. He didn't know where you were, but he went to the library to see if you were there. You weren't. I've called your cell phone all night without an answer. If you weren't home in the next hour, I planned to call the police."

My brain couldn't work fast enough to come up with another lie, so I stood there tolerating her tirade with my lips pressed together until I decided to go with the traditional teenage outburst. "I don't see why I have to tell you every little thing I do. I'm eighteen. I graduate in less than two months, and then I'm on my own. What's the diff between then and now?" I strode toward the steps, hoping to escape any more of her inquisition.

"Don't you walk away from me. I'm far from being done. Don't you realize the havoc you've caused us tonight? How could you do this to us, knowing we would be sitting here thinking of that rape two years ago, right here in the woods by this house? How could you let us worry ourselves all night long?"

I knew by the look on her face she was serious. She really had pictured me lying in the woods close to death, like the girl that had been found there when I was in tenth grade.

"You can't keep track of everything I do forever, Mama. I'm grown!"

"You were with Vince, weren't you? Do you know he doesn't even go by his proper last name? He's not listed anywhere. No one but you even knows where he lives, not even his drummer — Mike or whatever — because Tony tried every avenue he could think of, even that other girl — Pam — that he's apparently dating behind your back, but she wasn't home, and he didn't have her cell phone number."

I stood there on the verge of tears, saying nothing.

Mama continued. "They told me how he picked you up on his motorcycle yesterday, and Frank convinced me to wait, to not totally panic, to see if you'd gone off to be with him again.

"I've tolerated a lot over that boy, but this is the end, Dixie. You're grounded, and you're not seeing him again. You get upstairs and get ready for school, then spend a bit of time reflecting on what you've done. You will come home straight from school every day, and you'll be with a family member every moment of the weekend, beginning with Cindy. You can babysit her on Saturday while I run errands."

"You might like him if you got the chance to know him."

"I'm not in the habit of liking any boy who keeps my daughter out all night. I can't imagine what you were thinking, or maybe you weren't thinking at all, but that's about to change. Now get upstairs and take a shower."

I had so much I wanted to say. She didn't know Vince and I were going to get married. I was pregnant with his baby! We were going to be a family. But I couldn't spill all that until I had it worked out. I knew with Mama the best thing to do was comply until her temper wore off, and then she would talk civilly, so I trudged up the stairs as if I was contrite.

Tony gave me the evil eye when he came into the kitchen at seven to get some orange juice and a granola bar. "I used to think Maggie was dumb, but you've got nothing on her."

"You don't understand."

He shook his head and frowned, gulped down the juice, and walked out.

Maggie was a bit more vocal. "What were you thinking? Out all night? You were at Vince's, weren't you?"

I smiled smugly.

"You're stupid. All the stuff we used to talk about. Where'd all that go?"

I felt a pang at her words, a slice of guilt passing through like a shadow, but my head overruled. She was worse than my mother.

School wasn't much better. Heather and Tammy rushed up to me at my locker. Heather grabbed my arm. "Your Mama called looking for you last night. You should have told me I was covering for you, girl. Where were you?"

"You were with Vince, right?" Tammy asked as Amber approached.

I frowned and nodded. "I was out all night and Mama went berserk."

Heather's eyes bugged out. "You didn't! You spent the night with Vince? You didn't go home? Are you crazy or what?"

I imagined her running around the school with that news, so I lied. "I fell asleep on his sofa watching television."

Tammy laughed. "Like we believe that."

I made a face at her. "Think what you want."

Tammy yawned. "I've told you before—never date any guy more than three times. Guys are so predictable. Next he'll want you to move in, and there you'll be, stuck with some loser the rest of your life."

I emptied my book bag and pulled my physics book out of my locker. "Get a life, Tammy. He's not a loser."

"Sure. He's going to set you up in that brick mansion on the ocean and give you one of his cars to drive." She cackled at her own joke.

"Funny," I replied.

Amber stood between them now, listening to our exchange.

Tammy continued. "You won't catch me saddled with some

guy that expects me to live in a trailer and ride around on a motorcycle, messing up my hair."

I sighed. "We know, Tammy. But some guys have potential, you know. Five years from now he'll be a big hit, and we'll have the mansion and the cars and everything."

I slammed my locker closed and started up the hall.

Heather tagged along. "Ariana says he's a jerk."

It had been so long since Heather had mentioned Ariana, I hadn't thought of them still talking. "That's because he replaced her with Pamela in the band."

"I'm sure you realize it wasn't because Pamela is more talented—at least not at singing."

She dashed across the hall to her class.

Sam wouldn't talk to me. He'd been okay before, not caring too much that I'd ridden off with Vince after school, but something had changed overnight. At first I was relieved because I didn't want to deal with anyone, but after the first class or two his cold shoulder started getting to me. Who did he think he was? He said we were friends, but now it was like I'd broken some trust, some strange bond he'd built up between us.

I took the seat in front of him third period and turned around to talk to him. "What gives? You hang with me all week and now you ignore me?"

He didn't look up from the textbook he'd opened on his desk.

About that time, Kelvin Myers, this guy who's fairly good-looking but ruins it by thinking he's hot stuff, came strutting into class. I dated his best friend, Elliot, back in tenth grade, which makes my skin crawl to even think about now. I was a dork back then, and Elliot was the first guy that ever asked me out, so I flipped over him. But I wouldn't have anything to do with either one of them anymore. They seemed infantile nowadays, wrapped up in football and debate team and thinking high school was the epitome of life, as if the things that happened in the halls of this school would matter to anyone even days after graduation.

Kelvin liked to think he was some kind of stud, like every girl in the school had the hots for him, and liked to give the impression that most had slept with him, which was totally laughable. True, he nearly always had some girl to date, but no one could take his ego for more than a date or two, kind of the opposite of Tammy. Tammy chose not to date anyone more than three times; Kelvin couldn't hang on to a girl that long.

Kelvin did his usual. He stopped at the front of the class to make sure he had everyone's attention, then took a couple steps in my direction and started clapping. "Way to go, Dixie. Heard you got it on with motorcycle man."

Heat flushed up my neck and over my face. I knew Maggie wouldn't have told anyone, and Tony wouldn't have come up the senior hall. That left Heather or Tammy . . . or Amber. I'd had my differences with them in the past, and I'd come to expect them to make something out of the dumbest little comment if it suited them at the time. I had gotten over Tammy telling the girls that I had kissed Asby Jones, like that would ever happen. And there was the time Heather went around pouting, saying that I'd dissed her new outfit . . . everyone thought I'd insulted her when all I really said was I liked her beaded belt better than the gold one that had come with her new jeans. That was just a ploy so she could let everyone admire her new clothes. Sometimes they just didn't care whose life they tromped over if it suited their needs.

But this was different. Telling everyone I'd slept with Vince was low even for them.

I twisted around again to face Kelvin at the front of the room. I had to be careful about how I reacted. Anything I said would be repeated up and down the halls in a matter of minutes between classes. I stared him squarely in the eye. "What would make you say something like that, Kelvin? Run out of your own fake conquest stories, so now you have to make them up about other people?"

It didn't fluster him a bit. "I don't have to make up stuff about you, Dixie. Everyone saw you with him the other day, and today your best friend shared your little secret with the break crowd."

So—it was Heather. That's what I got for spending break talking to Mrs. Newell about the research paper. "Well, you can fantasize about it all you want, Kelvin. What happened between me and Vince is none of your business. He's not a dumb high school boy out to impress his friends, like you. We have a more mature relationship, one that you could hardly relate to."

Kelvin laughed. "Sex is sex; I don't care how old anybody is."

I made a face at him and turned back to Sam. He had been watching the exchange, his face red, his eyes clouded over, his placid demeanor lost to frustrated embarrassment.

"What?" I said to him. "You act like you have some hold on me. Get over it."

I would have gotten up right then and left school except I was already in enough trouble. Besides, Maggie had the car keys, and the teacher walked in and closed the door. So I sat there fuming through the entire class time and the rest of the day. I could hear people whispering about me. I didn't care.

They were all a bunch of losers. I was the one with a rock star boyfriend. The way I figured it, before all was said and done, they would all be admiring me.

Chapter Nineteen

SATURDAY MORNING I woke up feeling totally normal. I'd gotten over everything that had happened at school. In fact, I imagined I had never slept with Vince and the pregnancy was all a dream.

I kept my eyes closed and let the dream fill me. My stomach was still flat, and if I didn't move my head, the nausea wouldn't sweep over me. I could lie there and think about an ordinary life, like the one I'd had such a short time ago . . . when the most complex thing on my schedule was the next physics test or English paper.

I believed it for a while. I couldn't possibly be pregnant. It wasn't in my life plan. I intended to go to college to get a degree in something. I wasn't sure what, but I could work that out later.

I hadn't really envisioned my life much beyond that. Maybe an apartment in Columbia with a roommate. I would get a job after college, but not a serious career until I'd traveled to England and Spain and maybe Greece or somewhere fantastic.

As the vision unfolded, it dawned on me that until I saw Vince, I'd had no intention of settling down with anyone. Marriage hung out there like some distant plan in another lifetime that wouldn't have come into effect until I'd done all the playing I wanted. I had no desire to be like Heather, who sought an acting career, or Tammy, who figured a rich husband was the best path through life. And I wasn't a homebody like Maggie. She didn't care if she ever left town. She had settled into thoughts of going to college, then marrying Webb and living happily ever after in a little house in town.

I hadn't put that much thought into my future. College seemed like enough, with campus life to look forward to and life just stretching out ahead of me.

I enjoyed lying there fantasizing. I rewrote my life over and over again, each time with a different country to visit, a different city to settle in, a different lifestyle to enjoy.

But then my stomach leapt to my throat, and I dashed to the bathroom.

I splashed water in my face and stared at myself in the mirror until the nausea passed. My face looked different, rosy and healthy and full of more sparkle or something, despite the sick feeling in my stomach. I backed up and turned sideways. My stomach was still flat, or at least as flat as it had ever been. I'd always been a little fleshy, not trim and petite like Maggie, even though my arms and legs were more fit than hers because I'd been on the track team every year but this one and the city soccer team for years before that. Still, my belly was squishy. It always had been. Maybe it was a blessing, though, because no one would notice I'd put on a few pounds there and on my butt.

I twisted back and forth in front of the mirror. My boobs had gotten bigger, but no one would dare comment on that. Thank goodness we didn't have gym class anymore, so no one would know for sure. Except Vince, and he hadn't said anything about them being bigger.

Mama was waiting in the kitchen for me with a to-do list that included shopping, cleaning bathrooms, vacuuming, and dusting. I had no desire to spend my morning pushing a grocery cart around a store. "I thought you were running errands, and I was babysitting Cindy."

She put on one of those fake smiles meant to burn me, which it did. "I decided you can do both. Run the errands with Cindy. I have other stuff to do."

"Like what?" I know that was sassy of me, but I felt like crap.

Mama scowled at me but let it pass. She had better things to concentrate on. "Mrs. Graham invited me to go to a spa with her. Maggie is babysitting for her."

"A spa? Where?"

"Columbia. I'm sure we'll go out to lunch and do a bit of shopping, too, so I'll be gone all day."

I sighed. "Lucky you."

She grinned and walked off, pausing at the kitchen door. "By the way, Cindy knows what's up. I advise you not to try to dump her off somewhere."

"All right, already," I replied. "I get it."

I made a slight addition to the to-do list, one that Cindy wouldn't complain about. I took her to the park where the new slides and stuff had been installed after the fund-raiser. Mid-April, and the weather finally shone through sunny and clear, so it was a plausible reason to take her, in case I was questioned about it later on. While she was picking out food for her stupid fish at Wal-Mart, I called Vince and told him to meet me at the park.

Just as I hoped, Cindy ran off to play with other kids as soon as we got to the park. Vince was leaning on his motorcycle, waiting for me.

I headed toward the benches, but Vince walked past them to the swings, so I followed. I couldn't imagine he would really get on a swing, but he did, and pumped until he was soaring.

Despite the sunshine, the morning air hung damp and chilly enough to make me zip up my jacket and shove my hands in my pockets as I sat in the next swing, not swinging, just sitting and swaying a bit.

His voice came to me in waves as he whooshed back and forth. "I used to have swinging contests with my sister when I was a kid."

He'd never mentioned a sister.

"I always won," he continued, "until the day I jumped off midair and broke my leg."

"Smart move." I hooked my arms around the long chains of the swing and planted my feet firmly on the ground. I already felt nauseous without adding a swinging motion to my churning innards. "I bet you didn't swing for a while after that, did you?"

"Not till I got my cast off; then I was back at it, but I didn't jump off the swing anymore."

I imagined him as a little boy landing on the ground, screaming in pain as his sister slowed her swing and their mother ran up to find out what was the matter. It brought tears to my eyes. I thought it was the stress of everything going on in my life, but a large part of it was probably the hormones streaming through my body. I *wanted* to cry, but I forced the tears away. "Where is your sister now?"

"She's married, moved off to Georgia."

Maybe this was the opening I needed, except that his

swinging back and forth was making conversation slightly less than intimate.

He pulled himself to a stand on the swing without even pausing and swept by me like some jungle man on a vine.

"If you're not careful, you're going to break your leg again."

"This is nothing." He reached out and grabbed the next swing over, and swung his body around the plastic coated-chain, planting his feet on the other swing.

I laughed. "I didn't know you were a monkey."

"There's lots of things you don't know about me," he replied as he swung around and his feet plopped to the ground, "like I can't hang out with some chick who doesn't even swing."

"Please don't," I begged, feeling vomit rise.

He got behind me, and I braced myself for the thrust of his hands on my back. "Don't, Vince. You'll make me sick."

"Sick? You want to be sick? I can take care of that. Hang on."

He spun me around, winding up the ropes, and I knew what was coming. He was going to send me on one of those twirling rides that Cindy loved. "No! Don't!" I screamed.

"Don't be such a baby."

"I'll throw up. I know I will. Stop!" Anger resonated in my tone, but he ignored my pleas. "Stop it, Vince. Stop it!"

He twisted me around again. I could feel everything inside of me rising up. But he wouldn't stop.

"Please, no!"

He kept on.

"Stop it!"

I panicked. The words rose in me before I could stop them. "I'm pregnant, Vince! I'll throw up if you don't stop."

He let go of me and the swing and stepped back. The swing swung around, undoing the twist he had put into the ropes, his face flashing by me, shocked and white with his mouth hanging open.

I fell out of the swing as it came to a stop, and crawled to the grass where I curled up in a knot, holding my stomach with both hands.

He came to stand over me. "You're kidding, right?"

"No," I moaned. "I'm not kidding. I brought you here to tell you, but not like this."

"You can't be."

My eyes filled with tears, but I didn't let him see. None of it had gone right. It was supposed to be sweet and romantic, and he was supposed to hold my hand and tell me it was wonderful news because nothing could make him happier than having a baby with me.

He stepped away a pace and back again. "We've got to take care of it as soon as possible. We'll go tomorrow. No. Monday. You'll have to skip school."

I sat up, huddled in a ball, my entire future crashing around me like broken glass. "That's it, huh?"

"What other choice do we have? You're not about to saddle me with a kid."

It wasn't that simple. I admit the idea of having an abortion had flitted through my mind. How could it not, when the world tried to make it sound like the best solution? But it was different hearing it come from him. He wasn't the one that would have to "take care of it." I'd learned enough in health class and at church to know it wasn't just nothing. Some women never recovered from the trauma and guilt. And it wasn't like a tumor or a clump of lifeless cells like people tried to make girls believe. It was a baby. Our baby. Abortion wasn't something I ever thought I would even have to think about, and now it was staring me in the face like there was no other option.

I had to have time to think.

"I have to take Cindy home," I said, holding my sick stomach as I walked away across the park and called Cindy off the big slide. We headed to the far end of the park; I wanted to give him time to leave without having to talk to him again. I don't know if he followed at all or turned and walked the other way, because I didn't look back. I couldn't trust myself not to lose it in front of him.

My insides felt like they were being tormented by a tornado. My brain screamed in defeat. My heart wrenched with pain. Vince's reaction blew away everything I'd counted on.

I would have crumpled to the ground in despair, but I couldn't. I had to keep walking away. I had to focus on getting to the car and driving to the grocery store, forcing my feet forward one step at a time as my world melted away.

At the car I paused, my hand going to my neck to hold the heart pendant as I thought about Vince. But it was gone. I must have lost it somewhere in the park. I gazed across the wide expanse of grass and dirt between the swings and the jungle gym, thinking of how long it would take to look for it.

It was useless, not even worth trying to find.

Chapter Twenty

I SET MY sights on going to church the next day. I needed to have a heart-to-heart with God, to see if he would provide some miracle answer. Besides, Mama wouldn't let me slide two Sundays in a row. I was surprised she even let me go to my church without an escort, but I guess she figured she could call up any one of a dozen people to verify I was there.

I left a bit early. I had a craving for a Mickey D's egg-and-cheese biscuit, which was weird because normally I hated eggs.

My mind wasn't really on breakfast by the time I got there. It kept twisting around my dilemma, trying to figure out what I should do. I felt utterly confused, at the bottom of a barrel with no way to escape, which is why I wasn't paying much attention to where I was going when I passed by Annie Smith, the crazy lady with the big mouth, and bumped her leg by mistake.

"Excuse me," I muttered and stepped forward.

She grabbed my arm. "Why, ain't you Jessie's girl?"

The last thing I wanted was to get caught up in one of Annie's conversations, which was sure to turn to a plea for money—I was probably more broke than she was—so I nodded and turned away, but she didn't let go.

"Sit a spell."

"Got to get my breakfast," I said as I pulled away and headed for the back of the line.

Annie turned to talk to someone else, so I figured that was it; I was off the hook. I watched her from my slowly advancing position in line and thought of how desperate she was, about as low as you could get. She wasn't much different from a homeless person standing at a stoplight except she at least had the smarts to sit inside, warm in the winter and cool in the summer; and even though her shapeless blue dress looked like it came off the antique rack at the mission store, it was clean and not a bit ragged. She earned some money of her own selling stuff door-to-door — sometimes knife sets, sometimes books or vacuums. Right now, judging from what I could see in the canvas bag on the floor beside her, it was greeting cards and calendars. Knowing my mother, she'd bought some, especially if any had scenes of quaint cottages by the waterside, or snow-capped mountains. My mother was a sucker for pictures like that.

Annie's next victim was Ms. Perkins, a skinny lady in her mid-sixties with white hair and the same gold hummingbird broach on her lapel that I remember from as far back as my preschool library days. Ms. Perkins was one of those no-fuss people who operated on a constantly tight schedule, even though it was hard to imagine that there was much she had to take care of since her husband passed away ten years earlier and her children all moved away to other states.

"Ms. Perkins, I declare you look like a spring butterfly let loose in the dead of winter," Annie said.

Ms. Perkins smiled sedately, her crooked front teeth comfortingly familiar from all the years she'd greeted children among the rows of library books and shuffled them into reading circles on Saturday mornings. "Thank you, Annie. I do feel right springlike today with the sun shining so prettily."

"It promises to be a warm one. Them tiger lilies is raising their pretty orange-striped petals to the sky and praising God for the sunshine."

"For everything there is a season, isn't there?" Ms. Perkins said, and moved on.

"They surely is. It's the way of the Lord," Annie responded, more to the man approaching her than to Ms. Perkins. "He's with us all even now, ain't he Pastor Bob?"

Pastor Bob was a heavyset man in a hurry to get his hands on some breakfast. He didn't even break stride. "Amen, Annie."

It occurred to me as I watched Annie that she ought to be the most depressed person in the world, yet she bubbled with enthusiasm for life and had a smile for everyone who passed. She was like Maggie in that she *remembered* things about people. Despite the fact that she spent her life groveling and begging, she never seemed down.

As I collected napkins and a straw, Ms. Perkins passed back by Annie on her way out and deposited a cup of coffee in front of her. "God bless, Annie."

"Why thankee, Ms. Perkins. I'll be by later this week for another book."

It would make sense that Annie frequented the library, though I'd never thought of her as someone who would read much.

Pastor Bob reached into his bag and left a biscuit on her table as he exited.

Without consciously thinking about it, I found myself drawn toward her table.

"Have a seat, girlie," she said, and I did as I was told, wondering what on earth had possessed me.

I unwrapped my biscuit and sipped my orange juice.

"You got the weight of the world crossing your face, young 'un."

Was it that obvious? "I'm fine," I said. "Just hungry."

"I know that feeling," she said as she bit into her biscuit.

We munched in silence a moment till I couldn't hold back the words anymore. "How do you stay so optimistic?"

"Whatcha mean?"

I didn't know if she didn't understand the word *optimistic* or didn't realize how cheerful she appeared in her destitute life. "How do you keep putting on a happy face when you never know where your next meal is coming from?"

"Oh, that. Well, the Lord will provide. He always has. They's nothing easier than just giving your will up to Him and letting Him take over. They's nothing left to worry about after that. He takes care of it all. All you got to do is put one foot in front of the other, enjoy life as it comes at you, and show that same love to everybody else. What could be easier?"

Obviously she'd never been pregnant in high school. "Not everything is that easy. Some things have to be taken care of."

"They's nothing the Lord can't take care of. You just keep living, and let Him do the worrying. If you open your heart, He'll show you which way to go. It ain't always the easiest way, but if you listen to Him instead of the world, it'll be the right way."

I wondered where her words of wisdom had come from; what had happened in her life to make her sit back and let God take the reins?

I wasn't sure I had that much courage. In fact, despite my

Sunday morning mission of going to church, I wasn't sure I even had a heart open enough to hear whatever it was God had to tell me at that point. I figured He wasn't any too happy with the path I'd been walking down, and maybe He wouldn't be willing to help me out.

"You can't be doubting the Lord," she said, as if she were reading my mind. "You go talk to Pastor Bob, or Reverend John, or Father William, or one of the other fine men of God in town, and they'll help you see. I ain't got the words to explain it."

She took another bite of biscuit and a swig of her coffee and then started shuffling through her canvas work bag. "'Course I got the Good Book, and it's all in there. Listen up."

Great, I thought. I might be a youth leader at church, but that didn't mean I was into having a Bible lecture in the middle of McDonald's.

She flipped open to a well-worn page. "This here's from Ecclesiastes, chapter eleven: *When the clouds are full, they pour out rain upon the earth. Whether a tree falls to the south or to the north, wherever it falls, there shall it lie. One who pays heed to the wind will not sow, and one who watches the clouds will never reap. Just as you know not how the breath of life fashions the human frame in the mother's womb, so you know not the work of God which he is accomplishing in the universe.*" She smiled at me. "See there, God don't want you frettin' over nothing. Let Him take care of it all. You just do what you're supposed to do."

"That's my problem; I don't know what I'm supposed to do," I muttered, trying to resolve the part about the mother's womb.

"Well, let's see what else the good Lord has to say, then." She flipped around till her eyes fell on some text she had underlined in ink. "Psalm sixty-nine," she said, "verse six: *O God, you know my folly, and my faults are not hid from you.*" She looked up. "Well, I guess you knowed that He already knowed about your problem. Let's try again." She flipped pages and let them land open at will. "Ah, here's a good one to remember. Philippians chapter two, verse three: *Do nothing out of selfishness or out of vainglory; rather, humbly regard others as more important than yourselves.* Does that help? It always helps me."

"Sure," I replied, just to make her feel like she'd helped, but I didn't quite grasp how that had anything to do with my being pregnant. I thanked her anyway and tossed my trash into the can on my way out, thinking maybe I ought to go talk to Reverend John at church. Probably all he would say was, "Don't get an abortion," but maybe, just maybe, he would have some idea of what I should do.

Had I known what he was going to say, I would never have gone.

Chapter Twenty-One

I THOUGHT MY church was the prettiest church around. Located right smack in the middle of town on Main Street, the main building was red brick, but it had an ornate entrance with seven wide steps flanked by two palmetto palms and surrounded by azalea bushes that bloomed out in bright pink every spring. I'd always imagined I would be married in that church on a brisk day in March, and I would come out the door to pause on the steps for photos, my cheeks rosy with excitement and the chill in the air. It would be so romantic.

As I trudged up the steps, my heart sank. That scenario was nothing but a fairy tale.

I didn't hear much of what Reverend John had to say that morning, but I prayed. A lot. I kept asking God to fix my problem. I guess what I should have been doing was listening with an open heart, like Annie had said. Truth is I was too focused on myself to listen to anyone, including God. I just kept murmuring my own game plan over and over, wishing the baby would disappear and my life would be left like it had been just a few months earlier, without Vince, without any boyfriend, with nothing but graduation and college looming in the future.

I planned to talk to Reverend John after the service, but there were too many people milling about for coffee and doughnuts, and I knew from the looks of things he would be busy most of the afternoon, so I waited until the next day. I waited until Mags and the boys were inside the school, then I went back to the car and drove to the church. I just couldn't sit through another day without making some kind of decision.

I bypassed the front entrance and walked to the back of the building where the offices were located, through a wooden door that was probably a hundred years old, and into the main office. I thought Reverend John would be seated at his big mahogany desk doing whatever it is he did with his days: planning sermons or reading from the Bible or working on accounts or something. But he wasn't.

Farther down the hall, I found Mrs. Green at her desk. She was probably the better choice anyway since she was in charge of the youth group and was used to dealing with teens like me.

As I approached her desk, she looked up, her wrinkle-circled eyes wide with surprise for a moment. "Well, Dixie, what are you doing here at this time of day?"

I stood there, her sagging face staring at me, unsure where to start. I wondered if she even remembered what it was like to be a teenager. She had lived in a different century with different circumstances. She probably hadn't even kissed her husband until after they were married. Why on earth was I confiding in her? Because I didn't know where else to go. Because we had attended the same church for as long as I could remember, so I knew we shared the same beliefs. And because she was supposed to be a good Christian woman, which meant she should see my problem with love and understanding and help guide me. That was her job here—to act as a counselor to teens and guide them in learning their faith.

"I need some advice, Mrs. Green."

She waved me toward the leather chair to the side of her desk. "Well, have a seat, dear."

I wasn't too sure of how to start off, so I blundered straight to the point. "I'm pregnant, and I'm not sure what to do. You know—should I keep it? I have all these thoughts running through my head, and I can't make sense of any of it. I don't know what to do. I still have school to finish, and I wanted to go to college, and now this. I'm just so confused."

Her mouth hung open like a largemouth bass. "Why, Dixie Chambers!"

I realized right away she wasn't going to have much advice. I should have thought twice before I even opened my mouth.

"I don't rightly know what to say. How on earth did this happen? You're head of the youth group!"

"Yes, ma'am, I am. But I guess that doesn't keep me from being human."

"But, Dixie, we've talked about abstinence and God's commandments and . . . well, you're supposed to *know* better."

"Yes, ma'am, but it appears it happened anyway. The question is what should I do about it?"

She was shaking her head. "I'm going to have to call in Reverend John. I'll need his input, you know."

"He's not in his office."

"He never is. He's a busy man." She dialed a number and held her finger to her lips for me to be silent. "Reverend, I need you in my office if you're available, please." She paused. "Thank you." She set down the receiver and twirled her thumbs. "He'll be right here in a minute."

Obviously she had nothing to offer until he arrived, so I settled back in my seat and waited for him.

He strode into the room, his glance moving from me to Mrs. Green. "What can I help you ladies with today?"

"I think you need to sit down, Reverend."

He raised his eyebrows and took a seat in the leather chair opposite mine. "Sounds serious." He pulled up the sleeve of his black suit to glance at his watch.

"It is," Mrs. Green replied.

He turned to me. "What seems to be the problem, Dixie?"

I hung my head a moment, just long enough for Mrs. Green to take over. "She's pregnant."

I raised my chin and met his eyes. "I need advice. I don't know what to do."

Reverend John's face became as serious as a Sunday morning sermon. "I see."

"She's our youth group leader. . . ."

I couldn't understand why Mrs. Green was so hung up on that. What did youth group have to do with my problem?

"*Hmm.* Well, I'm glad you've been up front with us so we can handle the situation immediately. Do we have someone who can step in to take her place?"

"Melinda Watson."

He checked his watch again. "Fine. Take care of that."

My head swam as I tried to make sense of what they were talking about. Youth group? "I don't understand."

"Certainly you realize you can't maintain leadership of the youth group if you're pregnant. What kind of example would you be setting for the other girls?"

"But that's not why I'm here."

"Well, what?"

"I'm trying to decide what to do."

"Oh, I'm not qualified to give you counseling in that area, dear," Mrs. Green said as she made notes about the youth group on a pad of paper in front of her and then dug into her drawer, shuffled through a stack of cards, and pulled out a business card. "Here you go. Go visit the crisis center downtown. They have people trained in these matters, and they can tell you where to get proper medical attention."

I stared at the card. *Andrea Ford, The Crisis Center.* I would have laughed if I weren't on the verge of crying. Andrea Ford was the woman Frank dated before he married Mama. Even Maggie would have laughed at the irony if I told her.

Reverend John leaned forward and took my hand. "You must pray about this. Read Scripture and listen to God with all your heart. He'll tell you what to do. You could consider putting it up for adoption. The women at the Crisis Center can help you with that. You go talk to them, and we'll talk again afterward, okay?" He pulled out a BlackBerry. "Say Thursday after school? Around four? I'll put you down. Right now I have to get over to Cherry Oaks Rest Home. I'm speaking there this morning about the heavenly reward of salvation." He patted my hand again. "In the meantime, you do a bit of soul-searching, and we'll see where we are on Thursday." He paused at the doorway. "Have you told your mother?"

"No, sir."

"You should always confide in your parents, Dixie. How can you honor her as God commands if you don't share such news with her?"

I frowned. "I thought I could talk to you first."

"You best tell her about the youth group situation so there won't be a misunderstanding."

What was it with the youth group? This was my life we were talking about!

I followed him out the door and headed to the exit feeling like I was in a worse situation than before.

Chapter Twenty~Two

I RETURNED TO school just before the last bell so I could pick everyone up; Maggie would know I'd been absent from classes, but I hoped our lifelong friendship would keep her from telling Mama. If she kept quiet, I could forge a note to get back into school the next day; getting caught playing hooky wasn't at the top of my list of worries at that point. My whole body ached with the uncertainty of trying to decide what to do and where to turn, as I stared absentmindedly at the school, drumming my fingertips on the steering wheel, waiting for dismissal.

I wasn't the only one waiting in the parking lot, though. A movement by the corner of the building caught my eye. I wondered if it had been my imagination, but nothing moved. My eyes wandered up and down the rows of cars until I saw one that created a lump in my throat—the old blue Z that had dropped Vince off a few times, the one his creepy friend had ridden off in when I'd seen him hanging around band practice.

In my never-ending quest for a happy ending, I hoped it was Vince, that he'd hitched a ride with whoever it was that always drove that car, and he'd come to tell me he'd reconsidered our situation and wanted me and the baby.

No such luck.

Another movement by the building caught my attention, and I saw him — the creep — trying to stay out of sight as he smoked a cigarette and kept his eyes trained on the main exit. I thought maybe he was looking for me, so I crouched down in the car and waited.

It wasn't me he was looking for.

When the bell rang, kids poured from the building like milk sloshing into a bowl and over the edges as they rushed out in all directions.

Creepy guy didn't move.

Maggie and Webb weaved their way through the crowd like two foxes on the trail of a rabbit, their heads bent down, their bodies moving instinctively through the obstacles without conscious effort. They always seemed to be cocooned in their own world that way, so much to talk about, always heading the same direction with their noses together on the trail ahead of them. For an instant, I admired them and sensed the yawning gap of how I'd only felt that superficially with Vince. He didn't really know my heart. But then I lifted my chin and thought of how predictable the two of them were, how boring their lives must be, with every step planned out. They lacked spontaneity. They lacked carefree fun. At least, that's what I told myself. A lot of good either one had done me. How spontaneous did my future look at this point? Unpredictable for sure, but not spontaneous or carefree.

Billy approached, stopping halfway to talk to a friend, and I realized how much he had grown in the past year, not just in height, but maturity. I tended to think of him as a little kid, but he really wasn't. He stood on the brink of where my life had shifted from being invisible to being Miss Popular. Billy couldn't be classified as either one. He participated in sports without being a sports fanatic, but enough that he was really fit. I could see the young man emerging in him—broad chest, muscular legs, more chiseled features than he'd had a few years earlier when he still carried baby fat. As I watched him slap a high-five with one guy while talking to another and then waving to a third before continuing his trek to the car, I realized he carried himself with more ease than Tony and less self-consciously than Maggie, like a puppy in a field of grown dogs, totally oblivious to the growling and snarling undercurrents that accompanied the tentative tail-wagging. He probably didn't care a bit whether or not he was popular, so it came to him all the easier.

What had made me become so conscious of my standing at school? Was it different for girls? I didn't know, but I felt that *being popular* reigned like some constant rat race in the school halls, all the girls scratching and biting as they climbed over one another in the rush to the finish line. But what exactly was the finish line? Homecoming queen? Prom queen? Graduating with some status of being considered the beauty of the school (like I stood a chance of that with Heather and Tammy around) or just ahead of the pack in having boys traipse along at our tails with their tongues hanging out? Is that what I'd spent my high school years trying to prove? Is that what made Vince seem so appealing—being older, being a rock star, offering a hint of fame and status? What good was that going to do me at this point?

Tony finally came out, his hair as messy as usual, his thin shoulders slumped as if the world had defeated him, his steps flopping lazily one after the other . . . until Vince's creepy friend rushed up and pushed his shoulder. Tony, unsuspecting, stumbled sideways two steps before he caught his balance and turned with an expression that asked *What?*

Creep-o said something to him. I could see his lips moving as he stepped closer and closer to Tony, getting in his face. The way Tony looked back at him, I had a good guess of what string of cuss words he put back at the guy before turning and pushing his way through the last of the throng emerging from the school.

The creep gave him the finger and yelled something indecipherable, but didn't follow.

Loose papers scrawled with previous weeks' homework scattered to the floorboards as Tony threw his math book into the backseat of the car and ducked into his seat. "Let's get out of here," he said.

Sounded like the best idea to me. I revved the engine and pulled out, keeping a watch in the rearview mirror for the Z. "What was that about?"

Maggie and Webb were still in their own world. "What?" Webb asked.

"Nothin'," Tony said, his head craned around to see if we were going to be followed.

"What did he want?" I asked.

He didn't answer till we got home and the others were out of the car. "Vince is pissed that I'm not going to practice this week, but I don't give a crap. I'm not."

I shrugged as if it didn't matter to me, but I wondered why that had sent Creep-o out to the school. I knew Vince had a temper—he'd been furious when the other guitarist quit—but mad enough to send his creepy friend after Tony? It sounded ridiculous to me.

At the time, I didn't know what Vince was capable of.

Chapter Twenty-Three

I LAY ON my bed staring at the ceiling a long time as I tried to make sense of my future. It was too much of a decision to make on my own, yet I didn't want to go to some counseling center, either. I had no desire to talk to strangers or to Andrea Ford. They couldn't understand my life.

My head ached with the effort of thinking through what life would be like if I kept the baby. Where would I live? Obviously not with Vince. How would I support the two of us? College would no longer be an option, so what would I do with my life?

Even though those questions flew through my mind, I couldn't actually picture anything beyond the pregnancy. I didn't see myself with a baby in my arms. My head was filled with visions of everyone whispering about me. I'd be back to being Dixie the Dork. All the popularity I had enjoyed the last two years would be gone. I would graduate without a friend in the world . . . or at least at school, which was the same difference to me right then.

How could I give up everything I'd gained?

How bad would it be to get rid of *it*?

It was easy to think, but in my heart I wanted someone to convince me otherwise, to give some reason not to do it.

If I did have an abortion, would Vince and I become a couple again? Would he go to the prom with me and come to visit me at my dorm at Clemson in the fall?

The thought lifted my spirits, and the world drifted back to me in pieces. I could hear Billy talking to Frank in the family room about going up the road to Jasper's house. Mama was in the kitchen stirring something, the metal of a spoon clacking against the side of a pot or her big metal mixing bowl, and I knew the smell of some treat would soon waft around the house. I knew it was Mama in the kitchen and not Maggie, because I could hear Maggie outside hollering to Whizzer, playing fetch. Whizzer was meant to be Billy's dog, but Maggie spent a lot more time with him than Billy ever did.

I rose from my bed and went out to join her.

When we'd left the house for school that morning, the day had dawned with bright sunshine warming the dew off the ground, but as the sun dipped toward the treeline, there were dark clouds forming in the distance. Still, the warmth of the afternoon rays felt wonderful for the moment, and I was glad I had ventured outside. I settled onto the bench in the bottom corner of the yard, sitting sideways on it with my legs stretched out, and let the sun flush my face with its warmth.

Whizzer ran up and licked my nose.

I wiped away his slobber. "Thanks, boy. I needed a kiss, but you need to work on your aim. Most boys don't go for the nostrils."

Maggie threw the ball for him again and joined me on the bench, pushing my legs out of the way to make room. "Feels good, doesn't it?" she said with her face turned up to the sun. "We could put on bathing suits and catch about thirty minutes of sun."

Like that would matter to me. I wouldn't be showing my belly all summer . . . if I kept the baby.

I sighed. Maggie had made me face it again. I couldn't let it go for even thirty minutes.

She looked at me. "Since when does the idea of sunbathing make you frown?" She pulled the ball from Whizzer's mouth and threw it again. "Has Heather put a hex on tanning for fear of aging that perfect face of hers?"

"It causes skin cancer."

"Oh, and that's been a concern of yours since when? Geesh, I can't say anything to you anymore."

I took a deep breath. Honestly, when I thought about it, Maggie was the one person in whom I knew I should confide. She would have some intelligent way of looking at it and helping me decide what to do.

"There's just not a reason for me to sunbathe now, because I won't be sunbathing this summer."

"So? Neither will I. We'll have to have real full-time jobs to put money away for the fall. You know our parents can't foot the whole bill for two of us to go to college at once."

"They won't have to worry about it for me anymore. I won't be going."

"What? What do you mean?"

I sighed. "I'm pregnant."

She sat still as if the words needed total concentration to be absorbed properly. "Pregnant?"

"Yes, pregnant."

"You can't be."

I had argued that enough in my own brain; did I have to argue it into reality with her too? "Yes, I am."

Her face paled so that her zillions of freckles stood out darker than usual. "You can't be."

"I wish that were true."

"But what happened to waiting? We both said we would wait till marriage."

"*You* said you would wait."

"But Dixie . . ."

"Vince was different. I thought he was the one."

Maggie stood up and faced me. "Well, I've known for two years that Webb is my one and only, and I'm not sleeping with him."

I shrugged. "Not everyone is as perfect as you."

"I'm not perfect."

"Right."

She mulled over my problem. I could almost see the wheels turning in her head as she sat down again and stared into space. "Have you told them?"

"Who?"

"Your mother. My father."

"No. I may not tell them at all."

She turned to me, her eyebrows knit together. "Huh? How can you not tell them?"

"I'm trying to decide what to do."

"In terms of what?"

Why did she have to play so obtuse? "You know."

Her eyes almost bugged out of her head. "You're not consider-ing having an abortion?"

"Hush," I said, looking around. "Like, announce it to world, why don't you?"

"You can't seriously consider that. There's no way."

This conversation was not going as planned. I thought Maggie would be quiet and reflective, but I hadn't taken into account her strict black-and-white lines in matters of morality. Still, I thought I could get her to see it from my perspective. "What else am I supposed to do?"

"Have the baby, of course."

"I've thought about it a lot, but can you really see me having a baby? Being a mother? Come off it, Mags."

She pressed her lips together. Her eyes narrowed fire at me. "If you kill that baby, you're killing me."

"How do you figure?"

"Because I was that baby, except my mother was younger than you. She was only sixteen."

It was true. That's why Frank had married her, and then five years later, when Maggie was four, Tony was three, and Billy was a baby, her mother had committed suicide. She'd slit her wrists in the bathtub, with Maggie right outside the bathroom door. It accounted a lot for Maggie's attitude about life in general.

As I sat looking at her, I thought about her mother and how she must have felt when she first married Frank, still sixteen and so naive. She hadn't known how depressed she was going to end up. Depressed enough to kill herself and leave three kids mother-less . . . "So I guess that leaves me suicidal."

I shouldn't have said it. I knew before the words were out of my mouth, and I couldn't stop.

The look Maggie gave me cut me to pieces. "You are a total—"

She didn't have to finish the sentence for me to know what she meant. Her face said it all.

She stood up and stared at me with a look meant to shrivel

me into the ground. "What you are carrying is a child, not some thing you discard. What kind of church have you been attending all these years that it hasn't taught you that? I thought we shared values, but if you can even think of having an abortion, you're not who I thought you were.

"Sure, my mother committed suicide, but it was because she had postpartum depression and wasn't taking her medication. And she'd had three babies, not one. She hadn't even finished high school. Do you remember what we were like at sixteen? And she had the courage to have me. She may have been wrong to commit suicide, but she killed herself, not her baby. You tell me which is more selfish."

She didn't wait for an answer. She stomped off to the house and slammed the back door like a huge exclamation point at the end of her speech.

I could have sat in the sun for an hour afterwards, hoping the rays would burn a hole in my brain and put me out of my misery, but I had only stared into space trying to piece things together for less than a minute when Mama hollered out the back door. "Dixie, get in here!"

I knew as soon as I was in the door that Maggie had told them. Frank was seated at the table with his hands folded, and Mama was pacing back and forth behind him. The last thing I'd expected from Maggie was for her to snitch to my mama.

"Is it true?" she asked.

I sank into a kitchen chair and nodded.

"Was it that rock singer?" Frank asked.

I nodded again.

My mother growled deep in her throat. "I knew you were up to no good with him. I can't believe this! How far along are you?"

Everything in me was tied up in such knots that I couldn't speak, so I shrugged.

It looked like Mama's face was going to explode with frustration. "When were you supposed to have your period?"

I couldn't believe she asked me about my period in front of Frank. It's not like he was even my father. I looked from her to him and said nothing.

She leaned forward on the table like a cop at an interrogation and screamed at me. "How long ago?"

Tears welled up in my eyes. "About three weeks."

"Three weeks since it was due?"

I nodded.

"So you're about seven weeks along."

I shrugged again. I had no idea.

Her face relaxed. "At least it's not too late," she muttered.

"Too late?" Frank said. "For what?"

Mama gave him one of those sideways looks that meant *duh*. "Absolutely not. There is no way she's having an abortion."

Frank had forgotten how long Mama had been an independent woman. She could be sweet as sugar, but she had a steel backbone. She put her hands to her hips and fired her words like bullets. "She is my daughter, not yours, and I'll say what she does and doesn't do."

Frank pushed his chair back so hard it toppled over with a loud bang, but that didn't stop his reply. "You've already had more than your share of saying what she should and shouldn't do; that's why she's pregnant. I told you she needed a curfew, and you said, 'No, let her have her independence. She's grown,' you said, 'ready to take on the responsibility of being her own person.' Well look where that got her. Now she has all the responsibility she asked for. She is not having an abortion."

"Just because Mallory had a baby as a teenager doesn't mean you're going to convince my daughter to do the same thing."

His voice roared. "*I didn't have to convince Mallory.* We both wanted Maggie from the moment she was conceived."

I knew Mama would be upset about my being pregnant, but I didn't know she'd aim it at Frank. This reaction had to be something to do with Maggie's mama.

"How dense do you think I am? Mallory wanted you, not a baby, and she knew being pregnant was her ticket to the altar!"

Ah, there was a nugget of the secret I'd been missing. Mama really had still been in love with Frank. But why had she agreed to marry my daddy if she was still in love with Frank?

The questions flashed through my mind on some alternate side road to the highway through the present. I had to deal with my own life, not their past.

Frank returned to his true character, his voice calm. He picked up his chair, took a seat, and crossed his arms, not the least bit sidetracked or ruffled by Mama's accusation. "There is no greater blessing in the world than a child. How can you think otherwise?"

Mama, still red in the face, stared at him a long moment before turning the argument back to me with a wagging finger. "There's no way Dixie is ready to raise a child!"

"How do you know?"

"She hasn't even had a real job. She can't even do laundry on her own."

"Whose fault is that?"

"Oh, so now it's *my* fault because I didn't turn her into a slave, like you did poor Maggie?"

"Maggie isn't a slave."

"No, she just about had a nervous breakdown two years ago because of all the demands you put on her."

They had forgotten I was even standing there. I slipped away from the table and ran up the stairs.

Maggie gave me the evil eye, but I ignored her. I stepped over my piles of stuff, which Maggie had gathered up and piled on my side of the room, then flopped onto my bed to stare at the ceiling.

"Now you have them arguing."

I wiped at my tears and let anger rise up inside. "Not my fault."

"Yes, it is your fault. They've only been married nine months, and never in the two years time they dated did I hear them say a cross word to each other. In one day you have them screaming at each other."

I could have told her about Mama's comment about Mallory, but this wasn't the time for idle chatter. Maggie and I were on opposite shores, just like our parents. "They have different opinions on a very volatile subject. That isn't my fault. Your father needs to loosen up. Live and let live, and all that."

"Sounds like you and your mother have been listening to the same preacher. How can you possibly see abortion as letting anyone live other than your own egotistical self?"

I ignored her.

"If you do it, I'll never speak to you again."

"Good. You're a blabbermouth anyway. I can't believe you told them. If it breaks them up, it'll be your fault, not mine."

"I'm not the one who got pregnant."

"And what if you did? You think Webb would stand by you?"

"Yes, he would. We're already engaged."

It irked me to hear her say it. "Sure, you and your stupid four-year plan. You've been talking about it forever, but not Webb. Maybe he doesn't really feel the same way. Ever think of that? You never know what a guy is really thinking."

She looked down at her hands. I figured she was staring at her claddagh ring, an heirloom she'd inherited on her sixteenth birthday. She was supposed to move it to her ring finger as a wedding ring when she got married.

"What would you know about what Webb thinks?" she asked. "You stay so wrapped up in yourself, you don't know what's going on around here."

"I do too."

"Sure. Like you know some creep has been hanging around the playground at Cindy's school, and she came home crying about it a couple weeks ago? Or that Tony is all worked up about a girl he really likes, but he can't get up the nerve to ask her out?"

I shrugged like I didn't care. "What's that got to do with anything?"

"Because you don't know anything about what's going on with me and Webb, either. Webb and I are officially engaged. He asked me on Valentine's Day," she said.

I couldn't believe she hadn't told me. Maybe she had tried, but I didn't want to remember that. I wanted to be mad at her. I turned away. "Go jump."

She rolled off her bed and walked out without another word, presumably to go see Webb. She would tell Webb, and Webb would tell someone, and within hours the entire world would know I was pregnant.

I gazed out the window, but I kept feeling Maggie's picture of

Jesus staring me down. There were nights I loved that picture, but right then I felt nothing but spite. "I prayed," I hissed at Him, "and You haven't helped me. All those years going to church and leading youth group. What were those for? Don't You care? Haven't I done enough for You? And now that same church is kicking me out of youth group. What kind of thanks is that? Why can't You fix this problem? Why are You making me face this decision? My parents are fighting. Maggie isn't speaking to me. Where are You when I need You? What happened to that whole 'Footprints' thing, where You're supposed to carry us when times are hard?"

No voice boomed out from the heavens. No note floated down. No angel appeared. The only noise I heard at all came from below—Mama and Frank still having a heated argument.

My head throbbed as I listened to them. What I wanted more than anything was to be wrapped in my mother's arms and assured that everything was going to be okay, that she would take care of me and help me find a path through this mess. Instead, I huddled on the bed and stared out the window. As rain began to pelt the glass, tears ran down my cheeks.

The more I thought about it, the more I realized I had to take control. I wasn't Mama's little girl anymore. I had to handle the situation myself.

I pulled my suitcase from under my bed and stuffed it full of clothes. How many times had I used this bag for slumber parties and trips to the beach? I'd thought the next time I used it would be for a trip somewhere exciting after graduation and trips to Myrtle Beach during the summer and then for at least part of the clothes I would carry away to college. I hadn't foreseen this veer in the pathway.

As I pulled my favorite jeans from the closet, I paused. Half of what I packed would be useless. Already my butt was bigger, and so were my breasts. I had no idea how fast a woman put on weight and got a belly with pregnancy, but my tight jeans wouldn't last much longer. I threw them on the closet floor and dug out my favorite hip-hugger sweats, some T-shirts, and my hoodie. No doubt Heather and Tammy would wonder what was up with my dress code, but they would know eventually anyway . . . unless I followed Vince's plan.

I jingled the car keys in my hand, knowing that taking the car was going to leave Tony and Maggie in a bind, but I had no choice. I couldn't leave without transportation. They would work something out.

At the bottom of the steps, Cindy was sitting in the shadows crying. I bent down. "Don't cry. It's just a fight. Grown-ups fight just like kids. They'll get over it."

She pulled on my pant leg. "Tell them to stop," she pleaded.

Then she noticed my suitcase. "Where are you going?"

I didn't answer her. I shook her loose, turned into the laundry room, and slipped out through the garage.

Cindy followed me outside and stood watching as I pulled out of the driveway. My stomach felt sick and my heart ached. Maybe I should have been filled with anger toward my family, but instead I thought of my mother's twinkling eyes and sweet smile and how special we'd always been together. Time rewound in my head like a family video of birthdays and bicycles, of helping Cindy learn how to walk and playing Barbies with my mother, of last moments with my father before he died and long walks that spring with my mother as we cried and reminisced, of talking all night with Maggie, shopping in the mall, and baking Christmas cookies. And this year, in the few months since we'd become a family, we'd had Thanksgiving dinner with all the food and laughter we'd missed since Daddy died, and Christmas around the tree with corny Christmas carols, and Cindy jumping around all excited, wavering on whether or not she really believed in Santa, but giving in to at least pretending he was real because it was all such fun.

I didn't want to leave, but I had to. I had to take the situation on my own shoulders and take care of myself.

Unfortunately, I had no idea where I was going to go.

Chapter Twenty~Four

I WASN'T SURE what to do or where to go. I was out of the neighborhood and down the road before I pulled out my cell phone and buzzed Heather.

"Hi!" she answered. "Why weren't you at school today?"

"I played hooky. I had stuff to do."

"You spent the day with Vince, didn't you?"

"No. No definitely not. We had a fight on Saturday."

"Really? About what?" Her voice came across with that gasping sound she gets when she's about to get hold of something juicy.

I couldn't tell her. It was just too big to tell, especially on the phone that way, and spreading the news wasn't really what I was after anyway. What I needed was a place to stay and regroup. I thought Heather could put me up, but that would only be for a night. What good was that?

No good at all, but I didn't have many options. I had to ask someone for help. Maybe, just maybe, if I had a serious talk with Heather she would keep it a secret, and maybe she would have some idea of what I should do. She acted ditzy, but she really wasn't. She just knew how to work people to get what she wanted while staying totally innocent, as if whatever happened was their fault.

"Look, Heather, I can't tell you on the phone. I'm coming over."

"Sure!" she said. "There's no one here right now but me. My parents went out to the store."

I was glad she was by herself, that neither Tammy nor Amber was there. I couldn't tell them what was going on.

Heather met me at the door with a homemade milk shake for each of us. "You sounded upset, and you know there's no better cure than ice cream. Just don't tell Tammy. She'll kill me for not sticking to my diet."

Even as upset as I was, I welcomed the milk shake. My stomach was doing flips, and eating anything at all would make it feel better, but ice cream was supreme.

I followed her up to her room and sat on her bed with her. "I'm going to tell you something, but you have to vow not to tell anyone else, Heather. Not even your mama."

She shrugged. "Okay."

I stared at her. "I mean it. No one. This isn't something little. It's really, really major, and I'm trusting you to be my best friend in the world and not tell a soul."

She frowned as if I'd insulted her. "Well, duh. I am your best friend, aren't I?"

"Well, yes," I replied, "but sometimes . . ." I didn't say it. It would only cause her to get mad at me, and that wasn't the point. "Word's probably going to get around anyway, but right now I need total secrecy."

She stopped eating her ice cream and shoved her spoon into the cup. "You've got me worried. What is it?"

I just couldn't tell her. Even being best friends, I didn't think I could trust her not to tell the world. And after the reaction at home and church, I wasn't ready to face the whole world with my news yet. I stirred my milk shake. "I ran away from home."

She took a big slurp of hers, ready for some juicy news. "So what are you going to do? Move in with Vince?"

"No. I'm not even speaking to him now." I poked at the drippy ice cream like my spoon was a knife to Vince's gut. "I have no idea what I'm going to do."

"Then why did you run away?"

Why did I run away? To get away from Mama and Frank's fighting? No. It was more than that. I needed room to think. Space. A part of me just wanted to run and run and run, as if I could outrun my problems and avoid having to make a decision because there didn't seem to be a right answer. Make Mama mad or make Maggie mad. Of course I valued Mama's opinion more, but could I do what she and Vince wanted? Could I have an abortion? I couldn't think about it. I didn't want to think about any of it. I just wanted to bury my head in the sand for a while. That's what I was doing. Getting away from my problem. I just couldn't wrap my mind around the reality of what I had to face. Instead, I kept hoping some miracle would straighten things out.

"Look," I said, "I had a huge argument with my mama and Frank, and right now I need time to think. I need a place to stay."

"A fight about what?"

Heather's expression was so earnest, and I was so worn out from trying to work it all out in my head that I gave up on my resolve to keep it secret. She would find out about it anyway;

I was sure of it. My church knew and so did my family. How could I not tell Heather? "I'm pregnant."

Her mouth dropped open. "Serious?"

"Do I look like I'm joking?"

And then her whole demeanor changed. Her face lit up and she clasped her hands in front. "A baby! A baby!"

"Well, yes," I stammered, deciding not to add exactly what the dilemma was in terms of its fate. How could I when she looked so delighted?

"You are so lucky," she said.

That floored me. "Lucky? Heather, I'm not married. I'm not even talking to Vince right now, and my parents are at war over what I should do about it. How can you say I'm lucky?"

"Because I've always wanted a baby sister, silly. Why you know that I *love* children. I've been begging and begging my parents for forever, but my mama says she can't have any more on account of her having that operation, you know, that hysterectomy. She had some bad pains, and Dr. Watson—you know him, he goes to your church—he's Melinda's daddy. I don't much like Melinda; she's such a snoot. But Mama says he's the best doctor around here. 'Course he's the only gynecologist, isn't he? Well, he told Mama she had to have that hysterectomy, and that was back when I weren't nothing but an itty-bitty thing. So I've been hoping for years that we could adopt a little sister for me, and then I read about that little girl on the Internet. I'm just in love with her picture. She looks so sweet; I'm sure she'd be the perfect little sister, so I've been saving all those nickels and dimes to try to help her. I can't quit thinking about her. Even if we don't adopt her, I still have to help her. She's so precious. Anyway, that's why I've been saving up, you know." She scooted off the bed and dragged a huge jar of money across the floor and plopped it down in the middle of the bedspread. "She is one of those little girls in China. Do you remember when I talked about that in class that day? Some kids at this place have cleft lips and some have cleft palates. But she has a cleft lip. That's a slit in her lip or something. But she's still the prettiest thing I've ever seen. Big eyes and a round little face. Poor little thing. Maybe I should have just told everyone what I've been saving up for, but I just wanted it to be my little secret. They'd think it's silly anyhow, wanting my parents to adopt a sister for me. But this little girl—she needs an operation before she can be adopted, so I'm going to pay for her surgery. It's only five hundred dollars. Can you believe that? Amber spent more than that on her prom dress. I tried to get her to buy a cheaper one and give me the difference for my fund, but she wouldn't do it."

I sat there too stunned to interrupt her words as they tripped one over the other.

"Once that little girl has had the operation, she'll be fixed good as new. I'm hoping we can adopt her. My parents keep saying no, but if I pay for her operation, maybe I can change their minds." She leaned down and pulled a fancy, gold-embellished box out from under her bed, set it beside the money jar, and carefully pulled off the lid. There on top lay a picture of a Chinese infant. "See? Isn't she beautiful?"

It all sounded like some far-fetched story Heather would tell in class, not a real-life project that she would devote her heart to actually doing. "You mean you really want to adopt a Chinese baby?"

"Yes, really. Look at her sweet face."

I picked up the picture and thought of the little girl living halfway around the world. "I doubt your parents are going to rearrange their lives and adopt her just because you've raised five hundred dollars. They spent three times that on the laptop you got for Christmas and close to that on your iPod and the speaker system to go with it. What's it to them if you send five hundred dollars in change to China?"

She took the picture from me and set it back in the box as if it were breakable. "If they change their minds, it won't be because of the money. It will because of my effort and showing them how serious and dedicated I am to helping her." She slid the box back under her bed and put the jar of money back on the floor before joining me again. "But you're going to have your own baby."

"I don't want a baby! I want to go to college and travel and be a kid." I shook my head. "I don't understand where you're coming from."

"That's because you already have Cindy and Maggie. My house is so lonely."

"But you're graduating in a few weeks. You'll be off on your own."

She shrugged. "I still want a baby sister." Then she grinned. "Hey, maybe I could adopt your baby if you don't want it. That wouldn't take all that red tape or traveling to China or anything."

I rolled my eyes. "Heather . . ."

"Really. Then you could still see it whenever you wanted."

She was insane. "What if it's a boy?" As I asked her the question, I saw babies flitting by in my head, one a boy, one a girl. Was I starting to care whether it was a boy or a girl? Which would I hope to have?

"Oh, well. I'd really want a sister. When will you find out?"

I shook my head again, this time trying to get myself back to reality. "Look, Heather, I'm trying to make life decisions here, not plan out a nursery in some fairy-tale world. I have nowhere to live even. I need a place to stay. What am I going to do?"

Heather thought about it a moment. "Well, you might could stay with Ariana. She has an apartment by that park in Columbia, the one we used to go to on field trips. You know, Carriage Place or whatever it's called."

Yes! "That would be perfect, at least for starters. Do you have her phone number?"

She pulled out her cell phone and flipped it open with a look of importance. "Of course I do. I told you we're good friends."

She talked to Ariana a few minutes, explaining I needed a place to stay at least for a short bit till I worked out a problem, and hung up with a nod. "All set. She says you can't stay permanently, but she can put you up for a bit." Then she grinned. "Says she likes you. Guess I have good taste in friends."

I gave her a hug. "Thanks, Heather."

Who would have thought that it would be Heather who would come through for me?

Everything in Ariana's apartment had a used look to it, but it was spotless. An old futon sat against one wall, with a pretty flowered blanket on top and three handmade pillows. Books and magazines were stacked in precise piles on the hope-chest coffee table. An orange lamp stood in one corner, and a small patio table sat in the far corner flanked by two metal chairs. It was a world of yard sale finds brought together in eclectic harmony of sorts.

I set my suitcase down and plopped into what appeared to be a hundred-year-old armchair to greet her beloved dog.

He walked straight into my suitcase and bounced backward.

Ariana scooped him up. "Blackie is blind. You can't go leaving things just anywhere. Nothing can move. He has every step of the apartment memorized."

I reached for the dog. "I'm so sorry. Poor fella. I promise I won't leave my stuff lying around anymore." He sniffed my crotch and my shirt, licked my lips, then circled around twice before settling into a ball on my lap. He fell into an immediate deep sleep with snores that rivaled any old man.

Ariana rubbed his head. "He doesn't do much but eat and sleep anymore. I've had him since I was ten."

She stretched out on the futon, and we sat that way for a while looking for somewhere to start. "You can't stay here long-term, you know. It's not even big enough for one person, let alone two."

I glanced around for good measure. "I realize that. Only for a bit while I figure things out."

She nodded. "I'm still figuring things out myself."

"I thought you were doing what you wanted—singing and modeling."

"Sure, but not forever. Maybe if I was famous or something, but I've been driving this dream since I was little. All those pageants and talent contests. For what? A few lousy shoots and a handful of commercials. And the band? I had higher hopes than some local group. I always thought I would land a recording contract. It's too much work for too little return, and it's not going anywhere."

Is that how she saw Vince's future? Not going anywhere? Maybe I had been blinded by his enthusiasm. Not that it mattered now anyway. I wasn't part of that future. But Ariana had real talent, and Heather was sure she would be a star someday, otherwise she wouldn't have latched on to Ariana the way she had. Did Heather know Ariana didn't see herself becoming a star, let alone Heather, a newcomer to the whole acting arena?

If Ariana was having more serious thoughts about the future, maybe it was a good thing I was looking at things independently, away from Vince. "I thought you made fantastic money on the modeling."

"I do when I land a job, but it's not dependable. I'm going to keep at it, but I want to do something else as well, something more permanent."

"What?"

"Design school."

That sounded as risky to me as expecting to be a star. "So you're moving to New York or something?"

"No, nothing like that. Nothing big. I like to design jewelry and accessories, like belts and pocketbooks." She stepped over to a cabinet and pulled out a pocketbook made from an old pair of blue jeans and decorated with beads and rhinestones.

"Wow. I love it," I said, and meant it. I reached out and touched the beadwork. "My friends would really go for one of those."

She nodded. "There are lots of places to sell these types of things—little shops and stuff—and I can work on my own schedule, so there will still be time for modeling when shoots come around. I'm already producing a lot of stuff, but I'd like to get a degree in design too. I hope it will give me more ideas and a better foundation for really branching out into a business, instead of just having a paying hobby."

I didn't think it was the most secure kind of plan, but I had to admit it beat my plan—which amounted to finding a place to stash my suitcase. I took a roll of my talents: piano and soccer, neither of which looked too promising, especially with a baby in tow.

The television humming in the corner drew my attention. The volume was so low I couldn't really hear it, and I wasn't interested in watching it anyway—but it was easier to look there than at Ariana. I could tell she was waiting for me to tell her why I was there, why I had run away from home.

Ariana was staring at me instead of the television. It was making me crazy.

"What?" I asked.

"You're pregnant, aren't you?"

I blinked. "What makes you say that?"

"It just adds up. I know Vince's game. And there's not many things that would make a girl like you run away from a nice middle-class home. Anyway, my guess is he got you pregnant and now it's over between you two because he doesn't want it. Am I right? Because I can't think of any other reason you would run away from home."

I sat there like a zombie without a voice.

"I thought I was pregnant once, you know. In fact, I was about your age. Seems like forever ago."

I imagined Ariana as a senior in high school. She wouldn't have been anything like me. She would have been confident and sophisticated. It was hard to imagine her worrying about pregnancy. I considered it awhile, how her life would have changed.

Or would it have? Here she was two, maybe three years after graduating and still not doing much of anything with her life.

"Were you as scared as me? Did your parents reject you? Did your family quit talking to you?"

She shook her head. "It didn't get that far. I walked around in a daze for about a week thinking of what I was going to do. I had dated the guy for a long time, but when I thought I was pregnant, I suddenly realized I didn't want to spend the rest of my life with him."

That was pretty much opposite of me. I had wanted Vince more than anything in the world, and the baby was keeping that from happening. I wondered if she'd had the same thoughts as me, though, weighing her options. "Did you ever think of getting rid of it?"

"No, I couldn't let someone else raise my child. My mom would have gone ballistic. She is, like, so looking forward to having grandkids someday, she would have welcomed a baby with open arms. She wanted about ten kids; instead she got only me, so I could never give a baby away, unless I just let her raise it. I guess I thought she'd be right there with me, and we would do it together."

My question had gone right over her head. "That's not quite what I meant. I meant . . . did you consider, you know, not having it?"

"An abortion?"

I nodded.

"Vince's idea, right?"

I nodded again. I didn't bother to say my mother had echoed his thought.

"I knew from the moment I met him he was an egotistical idiot."

How much did she know about Vince? "I thought he was so cool. So awesome."

"Don't bet on it. I've known lots of guys like him. He's easy to define. I kept wondering how long it would take you to figure out what a self-centered jerk he was, especially given what all he's into."

I felt that puddle of misgivings rise from around my feet and fill me again, not just the uncertainties I'd had about Vince, but about the weird guy in black too. "What are you saying?"

She pulled her bathrobe closer around her and retied the knot of the belt. "You're clueless, aren't you?"

I felt a vortex sucking the life from my world as I stared blankly at her.

"He deals drugs."

I felt my face go white.

"Don't tell me you didn't know."

I shook my head.

"Didn't you wonder how he survived on the pittance the band makes? Or why that weird guy shows up at practices?"

"I thought he was some homeless guy Vince was helping out."

She laughed so hard she almost fell off her seat. "I can't believe you're that naive. He's Vince's cousin, but I don't doubt that he lives in the streets sniffing and shooting whatever he can get his hands on. All I know is that Vince is happy to keep him and his cohorts supplied."

"But he doesn't act like a drug dealer."

"What? You know, they don't all look like scumbags. I'm sure you have enough of them walking around your school to know they can be cool enough about it to keep their composure in public. The signs are still there. You never noticed Vince's glassy eyes or how odd his behavior is at times?"

A part of me had noticed and refused to catalog it that way. I had always excused his faults. I had even justified his actions. "How do you know all this?"

She got up and moved to the kitchen, reaching up into a cabinet for a glass. "Want some water?"

"Sure," I replied. "Tell me, how do you know he deals drugs?"

She tried to hide her face, but I saw the clouded look that passed over it. "I just do. Leave it at that."

I wondered if she'd been in trouble in high school. Or maybe she used drugs and that's what led her to Vince and his band. "Did you buy drugs from him?"

"I told you, I'm not going there. This is about you, not me. But you better keep an eye on that little brother of yours."

That threw me. I didn't have a little brother. Then I realized she meant Tony. "Tony? He doesn't use drugs."

"Maybe not before you hooked him up with Vince. It's like setting a kid in a candy store full of poison."

I shivered. Had I put Tony in danger? "Oh my gosh, you're serious, aren't you?"

She handed me an etched glass filled with ice water. Trust Ariana to have pretty glasses. "Yes, I'm serious."

"Tony has kept himself out of trouble in high school. He'll be okay."

Skepticism creased her brow. "Even a good kid can't turn away candy but so many times."

The thought constricted my heart. I thought of Tony's changing moods, his depression, and his comments about Vince. I felt sick with worry. Had I screwed up my life *and* his?

She settled back in the deep cushions of the red chair. "The point is Vince is a jerk and he wants you to have an abortion so you won't be a burden to him. As soon as it's over with, you'll never hear from him again, I guarantee it. I can tell you one thing: I never considered an abortion, and I sure wouldn't go that route just because some jerk of a guy was telling me to."

I could practically see steam coming out of her ears. She had probably been born with a stronger will and more independent nature than I had ever even come close to possessing.

Her face softened. "Well, honestly, maybe I did think about abortion for like ten seconds when the thought first hit me that I was probably pregnant, but not seriously. I could never do that."

"Oh."

"Have you ever seen pictures of what they do?"

"Not really."

"Well, before you even think about it, you'd better educate yourself on exactly what it is you're talking about doing. Just look online. It'll make you sick to your stomach."

Just what I needed, something to add to my nausea. Still, I filed the info away. She was right. I'd heard about abortion since elementary school, but I really had no idea how it was done. "They make it sound like it's nothing."

"Of course they do. How many girls would go to abortion clinics if they advertised the truth? Look at the options. They suck it out of you. They pull it apart. Or they burn it to death with saline solution, and you deliver a dead baby. And it makes a lot of women incapable of having a normal pregnancy later on. Is that what you want? I could never do that. That's me."

I didn't respond.

"I know it's scary when you're still in high school, but there's only a month or so left, right? The truth is that high school ends and real life begins. It might be harder with a baby, but not impossible. Just different. And there is adoption. That's something you have to work out. But how is carrying a baby around in your body for the next—what do you have left? Seven months?—how is that going to change life, other than maybe fewer dates?"

She made it sound like there wasn't much of a decision to make, but she didn't have to face a whole school of people gossiping or worry about graduating. It still seemed overwhelming to me.

Chapter Twenty~Five

I WENT BACK to school the next day. I hadn't really intended to, but Ariana woke me up at seven o'clock.

"Don't you need to get ready?"

It took me a minute to remember where I was and why. Reality hit me like a softball in the face; I was pregnant and had run away from home. "Ready for what?"

"School."

"I'm not going," I said and rolled over. The futon wasn't very comfortable. It was a cheap one with such a thin foam pad that I could feel every metal support bar. My body ached all over. I needed to sleep at least another couple of hours.

Ariana turned on the lamp beside me. "No way. You're not hanging around my apartment all day and turning into a drop-out. Being pregnant is no excuse for that. What are you going to do if you don't graduate?"

"What am I going to do even if I do graduate? I can't go to college now."

"Having a child doesn't keep you from going to college. My mom didn't go until she was twenty-eight, after I was born."

"Sure, I'm independently wealthy. I can afford college and

babysitters without even having a job."

"Don't be so lame. Lots of people work and go to school. Besides, there are all kinds of loans and scholarships, especially for independent girls with children."

I sat halfway up. Maybe there was some truth to that. I wasn't the only girl who'd gotten pregnant in high school. There were bound to be programs.

"Anyway, college or not, you've got to graduate."

"You sound like you're my mother or something."

"Truth is you're invading my life enough by sleeping on my futon. I can't have you hanging around all day. Get up, get dressed, and get out. Whether you go to school or not is your business."

Ah, the truth. I wondered if she got up every day at seven in the morning or only today to get me out of her space. I couldn't imagine what she did all day. If I were her, I would have slept till noon at least. She didn't have a photo shoot. What else did she have to do all day?

By the time I got out of the shower, she had two bowls of oatmeal sitting on the table. "I made breakfast. My daddy says this stuff sticks to your bones, keeps you full all morning."

Oatmeal?

I really wanted another egg biscuit from Mickey D's, but I ate the oatmeal anyway. My stomach was doing flips; I had to eat something, it was free, and she was right about it being filling.

"You better get yourself some juice this afternoon and whatever else you want to eat and drink. I can't supply you with meals, you know, and you have to eat right when you're pregnant. Have you gotten vitamins yet?"

I blinked. *Vitamins?* I was still trying to decide what I was doing, and she wanted me to take vitamins.

It felt strange pulling into the school parking lot knowing I'd come from Ariana's place instead of home. I didn't know what I was going to say to Maggie, or if she would even look at me. My stomach sat in my throat as I crossed the parking lot to the office to get an admittance slip for being absent the previous day and then headed to my locker.

Maggie was there with Webb, her arms full of books.

There was nothing to do but face her straight on. "Hi, Maggie."

She turned angry eyes on me. "Nice of you to take the car."

"I'm sorry. I didn't know what else to do. Did Webb . . . ?"

Webb didn't look any more pleased to see me than Maggie did, which didn't surprise me; they were joined at the brain. He leaned against the locker and looked me up and down. I knew what he was thinking. *Dixie pregnant.* "Yes," he said, "I brought them."

His smug look was more than I could stand. He used to be a total bum with no ambitions. Who was he to act like he was above me just because I was pregnant? "Well," I said, "considering she's brought you to school for the past three years, it's about time." I grabbed my physics books, slammed my locker, and strode away.

Halfway down the hall, tears formed in my eyes. Neither of them even cared where I had spent the night.

I didn't stay in the halls long enough to run into Heather and

Tammy until break. They were both surprised to see me. "We thought you were out again today. Were you sick?" Tammy asked from a safe distance.

I shifted my load of books to the opposite arm. At least that confirmed that Heather hadn't shared my secret with Tammy. I tossed her a quick smile, but I didn't really feel like talking. Tony, Maggie, Webb, and Heather all knew what was going on. I felt sure the entire student body would be gawking at me by lunch.

I brushed by them. "I just had stuff to take care of."

Heather poked Tammy. "She broke up with Vince."

I sighed. I wasn't in the mood. But at least she'd told Tammy something safe and not the real reason I was depressed.

"Oh!" Tammy wrapped an arm around me. "Is that why we're in such a gloomy mood today? Poor thing."

I didn't want her arm around me. I didn't want to even be near them. I wanted to go sulk in the park and eat a whole gallon of ice cream. In fact, the more I thought of ice cream, the better I felt. Now that it had come to mind, I craved it like a drug.

Tammy gave my shoulders an extra squeeze. "I thought maybe you had skipped school to go to the salon for a haircut."

Tammy freaked whenever a hair was out of place, and mine definitely needed cutting. Right now, I didn't care.

"Really, Dix, we need to get you in with Miss Sawyer. She is so fab. I mean look at my hair. She did a fantastic job on it. No one else has ever gotten the ends cut so precisely that they curled under just right."

Who cared about haircuts anymore? I had bigger problems, like getting a baby cut out of my gut. I glanced at the clock on the lobby wall. Only ten o'clock. It would be hours before school was over and I could go to the store for ice cream. I stepped away from the girls, slid a dollar bill into the snack machine, and bought some M&Ms.

"Dixie, what are you doing?" Heather screeched. "You can't eat that."

Not her worried about the baby's health too, I thought. "Why not?"

"It's bad for you," she stammered. "I mean, it will ruin your complexion. Chocolate is not on our list of acceptable foods."

"It's the best thing to eat when you're depressed. Didn't you know that? It has something in it that cheers women up." Probably not true, but it sounded good anyway. Not that I cared one way or the other. I intended to eat them just because I was craving them.

Lunch was as painful as break. I would have moved to Maggie's table, but she wasn't talking to me.

I don't know why that day was any different from all the days before, but it was as if my eyes were opened. Maybe it was because I'd had to grow up a lot in the previous twenty-four hours, and I was beginning to put a new value on everything around me. Whatever the reason, it seemed different. I'd spent the past two years trying to stay in with Heather and Tammy, but now I was seeing them with fresh eyes, more black-and-white than I ever had before—probably much like Maggie had. Maggie had gone through some hard times in tenth grade; she was always more mature than me, but she was forced to handle some pretty horrible situations that year with Heather and Tammy's friend, Sue. And then she was attacked by a crazy man. I had never really considered what that had probably done to her mentally. Instead, I had shunned her for being stupid at not jumping to Heather and Tammy's side like I did when they offered friendship and the chance to be popular.

As I sat in world cultures class that day, I began to understand how Maggie had viewed my friends for the past two years. Their inane conversation at break about their haircuts was bad enough, but as the day wore on, their attitudes just underlined their shallowness three times. Mr. Baire was discussing the economic causes behind the constant conflict in the Middle East, but Amber and Heather kept interrupting him with dumb questions.

"Mr. Baire," Heather said with her hand waving in the air. "Mr. Baire, why do you think Jesus was born there instead of in the States?"

Mr. Baire looked over the class, probably checking to see if anyone else knew how dumb that question was. Half the class sighed and put their heads on their desks in aggravation. It's not like we had a test that day; the rest of us just wanted to get through the lecture. Mr. Baire got a smug look on his face and replied, "Because there weren't any stables in the States."

Amber looked startled. "What? Why not?"

"Because Indians lived in teepees and didn't build barns."

The class snickered, and Mr. Baire returned to his lecture.

"But Mr. Baire," Heather said, "isn't it true He was really born in a cave, not a barn?"

"This isn't religion class. Concentrate, girls," Mr. Baire said as he tapped the dry-erase pen on the board. "We are talking about modern culture, not Jesus. Amber, look up here." He pointed to a map of the Middle East.

"Oh, a game. Can we play?" asked Heather.

I rolled my eyes. She really wasn't stupid. Why did she put on such an act? How had I never realized how dumb she sounded?

Mr. Baire returned her inane smile. "Certainly, Heather. All of you can play. Look at the map," he said, then continued with his lecture.

Sixty seconds later, Heather waved her hand again. "Mr. Baire, why are we staring at the map?"

Mr. Baire didn't even bother turning around. "So you won't interrupt me."

Duh.

Twenty minutes later, he asked for our essays on a current news item based in the Middle East. Everyone had them ready except Heather.

"Where is your essay, Heather?"

"I was going to bring it, really I was, but my father wouldn't let me use the computer."

"He used it all week long and wouldn't let you get your homework done?"

"Well, yes, sir. You see, he plays solitaire on it. It relieves his stress."

"Did you tell him you had an essay to write?"

"Well, not exactly. He was concentrating so hard, I didn't dare say anything. Besides, I had a phone call, and you know how I like to talk on the phone."

"You had a phone call that lasted all week?"

"No, silly. Just the one time I went to use the computer."

By this point, Mr. Baire's mouth had become a grim line. "Bring your essay in tomorrow, Heather, or you get a zero."

"Maybe you could turn it in to him as a text message," Asby said sarcastically.

Maggie giggled. Our eyes met, and she knew I was laughing

too. Heather and Tammy texted each other constantly, something Maggie and I had often laughed about. Somewhere beneath the hurt, we knew we were still kindred spirits. I just didn't know if we could bridge the gap to get back on that footing.

As I left class, I felt friendless. Just being around Heather, Tammy, and Amber made me feel like more of a failure. Amber had no plans other than a summer job. Heather would never make it to Hollywood. And Tammy was so intent on marrying a rich older man that she never faced the reality of making a living on her own. What were they ever going to do in life? I had to get a plan together. I had to make some decisions and take steps forward—one direction or the other.

Chapter Twenty~Six

A PLAN. THAT'S what I needed. But not until I had my fill of ice cream. I'd been thinking about it all day. I pulled out of the school parking lot aiming for the nearest grocery store but decided to head to one out by Ariana's apartment instead. The high school was on the opposite side of town from Mama and Frank's house, and the apartment was even farther, on the edge of Columbia. If I waited till I got clear of my hometown, I'd be less likely to run into anyone I had to speak to, and right then I didn't want conversation with anyone who knew me or might have heard about my situation.

Halfway there, I noticed my gas gauge was on empty. I didn't have much money left. If given the choice between gas and ice cream, though, I knew I'd choose the ice cream just as surely as old Annie would go for that perfume at Belk's. How could we be such weak creatures, giving in to our desires even when the choices in front of us were so plain?

The irony of that realization was a slap in the face. I'd done nothing but give in to my desires from the moment I first saw Vince.

Now I was stuck with a new reality. I had to get a job. I had to buy food and gas. Mama sure wasn't going to come to school and hand me money, and I couldn't count on babysitting jobs being steady enough to keep that much cash in my pocket.

I put three gallons of gas in my car—just enough to get to and from school for a day or two, really, since the apartment was so far away—and continued on to the grocery store as I weighed the value of a dollar like I hadn't since I was ten years old and saving up for a CD player. Twenty bucks seemed like an astronomical amount back then. A week ago I would have laughed at the thought, but at this point twenty dollars was my life savings.

As I thought about what I needed to buy, I caught sight of Vince's uncle's white delivery van, the van Vince had driven to practice a few times. It was parked at the side of a hardware store. I don't know why, but I pulled into the drugstore parking lot next door and sat staring at it, just thinking. Why had Vince been driving that thing, anyway? The answer was clear a few minutes later. He came out of the hardware store and carried something to a man's pickup truck, then returned to the store. I admit I'm slow, but after a couple minutes he came back out and retrieved a rake from an outdoor display and carried it back inside, and it dawned on me that he was working there. He had a job! A nine-to-five job at his uncle's hardware store. The implications slowly came to me—the band wasn't making enough money to support him, yet he'd given Tony a hard time about working at the grocery store.

The idea of Vince working as hired help at an out-of-the-way hardware store shattered my image of him. Not that I had a problem with any guy having an honest job. Maybe for that reason alone it should have boosted my opinion of him, but he'd come across so suave and egotistical, and I'd built him up so much in my head as being this big star that I felt deflated with disappointment. He wasn't who I'd imagined him to be. Were the other things true too? The things Ariana had said about drug dealing and such? Suddenly I felt like he was a complete stranger . . . and I was having his baby.

I pulled back out into traffic, my mind whirling, my spirit shaken, and depression settling over me. I needed ice cream — bad.

The day before I had noticed a little strip mall near the apartment that had a grocery store in it, and I pulled in, planning to shop there, but then noticed there was a Dairy Queen beside it. I weighed my options. A Blizzard or a half-gallon of ice cream? It made more sense to buy a carton, but my feet propelled me straight to the DQ. Once inside, though, I changed my mind. It was crazy to spend my money so freely. Instead, I waited till the customers cleared out, and got the supervisor's attention. It was time I started sorting out my priorities.

"Are you hiring?" I couldn't believe it was me, asking to work in an ice cream parlor. Heather would freak. Fortunately, this place was so far removed from home that no one I knew was likely to ever come in. Not that it truly embarrassed me to have a job like that; I'd just never pictured myself serving ice cream or flipping burgers or waiting on tables.

What would I like to do? We were supposed to be thinking about that all the time as seniors, and I'd barely given it any thought. I guess I expected the answer to float down in front of me someday like a neon sign, but my mind twisted around it while I stood there asking about scooping ice cream for a living. And suddenly it dawned on me: If I could *choose* what I did, it would be working at Parks and Recreation, teaching kids to play soccer and stuff like that. That's what I really loved doing.

I was so confounded by the realization that I almost didn't hear the lady's answer about the job.

"Sorry, I just hired someone last week, but Mary told me yesterday that she's looking for some help. I bet she would hire you."

I thought it was my wandering mind that made me miss some detail, because I had no idea who Mary was. "Mary?"

"Oh, down a few doors. You know, Mary's Boutique. Nice lady. She just had a baby. She thought she could keep running the shop as usual. I tried to warn her that having a baby would put a kink in her schedule." She laughed at her own wit.

Inwardly, I groaned. I'd already figured out a baby would do that, and I was only eighteen years old. "Thanks for the tip. I appreciate it."

Two doors down, I saw the sign for the dress shop. The front window had a mannequin in a blue dress, slightly more conservative than anything I would wear, but at least it wasn't a pair of ugly stretch-top pants with some gaggy matching knit shirt like most old women seemed to wear. I didn't think I could make myself sell something like that to anyone.

Inside, the sole salesperson stood behind a counter ringing up a sale. Perhaps she was the owner, Mary, who had just had a baby. She had narrow eyes rimmed by dark, thick lashes, and long thin arms with fingers to match. She moved with quick, precise movements, which made me think she had a tendency to be impatient like Mrs. Newell, my English teacher, who always seemed to bounce with extra energy. Mary, if that's who the salesperson was, and her customer were the only people in the store, so I wandered over to a jewelry display to make it less obvious that I was waiting to speak to her.

The jewelry wasn't too bad. Nothing too original, but not old lady stuff, either. The pocketbooks were better. She had a lot of unique ones, maybe made by some local designer, but not quite as good as Ariana's designs. Ariana used jewels and special stitching in the fabrics to add pizzazz.

I looked again at the dress in the window and thought of how much more appealing it would be with the right necklace and pocketbook, and maybe a gold belt around the waist. If I worked there, could I suggest such things?

"May I help you?"

The voice startled me. I turned around with a frozen smile on my face. "Hello. I'm Dixie Chambers. The lady down at Dairy Queen told me you are looking for help."

She eyed me up and down a minute. "How old are you?"

"Eighteen, ma'am."

She nodded. "Still in school?"

"Yes, ma'am. But I can work after school and all weekend."

"How about parties and ball games and the rest?"

"I need the money, really. I guess I've had my fill of the other stuff." As I said it, I realized I really had. I didn't have any desire to go to a party or a game now. I hadn't been in a while anyway because of Vince and his performances. Heather and Tammy hadn't invited me to go anywhere with them in ages. I was beginning to think Amber had become the third girl in their trio, replacing me because they expected me to busy with Vince. If it weren't for seeing each other at school, it would be a hard stretch to even call us friends. The only thing I had still been looking forward to was prom, but even that had faded away to being unimportant. Who in their right mind would invite a pregnant girl anyhow?

"Can you start right now and be here every afternoon the rest of this week?"

I hadn't had my ice cream yet. But there was more to consider than one ice cream snack. "Yes, ma'am. In fact, I'm out of school on Friday and Monday because of Easter. I'll work then, too, if you like."

"All right, then, let's get started. First we have to fill out some paperwork, and then I'll show you what you'll be doing."

As we got through the formalities and we worked around the shop, she explained more about herself. Her baby was only eight weeks old, and it was killing her to leave her with a sitter everyday. But she didn't want to lose her shop either. Her husband had taken off with someone else before he even knew she was pregnant, and she had no intention of sharing the news with him now, even if it meant not getting child support.

"I don't want to share her with him or anyone else," she said. "He was impossible to live with, and he'd spend the rest of his life making my daughter miserable, trying to tell her what to do all the time, like he did me. He never wanted me to have this shop, and then he couldn't stand it when it started making money."

I wondered how, when we'd only had two customers since I arrived.

"I'm thinking of bringing the baby here, keeping her in the back room. What do you think?"

A few months ago I wouldn't have had any kind of answer for her. What thoughts had I ever given to babies? But the question didn't seem all that odd to me now. I could be trying to solve the same kind of problem myself. I hadn't thought a bit about what I would do with a baby after it arrived. Where would I live with my child, who would take care of it while I worked, and how could I possibly continue my education as Ariana implied I ought to? She made it sound like it would all fall into place, but Miss Mary made me really think about it. Where would I find a babysitter? I hadn't even considered the idea that it would bother me to leave my baby with someone else, not when I kept considering . . .

Miss Mary paused in hanging up a new pack of shirts to hear my answer, and there I was lost in my own problems.

"What's the point in having your own store if you don't do what you want with it?" I said. "I'd bring her down here and start carrying a line of expensive girl's clothes. You know, not ordinary mall stuff, but those really fancy ones with lace and ruffles."

She brightened all over. "What a fantastic idea." She shoved the last shirt onto the rack and pushed open the door to the back room. "I could easily fit her crib back here. She sleeps most of the time right now anyway."

"The only thing I would worry about would be someone snatching her when you're busy. Of course, if you cleared out the whole room, reorganized it and all, you could fit an old chair and lamp and stuff back here, with a nice area rug on the floor and a toy box, and let the babysitter watch her right here. Then you can sit with her when you want, but you're free when customers need you."

She nodded as she envisioned what I was saying. "I knew there was some reason I hired you on the spot. You must be some kind of messenger from God, answering my prayers."

I laughed. "Believe me, I'm not on God's list of angels."

That brought a worried look. "Are you in trouble for something?"

I didn't want to tell her. I wasn't ready to make public pronouncements yet. Saying something at church had given me a taste of where that could lead. I shrugged and turned back to the rounder to straighten out the sleeves of the shirts. "Not with the law or anything. I've just had a major fight with my parents, and they aren't speaking to me."

She stood in front of me, hands on her hips. "Have you run away from home? Is that why you need money so badly?"

"Not like you think. They know where to find me. My stepsister and I are in the same classes at school, and yes, I'm still going to class. I've just moved in with a friend until I work out what I'm going to do after graduation."

"End of May?"

"What?"

"Graduation. It's the end of May, isn't it?"

"Yes, ma'am. May twenty-third."

"It will be here sooner than you think. The azaleas are blooming in my garden."

I agreed with her there. Everything seemed like it was coming faster than I could handle.

Chapter Twenty-Seven

BY THE END of the week, I had told my teachers about my new job and bowed out of yearbook staff and art club. I settled into a routine of working every afternoon. My first paycheck was due in the morning, not a day too soon either. I'd been eating ramen noodles all week for supper and Total cereal for breakfast. Maggie had seen me skipping lunch and knew instinctively that I was broke—I never seemed to have money in my pockets the way she did—and was kind enough to buy me lunch every day. "You have to have something nutritious, no junk food," she said as she thrust money into my hand. I took the money without argument, but inside I was a mess of emotions. I knew in my heart that Maggie was right about the baby, but I was afraid to face that reality, especially with Mama and Vince intent on abortion as the only option. If it weren't for Maggie and Ariana, I probably would have caved under their pressure because it seemed like the easiest solution—to eliminate the problem rather than face it. Instead, I kept ignoring the reality that I had to take measures one way or the other. I had to quit walking around in a daze and come to some decision.

Amazingly, Heather and Maggie both kept my secret. If there

had been gossip about me, I would have known by the looks, if not direct comments, people gave me, and no one had said or done anything. I thanked Heather in the bathroom midweek. "It means a lot to me that you haven't said anything to anyone."

She hugged me. "I'm your best friend, silly. You can count on me."

That made me feel bad for having mean thoughts of her so recently, of thinking of her as a birdbrain with no realistic goals.

An hour later, she proved my first expectations true. Amber walked into lunch with an odd look on her face and leaned into me. "Is it true?"

My heart sank.

She took my silence for assent. Her face crunched up into disgust, with her nose wrinkled and her lips pursed together. "Too bad for you."

"Thanks, Amber," I replied.

I picked the sandwich up off my plate and left the lunchroom, munching as I went.

I passed Heather. "I thought you didn't tell anyone."

"I didn't!"

"Then how did Amber find out?"

"Oh," she said, "Amber's different, isn't she? I mean, she's one of us."

So Amber's inclusion was official. I gritted my teeth. If Amber knew, no doubt Tammy knew too.

Maggie hadn't asked where I was staying, and I didn't volunteer the information. Since she saw me in school everyday, she would let Mama know I was okay. She could find me there if she really wanted me. They probably thought I was living with Vince. If only they knew.

I developed a routine of sorts. After school, I worked at Mary's Boutique until seven and then headed to Ariana's apartment to eat, get my homework done, and collapse into bed. I hadn't expected pregnancy to drain me so much; the need for sleep dragged at me constantly.

On Friday I was alone in Ariana's apartment, sitting on the futon, trying to catch up on homework so it wouldn't be hanging over me while I worked full-time during the long weekend. I heard a rap on the door. I had no idea who it could be — Ariana had landed a photo shoot in Atlanta and was gone until Sunday morning, but I thought maybe she had friends who didn't know her schedule. I sat still a moment, my cautious side telling me to ignore the knocking and wait for whoever it was to go away. After all, I was alone, and I certainly wasn't expecting company; no one knew I lived there, not even Vince. It could be anyone at the door.

The knock came again, bringing Blackie out of his deep sleep in his dog bed to yap five times in a row before he forced himself to stand and hobble toward the door. "Anyone there?"

It was a woman's voice I vaguely recognized. I eased myself to a stand to keep from making any noise and crept to the doorway to peer out the peephole. It was Annie, the lady who begged for food at McDonald's. I held my breath a moment, trying to decide what to do. I didn't really want to talk to her. No doubt she was looking for a handout, and I had nothing to give.

Not true, I reprimanded myself. I had just put on a pot of soup to heat up for supper. Ariana kept telling me I ought to be eating more than broth and noodles, but some nights it was all I could stomach. There was no reason I couldn't share it. I wouldn't eat it all.

Annie knocked again.

I sighed. The way my life was headed, I could easily end up in as bad a spot as old Annie, hoping someone would share food with me.

I opened the door. "Hello, Miss Annie. Come on in."

She stepped into the small room without so much as a hesitation. "I don't know how I knowed it, but I just knowed you was living here. I guess the good Lord done told me in His own way."

I shut the door behind her. "You mean you were looking for me?"

"Well, not exactly. I'm out selling these here packs of assorted cards. You know, birthday, get well, congratulations, and, of course, sympathy cards, but landsakes at your age I hope you ain't needin' that kind of card. Would you like to look at 'em?" She fished in the canvas bag she always had slung over her shoulder and handed me a box. "Like I was saying, I was out selling, took the bus 'cause I done been to every house in town, and I just knew I ought to knock on this door. I had this inklin' you was here."

"I guess you gave up on vacuum cleaners."

"Oh, I still sell 'em sometimes, but they got to where they was hurting my back a mite to haul around, so I jumped at the chance to hook up with these cards. Becky Sue Sawyer got me started. Do you know Becky Sue?"

I shook my head; the name wasn't familiar.

"She's new in town, and she joined that Bible study group I'm in."

That rang a bell. Miss Sawyer — the new hairdresser Tammy had mentioned.

"Anyways, I just love to hear her read Scripture. She's got a voice smooth as molasses being poured, and we all mop up her words like we's biscuits."

"Look, I've got some soup that's about done. Would you like to share it with me?"

"Oh, don't you know I would. It's been a long day out there today, and they's a storm a-brewin', and I just knew the good Lord was gonna find me something to comfort these old bones."

I waved her over to the little glass table Ariana had placed by the kitchen window. "Sit down and I'll get it."

She settled herself at the table with her heavy canvas bag at her feet overflowing with the assortment of odds and ends she carried around, and pushed the frayed shawl off her shoulders onto the back of the ladder-back chair. Her half-blonde, half-brunette hair hung to her shoulders, puffed out around her face in total disarray. To see her smile at the arrival of a mere cup of soup, you'd have thought she was a queen being served prime rib.

"Ain't this lovely," she said.

She waited for me to take my seat and then bowed her head. "Heavenly Father, we give you thanks for providing this meal and ask Your blessing upon it. Amen."

I'd expected a longer prayer than that and looked up somewhat surprised, but she didn't notice. She'd gone immediately to spooning up her soup. After a few mouthfuls, she laid her spoon aside. "Oh, I done forgot why I was even hoping to find you. How ungracious of me, especially after speaking to the Lord." She pulled out her Bible, laid it on the table next to her bowl, and turned to a page she had marked with a string.

"This right here," she said. "It's from Jeremiah. Do you recall reading his words of wisdom? Well, right here in chapter one is what the good Lord told me to say to you: *Before I formed you in the womb I knew you.*" She caressed the page a moment with her eyes closed, then packed the book back into her bag. "It's a wondrous feeling to know that God Hisself had His hand on our creation from before we even existed, ain't it? I expect that's what God wanted you to know. Was you having doubts about Him loving you? About you being one of His children? Was that it?"

I stared into my soup. She had no idea He was telling me He had His hand on the creation in my uterus.

"Well, darlin', there ain't no need for any doubts 'bout God loving you. Like the Good Book says, He knowed you way back then. He created you for a purpose. I'm thinking maybe you need to still your heart and listen to Him a piece. He'll tell you what you's supposed to do, whatever it is you can't decide on."

I had contemplated taking things into my own hands. It was a mirror being held up in front of me, showing me how selfish I was being.

The thought startled me. Isn't that what she'd read to me last time? To not be selfish or vain? Was that the bottom line as to why I was considering an abortion? I was afraid of being ridiculed. I was still hoping to get Vince back. I was terrified of figuring out how I would raise a child.

Everything Annie had quoted to me was meant to offer me assurance. How had she known? All I could figure was that God really had led her to me. If I believed in Him as I had professed in church and youth group for as long as I could remember, I had to open my heart to the possibility that God could use someone like Annie to bring me a message.

My hand went unconsciously to my belly. *He already knows you and loves you, and I've done everything in my power to ignore you, to deny that you even exist.*

"You gonna be sick, young 'un? You look kinda pale."

I bit my lip. "No, I'm okay." I reached my hand out across the table and touched her arm. "Thanks for coming today, Miss Annie. You don't know what it's meant to me."

"Me too." She grinned so wide, I could see the space where she'd lost a tooth. "This soup is just what my soul needed today. The Lord sure is good, ain't He? Providing what we need every single day. We just got to let Him carry the cross. Seems like it shouldn't be all that hard, but it sure trips some folks up."

I nodded.

When she'd eaten every last drop, I fished my last ten dollar bill from my pocketbook and pressed it into her hand. "I'm so glad you brought those cards. I needed a card for my sister's birthday and a congratulations card for someone else."

"You take care, young 'un. I'll be praying that the Lord eases your mind."

"You've already done that, Miss Annie, but keep on praying for me anyway."

That night I had a dream. I saw Jesus sitting on His throne in heaven with children gathered around Him. One was standing off to the side a bit, sad and forlorn, a little boy with sandy hair and bright blue-green eyes like the sparkling ocean on a sunny day. He looked at me as if his puppy dog had just been hit by a car, then turned and moved to Jesus' side. He laid his head on Jesus' knee, and Jesus caressed his head.

What's wrong with him? I asked in my dream.

Jesus wept. *He is the child you rejected and threw away.*

I woke with a start and stared at the ceiling, my heart pounding. That poor little boy. My little boy. How could I ever face him in heaven? How could I ever live with myself, knowing I'd refused to open my heart to that cute little boy, one of God's special creations, my own son?

I got up and opened the box of cards I'd bought from Annie, sorted through them, and pulled out one with a teddy bear holding balloons. It had Congratulations written across the top. I sat at the table, pen in hand, and wrote on the inside:

Vince,
Congratulations on the upcoming birth of your child. You're
going to be a father whether you like it or not.

I hesitated over how to sign it. Love? No way. In the end, I simply scrawled my name and shoved it into the envelope.

Chapter Twenty-Eight

I FELT WEIRD walking down the school halls on Tuesday, because I was sure that the news of my pregnancy had spread by now. Everyone in school would know. After the gossip about Vince, there wouldn't be much doubt in anyone's mind as to whether or not it was true, even if I didn't admit it.

But I had a new resolve to plan out a future that included my baby. The more I thought about the little person growing inside me, I couldn't believe I'd ever even considered any other alternative than keeping it. Who was Vince to think he should be able to flush away our child? The enormity of having almost raised my hand against God, of committing murder, not in self-defense but against my own flesh and blood, astonished me.

Sam hadn't talked to me much since the whole Vince-sleepover rumor, but he must have sensed something had changed. He approached me during break.

I no longer hung out with Heather and Tammy in the atrium lobby where classmates mingled for break. Instead I slumped against the wall across from my locker to work on homework. Surprisingly, I realized I could get quite a bit accomplished in the time I used to spend in useless chatter—which meant I would be able to crawl into bed all the earlier at night.

Sam stood over me a minute, then dropped his books to the floor and sat down. "So what's up?"

I glanced up from my notes. "You're speaking to me again."

"I thought about a lot of stuff over Easter."

I had done a lot of thinking during Easter too. It was a lonely Sunday without family or church, but good for reflection about the Resurrection and forgiveness and all that. I'd had a long talk with God.

Sam continued. "I had no right to judge you."

"You're right about that," I agreed.

"I hear you broke up with motorcycle guy."

"What of it?"

He shrugged.

I went back to testing myself on vocabulary, covering up my notes and repeating definitions in my head.

"I hear you ran away from home."

I gave up on the definitions. "I didn't run away. I moved out."

"Where are you living?"

"With a friend. A *girl*friend, if it matters."

"Oh," he said. He sat quietly a moment, gathering courage I think, and then said, "Would you go to prom with me?"

I didn't want another boyfriend. Somewhere during the weekend, I'd come to resolve that as strongly as I resolved to keep the baby.

But I could use a friend.

"Sam," I said, keeping alert for any change in expression, "are you asking because you want to be my boyfriend or because you want to be my friend?"

He didn't answer for a couple seconds, but gazed back at me just as intently. "I can't be your boyfriend, can I?"

I shook my head. "No, you can't. No one can. I have to be by myself for a while, and I don't want a relationship like that with anyone. But even if I did, I want you to understand I don't feel that way about you. You're a nice guy. You have a lot of wonderful attributes. You're honest and quiet, and you're not egotistical or out to impress anyone. I like that about you. But I'm not in love with you. Can you live with that?"

I could see in his eyes that he couldn't speak, but he nodded.

"What I really need is a good friend who won't talk to anyone else about me."

He laid a hand on my shoulder. "Friends only, I promise."

The sincerity was still there in his face and eyes and the relaxed demeanor of his body, and I knew he meant it.

"I'll think about prom," I said. "I've got a lot on my mind right now, and prom just doesn't seem very important anymore, so I'm not sure I even want to go. I'll let you know tomorrow."

"Tell me what's wrong."

I searched Sam's face. He had this steady gaze and softness that was so unthreatening, so trusting . . . but I'd learned to be cautious. I looked up and down the hall. No one else was around. It was safe to talk.

I sat up straight as if it would give me extra strength, took a deep breath, and whispered. "I'm pregnant."

Tears welled up in my eyes as I admitted it, then my shoulders sagged and shook. Sam pulled me close and let me cry into his shirt. "I wondered if that's what it was."

"What made you guess that?" I asked in muffled sobs against his chest.

"My aunt is pregnant. Every time she comes to the house, she and my mother make a fuss over every change they see, and . . . well . . . you've changed in the same ways."

I looked up to see him blushing. How could Sam have noticed the changes in my body when Vince hadn't? But then again, Sam's silence seemed to open his eyes more, making him notice everything that happened around him.

I sat up and brushed away my tears. "I'm glad you're my friend, Sam. I really need a good friend."

He smiled. "Me too."

The bell rang, so we gathered up our things and headed to class, knowing without saying it that we would talk later.

Heather saw us walking down the hall together and dashed up to my side, pulling me over to whisper, "What are you doing? Don't tell me you're going to date Sam?"

Her sweet berry perfume overwhelmed my senses. I tried to hold my breath. "We're just friends, Heather."

"You can't just be friends with a guy, especially not a leech like him. He'll follow you around like he owns you or something."

"Actually, he's a nice guy. I like that he's quiet. He won't go around spreading stories."

She totally missed my insinuation. She didn't understand the value of silence.

Her stance — hand on hip and pouting face — registered her disgust. "He doesn't have to say anything to anybody. Just being seen with him is going to ruin you."

"If it worries you that much, you can keep your distance."

"Ugh!" She tossed her hair over her shoulder like some mark of honor. "Like you would choose to hang out with him instead of me and Tammy?"

"I'm not choosing one or the other. I'm just saying he's my friend, and if that bothers you, you don't have to associate with me anymore."

"After I hooked you up with Ariana? That's gratitude."

"Look, Heather, I'm really grateful you called Ariana for me, but that doesn't mean you can choose who I can and can't talk to at school."

"Well, I'm not hanging out with Sam."

The tardy bell pealed, and I stepped into the classroom, leaving Heather in the hall wondering whether or not she'd won.

Chapter Twenty-Nine

VINCE SHOWED UP at school again the next day. It was like *déjà vu*, me walking out with Sam and Vince standing by the car waiting for me. Except this time Sam didn't turn and walk away.

I touched Sam's arm and gave him a look that meant I needed to say my piece. He frowned and furrowed his eyebrows, and I knew he understood but didn't like it.

"So," I said to Vince when I'd gotten within a step of the car, "what brings you here?" Looking at him, armed with everything Ariana had told me, I could tell he was high. How had I ever taken those glassy eyes as just being dreamy? Now that I knew the truth, it was so obvious. His eyes looked glazed from whatever it was he was on.

"We need to talk," he said.

"Really?" A touch of sarcasm reached my voice. "Did you bring more wine and cheese?"

That didn't go over well. A look passed over his face that probably meant he was mad, but he recovered quickly and reached for my hand. "We need to work this out, Dixie. Figure out what we're going to do."

Students walked past us with little more than a glance as they made their way to their cars, piled in, and left trails of exhaust as they headed down the road. But Heather, Tammy, and Amber had come to stand within earshot, with their eyes wide and whispers passing back and forth between them. I thought of them more as interested bystanders than allies. Other kids convened behind them, stopping on their way across the parking lot, some leaning on car hoods, some just standing and gaping at us — we were gossip being played out in front of them, a continuation of *Dixie and Motorcycle Man* to keep them entertained the rest of the week. At my expense.

I ignored them. I stared into Vince's glassy eyes, trying to decide where this strategy was taking him. Soften me up, get me back at his side so he could make sure I had an abortion? "Figure out what we're going to do?" I repeated. "You mean you really want to work things out?"

"Of course."

A tiny glimmer of hope still lived inside me, crazy as that sounds. It flared at his words and coursed through my veins. I flushed as I pushed it to the ultimate question. "Are you going to marry me?"

"What?" For once, I saw real shock cross his face.

Heather stepped up and squeezed my arm, whether in excitement or what, I wasn't sure, but I could hear girls whispering all around me, probably as shocked at my question as Vince was. I was in neck deep, so I asked it again, this time even louder, as if he were a deaf old man. "Are you going to marry me?"

"Uh, well, I think we just need to talk first."

"About what?"

"You know."

I was getting into the act by this time. I tossed my hair back as if I were Heather and rolled my eyes like Tammy when she was exasperated. "Do you want to get back together or don't you?"

"Of course I do."

"You do?"

The crowd of onlookers didn't give him any pause; he went into acting mode as if we were alone in bed together. "Things aren't the same without you. You know you're my girl."

"Really? Then what is Pamela's part in this play?"

"Huh?"

I figured I might as well give everyone their money's worth. They already had enough fuel to make up more than I could ever reveal. Maybe I'd get a few sympathizers if I played all my cards. "You know, Pamela—the girl I caught you in bed with. Do you remember her?"

He shifted back and forth on his feet, the crowd holding their breath to see how he would answer that one. "Pamela is my lead singer, Dixie."

"Oh, right. I forgot. Somewhere it's written that you can sleep with someone other than your girlfriend if it's to get them to sing in your band."

"Well . . ."

"I wonder why Ariana didn't have to sleep with you?"

"Actually . . ."

I felt like I was going to be sick. "Don't tell me that, Vince. Not her. There's no way." Ariana was too sophisticated, too independent. There's no way she would have stooped to sleeping with Vince. She'd insinuated that she didn't even like him. I shuddered. "Not Ariana, ever. Not even in your dreams."

He shrugged.

I grimaced as I pictured them together and then considered

what others had done to belong. Like Judy. I couldn't figure out why she was in the band. She acted like she didn't even *like* playing keyboard.

I pushed the thought away to ponder later and crossed my arms as I stared him down. "So what are you getting at? We ought to get back together, but you can still sleep with whatever new band member you want?"

"Don't be stupid. You know I care about you."

"No, actually I don't know that, Vince. Why don't you just leave, go on and forget about me. You obviously have more girls waiting in the wings. You don't need me, and you sure don't want me."

He looked over his shoulder at the kids listening and dropped his voice a notch, trying to keep it private. "That's not true. We had a good thing going."

"Had. Past tense. But you never really meant any of it. I was just a girl passing through your life."

"Admit it; you still want me."

Maybe he'd taken acting lessons along with voice as a kid. Come to think of it, every performance was an act. Maybe there was no *real* Vince. Maybe everything about him was a false image, something acted out for the moment. "You're a double-crossing jerk. Just go! Leave me alone."

"I came here to ask you to get back together."

I kept thinking of Pamela that night, and his reaction to the pregnancy, and all the nights I'd waited by the phone to hear from him. He only did what suited him at the moment. "Get back together in what way? So you can see me when it's convenient and have Pamela or some other slut behind my back?"

"It's your fault you interpreted—"

"Everything's my fault, isn't it? It's my fault! It's my fault I met you. It's my fault I thought you loved me. It's my fault I slept with you. And no doubt it's *completely* my fault that I'm pregnant."

A gasp of whispers rippled through my classmates, but I didn't care. At least I was the one spreading the news instead of Heather or Tammy.

"You didn't tell me you weren't on the pill."

Maggie arrived at last, having pushed her way through the crowd and made it to my side.

Having her there boosted my confidence, filling me with words she would have spouted. "Oh, is that how it works? We girls are just supposed to be prepared in advance—in case one of you horny guys decides you need sex?"

"No one forced you."

If ever I felt eyes burning into me, it was right then, as I faced up to what I'd done and admitted it in front of all my classmates. "You're right, there. I was an idiot. You didn't force me, but I'm not stupid enough to walk that path twice. I'll never look at any guy the same way again. I'll never *believe* any guy when he says he loves me, or trust that he'll be there when things go wrong or when I need him the most.

"I gave you my heart, Vince, and you broke it. I won't give you a chance to break it again. Unless you can tell me that you're ready to commit to me and this baby, and I mean a lifetime commitment, then we don't have anything to talk about."

Maggie leaned into me at this last bit to put in her own piece. "He doesn't want you, Dixie. He wants Tony back in the band. Isn't that right, Vince?"

Vince turned on her. "Shut up."

It only took me a second to digest what Maggie was

implying. If Vince didn't get back together with me, Tony was going to quit the band and Vince would be without a second guitar. "Oh, that makes sense. You can't sleep with Tony, so I was the next best thing. Is that how it is? How could I have been so pathetic?"

"That's not how it is."

From somewhere behind Maggie, Tony's voice rose above Vince's. "Give it up. I'm not coming back to your band. It ain't gonna happen. I'm with a new group."

Vince glared at him. "But if I get back with Dixie . . ."

Tony pushed past me. "I just said that to get you off my back because you won't let it go. I really don't care if you're dating Dixie or not. I'm not interested in your band anymore. I been telling you that for weeks. Take a hike."

"You can't be serious about playing in that little *church* group instead of rockin' with me?"

"It ain't all about you, man."

I know my mouth was hanging open in shock. Had he really dated me, slept with me, just to ensure that Tony would play in his band? I could believe he slept with Pamela in exchange for giving her the lead singer position; that showed her stupidity. But to think he was only using me to keep Tony in his band was disgusting. About ten cuss words rose in my head and came close to spurting out my mouth before I threw my bag in the car and climbed in. "Go away, Vince. I don't ever want to see you again."

Everything in me shriveled up. All my bravado had been spent. I felt like a shell, emptied out. I slammed the door shut and revved up the car.

Sam's sister, Sophie, a tiny tenth-grader with more daring than the most outspoken senior, was pushing between people to reach

Vince. I wondered what she was going to say to him but was too exhausted by it all to listen. I pulled forward slowly as the crowd parted to let me through, leaving Sam, Heather, Maggie, Webb, and Tony staring after me along with everyone else.

Whatever Sophie said to him would come back to me, I was sure, right along with everything else. My life had become a war zone on an open playing field.

Chapter Thirty

SCHOOL WAS TOUGH the next day. Every eye was on me as I moved through the halls. Even the teachers were talking about me. It wasn't like I was the only girl in school who'd ever gotten pregnant, but such news always created a ripple of gossip and speculation. Everyone loved to have dirt to talk about. The difference was that this time it was me. I admit I had done my share of whispering and pointing at other girls and never gave a thought to how it made those girls feel, or how it might affect their decision as to what to do with their babies. Half the girls in class could be sleeping around, and hardly anyone even cared — but let someone get pregnant, and suddenly they were guilty of some horrible act.

I tried to keep it all in perspective. School would be over before I would even be showing much, and after that I wouldn't care what any of them thought. Everyone would wander off to their mediocre lives, get degrees in boring subjects, get married and have kids, and turn into middle-aged people just like Mama and Frank, and in the long run, who would remember or care that I had a baby at eighteen?

I told myself all that, but it was still hard seeing the expressions on kids' faces when they looked at me. It seemed like the entire world was enclosed within those four walls, and everything I'd grown to be during high school—popular, pretty, smart, a girl who was admired and would accomplish things in life—all that seemed to be disintegrating. In one week I had slipped to the bottom of the totem pole, back to where I'd been at the start of tenth grade when I was an invisible nobody, except I had a new label now, one I preferred not to think about.

At break, I was called to the guidance counselor's office. It wasn't hard to guess what she thought she needed to counsel me on.

Miss Nancy, a heavyset black woman with skin the color of coffee and eyes like black marbles, greeted me warmly with a sweep of her arm toward a worn-out, vinyl-upholstered chair that had long lost any appeal. She took the chair beside me instead of the one behind her desk. "I'm hearing talk about you today," she said.

I nodded and stared at her hands folded quietly in her lap, each finger bearing a ring, some silver, some gold, all with different color gems of some sort. My eyes remained trained on the sparkling jewels as my mind raced ahead. I knew I wouldn't be kicked out of school for being pregnant; I'd seen other girls walk this path. But what happened behind the scenes that I'd never heard about? I couldn't really deny my condition, though. Not when the entire school buzzed with the news. I figured I might as well admit it and get the consequences over with rather than worry about them later. "Well, it's true. I'm pregnant."

"Have you told your parents?"

"Yes."

"Good, good. It's always best to be up front with your parents."

"Not really."

She leaned toward me, resting her elbow on the arm of the chair. The sweet smell of lavender drifted around me. "What do you mean? Were they not supportive?"

Of all the rings on her fingers, I liked the sapphire the best. I liked the deep rich color of it and wondered if it was her favorite too, because she kept touching it with her other hand. It made me think of Maggie with her claddagh ring, following her plan, making sense out of her life, and me with nothing on my fingers, not even a class ring to show that the guy I'd slept with cared enough about me to consider me his girlfriend. My fingers were chubby, white, and bare. I folded them together, one fist inside the other, and looked up at Miss Nancy's calm face, her gold tooth shining in the center of her smile. Did I want to tell her what happened at home? Would it do any good? "They got into an argument about it, about what I should do."

"Ah, I see. And have you come to a decision? Or are you all still discussing it?"

I set my mouth in a grim line, ready to be on the defense. "I'm keeping my baby."

She nodded, whether in agreement or not I wasn't sure, but she didn't say anything for or against my decision. "Have you seen a doctor yet?"

I felt like an ignorant kid. *Duh.* I was an ignorant kid. How could I possibly be on the way to motherhood? "No, not yet. I guess I need to."

She heaved herself to her feet and moved back to her desk, shuffled through a drawer, and pulled out a pamphlet with a bold red header: *You and Your Pregnancy.* "This has the phone number for the health department and explains a bit about prenatal care."

As she placed it in my hands, I realized how real all this was. It wasn't just images of some future child, or some argument between me and Vince. It was real. I was pregnant and I had to deal with it. I had to go to the doctor, get on vitamins like Ariana said, and start paying attention to all the changes in my body.

"You read this," she said, "and in the meantime, I'll set up an appointment for you to talk with the school nurse. She can answer some of your questions and help you make an appointment with either the health department or a doctor, depending on your insurance."

Depending on my insurance? Did I know anything about what health insurance Mama had? Could I even use it since I'd run away from home? Or would I be joining a line of women seeking medical care down at the health department? I had no idea. I had more to sort out than I thought.

My confusion must have shown. She put a hand on my shoulder. "It's not as complicated as it sounds. You just need to start treating yourself like you're pregnant, pay more attention to your health. But the first thing you need to do is have your pregnancy confirmed with an official test."

"I did a test."

"At the health department or by your doctor. Then, if it's positive, the nurse will write you a note to be excused from class when you feel sick or have to pee or just can't stand sitting anymore."

"Serious?"

She laughed. "Sounds good, I know, but you'll appreciate what it really means as time goes by."

I already had an inkling of that. Getting through school days with my stomach churning had been hard. It was nice to finally have something going my way. "Thanks."

"You come talk to me anytime, Dixie," she replied.

As I walked down the hall, I didn't even bother to hide the pamphlet in a textbook. There couldn't possibly be a soul in the entire high school that hadn't heard about it by this time. Anyone who missed it after school would have gotten the goods on me during break, as kids caught up on any gossip they missed the previous day. My after-school drama would top that list.

There were still a few minutes of break left, but I didn't feel like walking into a crowd of piranhas. I took a seat in English class and stared at the board, figuring no one would actually have the nerve to say anything to me about it. Most students preferred to talk behind a person's back than to actually say anything to her face. But there was an exception—Sam's sister, Sophie. She appeared at the door and ran to my side.

"I finally found you." She drew in a deep breath, as if she'd run around the entire school.

"Sophie, what are you doing on the senior hall? You're going to get a tardy."

She shook her head. "No sweat. Miss Meeks likes me. I'll tell her I was running an errand. Anyway, I had to come tell you that you rock. I love what you said to that guy yesterday, and I'm telling every kid in the school where they can get off if they say one bad thing about you. You're great."

That made me smile. "Thanks, Sophie. You and your brother, you're both all right too."

She grinned and ran back out the door, her tennis shoes plopping hurriedly all the way down the hall, until the sound disappeared into the crowd of seniors returning from break.

At least I still had two friends at school, even if one was a tenth grader.

Heather caught me between classes. "I tried calling you three times last night, but you never answered your cell phone."

"Sorry. I turned it off. I didn't feel like talking to anyone."

"But Dix, come on. I'm your best friend. What gives?"

I couldn't believe she was that ignorant. "Heather, you told Amber! That didn't exactly put you on the top of my list of confidantes."

She waved one hand at me. "Oh, don't be silly. I had to tell her and Tammy. We're all best friends. Anyway, I've got the most exciting news for you."

I couldn't imagine what that was, and I was less than enthusiastic about hearing it. It was bound to be some dumb, frivolous bit of fluff, probably about the prom next weekend. "What?"

She looped her arm through mine. "Well, I begged and begged my parents to adopt your baby, but they said no. They just totally couldn't get it. They refused to adopt my little Chinese girl too, though Daddy did give me the rest of the money for her operation . . . so once that's done someone else can adopt her. I'm glad about that anyway."

I missed half of what she said. I was still back on the part about her parents adopting my baby. "You can't adopt my baby, Heather."

"That's what I said. My parents said no. But the good news is that in my search for a couple to adopt my Chinese girl, I found two couples that want her, so I told one of them about your baby, and they want to meet you. Isn't that great?"

I looked at her like she was nuts and slowly shook my head. "No, that isn't great. I didn't say I was putting my baby up for adoption."

"But you said you didn't know what you were going to do

with a baby, so I figured this was the perfect solution."

"I'm keeping my baby."

"Keeping it? Like being a mom and everything?"

The clock was ticking away; I had to get to my next class. I took a step in that direction. "Yes, Heather. I'm going to be a mom." As I said it, my body flushed at having said it aloud, at facing the daunting future ahead of me. *I was going to be a mom!*

She walked along with me, weaving between students. "Are you sure? You said you didn't want the baby, and this couple is really excited."

"Yes, I'm sure. I want my baby. It just took me a while to figure things out. You just never can tell about people, can you?" I was learning more and more how true that was. I didn't know Vince. I didn't really even know myself—I was just learning who I was and where I was going, as if I'd never really connected to that face I'd seen in the mirror for the past eighteen years.

Tammy came running up and grabbed Heather's elbow. "There you are."

"She's keeping it. Can you believe that? Dixie—a mom."

Tammy looked me up and down. "Better you than me. It's gonna cost a rich man a lot of money to make me have a baby."

Tammy and her millionaire-husband plan. Well, who was I to say it was such a bad idea? I'd taken the opposite turn, becoming an unwed teenage mother.

Tammy hooked arms with Heather and eyed her in a way that I knew meant she was disentangling herself from me. "Come on, Heather. I've got something to tell you."

Since when didn't she include me?

Since she found out I was pregnant and was no longer up to her standards.

At the end of the hall, they stopped to talk to Amber, their heads bent together in secrecy, with frequent glances in my direction.

My heart felt full of lead as I turned away. I knew without another word from Tammy or Heather that I had been replaced.

I grabbed a vending machine sandwich at lunchtime and slumped in the hall again to work while I ate.

Sam arrived a few minutes later with Sophie at his side and joined me on the floor. There I was, seated in Loserville, my entire list of high school triumphs gone. But as I sat there with the two of them, munching on my sandwich and listening to Sophie chatter on about hoping she could help me with the baby, my heart warmed to them both. Here were two sincere people who cared enough about me—someone who had never shown a minute's attention toward them—that they not only stood by my side as friends but defended me while my two "best" friends ridiculed me and turned away.

Chapter Thirty~One

GRADUALLY, AS WE had time throughout the week, Miss Mary and I reorganized the back room, moved the stock to one side, cleared out all the empty boxes, and moved her desk and filing cabinet to the wall behind the cash register. When I arrived Saturday morning, she had a couple teenage boys moving in a secondhand sofa and a rug, just as I had suggested. The crib was already in place, and her baby, Angelica, was lying in it, sleeping through the ruckus. A rocker had been placed in the corner, with a standing lamp beside it.

"What do you think?" she asked.

"Wonderful," I replied. It was a bit cramped and old-looking, but my standard of living had dropped somewhat since leaving home.

"A construction friend of mine is making me a toy box out of scrap lumber this weekend and said he'd bring it around on Monday."

Joy radiated from her, and the stress I'd seen just a few days ago had eased from her face. I wish my problems were so easily resolved. I had prayed a lot since Annie's visit, hoping God would give me some sign as to how to resolve all the issues in my life, but

I decided I could only take it one step at a time. If I'd helped Miss Mary solve her problem, surely I could do the same for myself.

As the boys finished up and she paid them, I noticed there was one thing missing. "Where's the babysitter?"

She grinned. "I figured with two of us here on Saturday, we can handle the store and one small baby."

Half an hour later, as I finished ringing up a customer's items, I heard Angelica's whimpers over the baby monitor we had sitting by the cash register. Miss Mary was helping a woman coordinate a skirt and blouse but turned at the noise. She never said a word. She raised eyes at me with a slight tilt to her head that clearly asked me to tend to the baby.

It wasn't like I hadn't seen a million babies before at church and the grocery store and wherever, but I hadn't ever babysat a newborn. The kids I watched were at least two. Most were between four and eight.

Her little noises sounded like a kitten. I bent over her. Little bubbles of saliva formed around her mouth. As I lifted her to my shoulder, her tiny body conformed to mine, and emotions stabbed through me. She was so precious, so helpless! I told myself it was hormones as tears seeped from my eyes, but it was more than that. She was so darling!

Miss Mary joined us a few minutes later, finding me rocking Angelica in the rocker, the tears still falling. I couldn't even wipe them away with the baby in my arms. Miss Mary came forward and pulled her from my arms and handed me a tissue. "You're pregnant, aren't you?"

"How did you know?"

"I wasn't sure until now," she replied.

I stood up and let her have the rocking chair. "She's so adorable."

"It's a bit overwhelming, isn't it? I remember when I was at your stage. I cried over the stupidest things. A dead bird on the road. A broken dish. Even things that made me happy, like hearing from my brother who lives in California. It's normal."

I hung my head. "I was thinking about how I almost . . ." I couldn't even finish the sentence. I couldn't tell her.

She didn't want me to. "We have all kinds of crazy thoughts. Life can be confusing. But don't worry. Everything is going to be fine."

I managed a smile. "Now who sounds like a messenger from God?"

"He does have a way of bringing people together at the right time, doesn't He?"

I thought of Annie and nodded.

"Now I know who I've been saving those maternity clothes for. I almost traded them at the mission store for the sofa, but something told me I needed to hang on to them. We're about the same size. They'll fit you perfectly."

I can't say we shared the same taste in clothes, but I wasn't about to turn down her offer. I barely knew where my next meal was coming from, let alone a maternity wardrobe.

I returned to the front of the store to work on the window display. Miss Mary had given me free reign to dress the mannequins and loved the flair I added to them with accessories, especially after a few customers had come in and bought outfits based on my fashion sense. I smiled as I hung one of Ariana's pocketbooks on the arm of one of the mannequins. I had convinced Miss Mary to carry a dozen of Ariana's designs on spec, and three of them had sold the first day. The more I worked there, the more I was thinking of how much I loved fashion and that maybe Ariana's plans for design school really weren't that far-fetched. Maybe I could go into design, too, but designing clothes or advertising layouts for fashions or something along those lines. I planned to research it, to see what various degrees were offered for that sort of thing.

I had just finished the display and was heading to the back to check on Miss Mary and the baby when the door jingled with the arrival of a customer. It was Maggie.

I stopped halfway across the store, my mouth hanging open, I'm sure. "How did you know I was here?"

"Jessie asked me and Webb to follow you home after the first night you were gone to see where you went. She wanted to make sure you weren't in a bad situation."

Spying on me. That would figure. "Okay. So here I am. I got a job. Surprised?"

"Not really." She moved around the store, touching fabrics and letting necklaces dangle between her fingers. "Decent job too. Better than flipping burgers, though since it closes at seven I'm assuming you don't get many hours in."

I shrugged. "So you came to tell me what you think of my job?"

She stopped fiddling and turned toward me. "No. I came to tell you that Cindy is in the hospital, and they don't know what's wrong with her."

"What do you mean?"

"She keeps vomiting. Can't keep anything down. Running a fever. Nothing is working."

I had been so absorbed in my own problems, I hadn't thought of Cindy since I'd left. "How long has she been sick?"

"Days. We thought she was just upset by the fight and you

leaving, but it's gone way beyond that."

"You could have told me."

"I'm here, aren't I? It's not like it's a short drive out here."

"You could have told me at school."

"They didn't take her to the hospital until today."

I drummed my fingers on the counter, trying to decide what to do. I couldn't leave. I had six hours left to pull. "I'll go to the hospital as soon as I get off work."

She nodded and left me standing there, staring out the window, thinking of my nine-year-old sister. No, not nine. Ten. Today was her birthday. Suddenly I missed her like crazy. Her pixie face, so like Mama's, and her beautiful blonde hair, so much fuller and softer than mine, and that cute way she had of smiling with one eye squeezed almost shut. Cindy had been like a baby doll to me all the years I was growing up, yet this year we'd done so little together. What if she didn't get well?

I paced around the store fidgeting with displays and watching the clock slowly tick the time away.

My visits to the local hospital had been few. The worst was when my dad was diagnosed with lung cancer. I went with my mother several times to take him in for treatments. He came out sick and exhausted and didn't seem like my father anymore on those days. Then I went to visit a girl from school who was in intensive care. She stayed there for like a month. Maggie and I took her a bundle of pictures and letters the class had made for her. Maggie visited her almost every day, but I didn't. I couldn't stand the smell of the place. It made me think of my father's death, and I just couldn't handle it.

I hadn't ever really thought about it before, but the first time I remember ever going to the hospital was when my mother gave birth to Cindy. I was eight at the time. I looked in that nursery window trying to pick out which baby we might be taking home, but Daddy said he didn't see her in any of the basinets, so he led me to Mama's room. She patted the bed for me to climb up beside her because she had Cindy in her arms, wrapped up in a pink blanket. I gazed into that scrunched-up little face thinking she was the ugliest girl I ever saw, wondering how I was going to explain her red, wrinkled face to all my friends. I had no idea how beautiful she would become or how much I would love her. It was hard to imagine what life would have been like without Cindy, especially after Daddy died. Mama and I wouldn't have filled up the house by ourselves.

I was wiping away tears by the time I found out Cindy's room number and made my way up the elevator and down the hall.

Mama was sitting by the bed, her head bent into one hand, with the other hand stretched out, holding Cindy's limp fingers.

She raised her head and gave me one of those weak smiles that meant *hello, but things aren't good*. It didn't matter what was going on between the two of us; Cindy was all that mattered at that point.

"What has the doctor said?"

"She's on intravenous fluids to get her hydrated, and they're monitoring her. They don't know what else to do. She's not responding to antibiotics."

"She has to get better, Mama. I just can't imagine if she doesn't."

Mama nodded.

I bent over the bed and touched Cindy's still arm. "I was thinking of the day she was born," I whispered.

"Me too."

That didn't surprise me. Mama and I had a way of knowing each other's thoughts sometimes.

"She was a miracle in our lives, you know," Mama said, and I could see she was fighting tears too, or she'd been crying so much there were only dribbles left. "I had three miscarriages after you were born, and the doctor finally told me I would never carry a baby to term again. Then she came along. I stayed on pins and needles, praying every day, the whole time, so sure I was going to lose her like I had the others. She was born early, but she survived, my angel girl."

Emotions rolled over me, and I couldn't stop the tears. "I remember you being in bed a long time, but I didn't know that was why, Mama."

"You were too young to understand. We didn't want you to know about the others. Two boys and a girl." Her mouth, nose, and eyes wrinkled up as she made an effort to shut back the storm of tears.

I glanced at Cindy, then sat on the edge of the bed. "I'm not having an abortion, Mama. I'm going to keep this baby."

She nodded, and I knew she had been through all the trials and fire with God that I had recently traveled. I imagined it was the hours at Cindy's side, thinking back to the babies she had lost and how precious Cindy was to her, but I didn't need her to explain it to me. I didn't need to know how it was that He managed to bring her to her knees and change her stance. God had opened our eyes and our hearts, and that's what mattered.

All my life I'd thought I'd had such great faith, that I was such a good Christian, so it shocked me to realize I had been mostly mouthing the words, not living it in my heart. I could quote a Bible verse as well as anyone, but then just went on my merry way, not worrying about reflecting Jesus in what I said and did. I had to admit that Maggie had me there. She didn't fake it with verses or preaching; she lived her faith. In everything she did, she weighed what life put in front of her with what God would want. She wasn't perfect, but she was a lot closer to it than I was. It was time to follow her example.

It was time to get back to church, maybe at Maggie's church instead of the one that had rejected me when I most needed support.

It was time to start praying again, praying Cindy would get better, praying for the baby growing within me and for me and Mama to get back to being each other's pillars like we'd been since Daddy's passing. And for Maggie.

I closed my eyes and offered up a prayer asking for guidance, opening my heart to God without reservation, without trying to control where He might lead me. When I opened my eyes I suddenly missed Maggie with such force, my stomach contracted at not having hugged her at the store or told her how much she'd meant to me through all the years of my life. *She* was my best friend, not Heather or Tammy or even cute little Sophie.

Chapter Thirty-Two

THE BOUTIQUE WAS closed on Sunday, so I spent the day at the hospital with Cindy and Mama. Mostly our moments were silent, both of us lost in thought, or we talked about silly things that didn't matter, but she finally asked about the baby. Had I been to the doctor? Did I have a due date? I told her my appointment was in a couple days. I thought about how much better it would be if she were with me, sharing her knowledge and keeping me company, but I didn't ask. I didn't even ask her about the insurance. I couldn't walk out of her house and then demand benefits that I'd given up.

What I really wanted was for everything to go back to normal, for Mama to take care of me like she always had, to hold me and make everything better.

She did finally hug me when I was leaving the next day. The doctor had just announced that Cindy had turned the corner and would likely go home in the morning. It was as if it released a floodgate in Mama. When he left the room, she started bawling again and took me in her arms. "I love you, Dixie. Please don't ever doubt that."

I couldn't speak without crying, so I nodded and left.

Mama showed up at the boutique a few days later, coming to stand just inside the door with a confused, disoriented look about her, her pocketbook clutched to her chest and her coat hanging open at an odd angle.

I rushed across the store and pulled her to one side, near the display of evening gowns. "Mama, what are you doing here?"

She relaxed into a smile at the sight of me. "Dixie," she said, and touched my face with the whole of her hand. I thought she was going to cry, and I glanced around to see what Miss Mary might be making of the scene. She was seated at her desk in the corner with Angelica in her lap. She smiled warmly at us before turning back to her work. I'm sure she had one ear open, though, so I lowered my voice to a whisper. I had no idea why my mother had come. "Is Cindy sick again?"

"No, no. I came to see you. Can you take a dinner break?"

It was only five o'clock. "No, Mama. I only work from 3:30 till 7:00, so I don't get a break. What's wrong?"

"Well . . ." She shifted her weight from one foot to the other as she eyed a customer browsing through the dress rack.

"It's okay, Mama. We can talk here. That customer is a regular. She'll let me know when she's ready."

She dropped her voice so low I could barely hear her. "Well, Frank and I were wondering . . . well, if you're not marrying that boy, what are you planning to do?"

"I'm definitely not marrying Vince. It's over with him."

"Then what will you do? Have you made plans?"

If I had been Maggie I would have had a plan, but I seemed to sail through life one day at a time with no idea where I was headed. I shrugged. "Not yet. Not really."

"Then come back home. We'll still expect you to work, to pay for the baby's needs, but there's no sense in you paying rent when you don't have to."

"Actually, I'm not paying rent. I'm just staying with a friend. But it's only temporary. I can't stay there for long. I'm sleeping on her futon and living out of one suitcase."

"Good. Then you pack up your stuff tonight and come home after school tomorrow."

"I have to work, Mama."

"Oh, of course you do. Well then, you may as well pack up and come home tonight. I'll keep a plate of food warm for you."

It sounded good in theory, but after she left I tried to picture myself raising a baby in my mother's shadow. What choice did I have?

When I got off work, I threw my stuff back in my suitcase and drove home. It was eight thirty by the time I got there because Ariana wasn't home when I left, and I had to take the time to write her a note, thanking her for her hospitality and all that. I ended it kind of open, in case things didn't work out once Mama laid out her idea of *details* regarding what it would mean to live at home again. For starters, I figured I would never be allowed to date again.

The house seemed noisy after the silence of Ariana's apartment. Billy was sprawled on the family room floor watching television, his school books spread around him. Guitar strums floated down from Tony's room. Mama and Frank were in the kitchen, their voices coming to me from the open swinging door. They were standing by the counter holding hands.

I hadn't been gone all that long—just two weeks—but I felt like it had been six months and I was a stranger coming back among them. I stood just inside the kitchen door. "Hi."

Cindy got up from the table and hugged me. "Dixie! I'm so glad you're home. Will you sleep with me tonight?" She still looked pale, and thinner than usual, but her smile had returned. "I have so much to tell you. Is it true you're having a baby?" I pulled her into my arms, and she prattled on, her voice more languid than usual. "Mama says I'm going to be an aunt. How come God let you have a baby without being married?"

Her warm body felt good next to mine. I was glad to be back with her. As I looked into her eyes, I realized everything I had done would have a lasting effect on her. What would she think of my having a baby? How would I measure up against Maggie now? Maggie was so perfect, a much better example of a big sister than me. I would have to make it up to Cindy in other ways, and tell her someday how wrong I had been to get involved with Vince. But all that could wait. "Yes to sleeping with you, at least until you fall asleep, if you get all your homework done and get your jammies on before I flake out."

She dragged me to the table where she was finishing up her math homework. "I just have to do these times tables, and then I'm done."

Mama gave me a hug and took the seat beside me.

Frank nodded at me and headed for the door. "I'll get Maggie."

Mama hurried Cindy through her problems and sent her

upstairs while I sat wondering why Maggie was being called down.

Pounding steps that didn't sound at all like her or Frank rushed toward the kitchen. It was Tony. "Well, about time you brought our car back. Where are the keys?"

"Hello to you too."

"Gretchen is waiting for me, and it's going on nine o'clock. Her mama won't let her stay up past ten on a weeknight."

"Who's Gretchen?" I asked, but he snatched the keys from my hand and ran out.

"Gretchen Wyatt. A new girl at church," Maggie replied as she entered and took a seat beside me. "Apparently the love of his life. I told you that you were clueless about what was going on around here. He's been crazy over her for a month."

In all the years I'd known Tony, he'd only begrudgingly attended church on threat of no food on Sunday if he didn't go. How ironic he'd met a girl there! God was probably having a good time with that one, as opposed to me, the into-everything-at-church girl, who got used by a rock singer who probably didn't even believe in God. Funny, I'd never even asked him. In hindsight, my priorities were slightly skewed.

Maggie laid a stack of papers on the table. Knowing her, she'd drawn up a contract for me to sign. *No more boyfriends. No more sex. No rock bands. No drinking.* I shoved the ugly thought away. I'd already made all those resolves to myself without her having to say anything, so there was no need for me to get riled. I just resented her still being on track with her four-year plan while I was running down some uncharted path into the unknown.

I tapped my fingers on the papers, ready to grip the bull by the horns. "So what have we here?"

"Room layouts."

I laughed. "Has Andrea been stopping by or what?" Frank's old girlfriend had made plans to renovate and rearrange the entire house before Frank dropped her.

Maggie laughed too. "No, but maybe we should consult her."

Mama frowned at us both. "Girls, no need to make fun of your elders. Andrea's heart was in the right place."

I giggled again because I knew she was just saying it for Frank's benefit. "Seriously, are they room designs?"

"We'll get to that," Frank said, taking a seat across from me. "First we have to lay down some ground rules and decide if this is going to work."

Oh, boy. I knew that was coming. I leaned back in my chair. Frank had never shown signs of being the strong, fatherly type. Maggie, Tony, and Billy weren't rebellious at all, so he'd never needed to come down on any of them. Whatever he had suddenly been inspired to say, I didn't have much choice except to listen, because I sure didn't have the money for an apartment. "Okay. Shoot."

His arms were folded across his chest; his face was set in serious mode, which I thought was rather funny, considering he had been in my shoes eighteen years earlier with Maggie's mom.

"You will be totally responsible for the baby. Just because you'll be living here doesn't mean we're raising it. It's your child, not ours, and you'll have to understand that straight out."

"We'll help, of course," Mama interjected, "but you'll be the one doing the night feedings and dressing her in the morning and all the rest."

"Or him," Maggie said. "It could be a boy."

My head started to spin.

"You look ill, darling," Mama said. "I bet you haven't eaten. I forgot I had your plate warming." She pulled a plate of chicken, mashed potatoes, and green beans from the oven. The smell of the home-cooked meal rose to me like a sweet promise. I dove right into it and relished every mouthful. It seemed like forever since I'd had mashed potatoes with gravy. At least living at home, I would be fed!

"We'll be here," Mama said, watching me gulp down the food. "We just want you to realize it's your child, and ultimately it's your responsibility."

How many times did they think they had to say it? "I get it already."

"Have you settled things with that boy?" Frank asked. "He doesn't want to be any part of the baby's life?"

I shrugged. "The only thing he says is to get an abortion."

Maggie frowned. "I should have figured it came from him. What a jerk."

I concentrated on my green beans.

"Either he's going to pay child support, or he's going to sign over all parental rights to you. You'll have to make that clear to him."

The chicken was delicious. "I can tell you the answer to that without asking. May I have some iced tea, Mama?"

She got up and filled a glass for me. "We just don't want him showing up a year from now or five years from now saying he wants to be part of the baby's life. That could be disastrous for you. Think if you marry someone else, and that guy shows up on your doorstep one day."

Did I have to think that far into the future too? Did I have to consider that Vince hadn't just ruined my carefree college days, he may have also ruined some future marriage I hadn't even considered? I stared at her with a blank expression, then slurped down half the tea. I hadn't realized how thirsty I was. The constant nausea I usually had was beginning to subside, and I realized that some regular home-cooked meals would do me good. "So do you have some paper for him to sign or something?"

"I'll find out if there's something like that we could have written up. I'm not sure."

I was wishing I had more chicken and fewer green beans, not that they weren't good too, but I suddenly craved chicken like this was my last meal on earth.

"The next concern is a babysitter," Maggie said, "since you'll be working and going to college."

I raised my eyes from my plate. "I will be? I mean, I can still go to college?"

Frank watched me pick at the bones while I talked. I must have looked like Billy and Tony going after that food, which was highly unusual for me.

"You should be due in October or November, right?" Maggie asked.

Was I due in October? I realized how clueless I was about everything. I hadn't thought anything through. I'd been in panic mode, turning in circles and not thinking seriously about any of it. I must have gotten pregnant the end of February, so I nodded like I'd known that all along.

"That leaves the fall semester out," Mama said. "You're likely to be miserable at the end, and then you'll have a few weeks when you really can't drive, and the baby will need you around the clock—"

"So I checked on summer courses at USC," Maggie said. "I figured you'd rather go there since it's within driving distance and you can live here at home. Anyway, you can get freshman English and math out of the way, and if you do the same next summer, you'll still graduate in four years."

Maggie with the plan, as usual. I felt like my entire life had been plotted out during the short time I'd been gone.

"Anyway, you'll need a babysitter while you're working," Maggie continued. "I talked to Mrs. Graham, and she says she would love to do it. She says she loves having a baby in the house."

Mrs. Graham was our next-door neighbor. Maggie had baby-sat her daughter, Kimberly, since she was first born, and now her little brother Bryce, born last year. "Kind of strange, you babysitting for her all these years, and now she's offered to babysit for me. But I'll only need a babysitter during classes. I'm pretty sure I can take the baby to work because Miss Mary has a nursery in the back of the store for her baby, Angelica."

Maggie leaned forward on the table. "Really? That would be great. You'll have more time with him."

"Or her," Mama added.

That was true. No carting my baby off to a day care center somewhere across town. I had actually worked out something about taking care of the baby without even realizing it.

"Now to the ground rules," Frank said. "No dating anyone we don't approve of, and if you do date, you can't just expect us to babysit at night. If we're free and willing, we will, but you will not take it for granted that we're here to serve you and the baby."

I nodded. What else could I do? Besides, I had no desire to date anyone at that point. I foresaw nights of being exhausted between college, work, and a baby.

"You will continue to help with chores around the house."

I nodded again as I picked at the last of the beans.

"You will contribute a portion of your earnings to family expenses to cover the baby's supplies, doctor appointments, and whatnot."

"Okay."

"The rest goes into savings so you'll eventually be able to afford a place of your own."

I nodded.

"All right, then," he said, and relaxed as if he'd been expecting a fight that he'd somehow escaped.

Maggie spread her papers out on the table. "Now for the fun stuff: the bedroom."

She had drawn a layout of the room with the old furniture rearranged and baby furniture added. "We thought about finishing the attic, but Daddy said that would cost too much, and anyway, I'll be gone to Clemson by the time the baby arrives, so you can have the room to yourself."

"I thought Billy was supposed to move into our room in the fall. He's had to share with Tony for the past year." Originally, Billy, Tony, and Maggie each had their own rooms. When Mama married Frank, Billy moved in with Tony, Cindy took his room, and I moved in with Maggie.

Mama spoke up. "We all talked about it and decided they could tolerate it for another year until Tony goes off to college. It's not that big a deal. Lots of brothers share rooms. Besides, I think Billy has enjoyed sharing with Tony. It more or less forces Tony to spend a bit of time with him."

I hoped that didn't come back to haunt me. Tony was bound to be mad about it. But I let it go. If they had worked it out, the best thing was to leave it be and see how it went.

I glanced at Maggie's drawings. She had it all worked out with our beds rearranged, hers bunked with Cindy's, and our room rearranged with a crib and changing table. "You moved your bed into Cindy's room?"

"Well, I will be home on weekends sometimes, and I'll need to sleep somewhere. Cindy says she doesn't mind."

I leaned back, my plate practically licked clean and my entire future planned out.

Somehow it all seemed too neat and tidy. Something was bound to disrupt it all.

I should have figured it would be Vince.

Chapter Thirty-Three

WHEN I HEARD a rap at the front door a few nights later, I didn't think much of it. Billy jumped up to answer it. I stayed in Frank's recliner and kept reading my history textbook. I needed every minute after work to study and still get to bed at a decent time, which my body would have liked to have had about two hours earlier than I managed. The pregnancy had me so tired I had to keep forcing my eyes to stay open, and it was only nine o'clock.

But school was almost out. I'd passed on the prom, much to Sam's disappointment. Instead, I took pictures of Maggie and Webb with Tony and Gretchen as they headed out as a foursome. Honestly, I was relieved to fall into bed at eight o'clock while they were just beginning to dance.

Now I was in the homestretch. If I could just get through a few more days, then exams, award ceremonies, and, finally, graduation, I would be home free. The thought kept me going.

The strange voice at the door broke my concentration; I didn't recognize it. The girl had a nasally grate to her diction, and puffy, ragged black hair, black-framed eyeglasses, and a red billowing skirt that made her look as if she were a gypsy or something. I had no idea who she was, but she was asking for me.

I stood up, wary about what she might want. That's when I saw the boy behind her, the scruffy guy in black, the one that hung around waiting for Vince at practices and performances.

Maggie, stretched out on the floor with her textbooks, looked from the girl to me with huge questions written across her face: Who is this, and what have you brought upon our house now?

Mama and Frank weren't home, or I would have sent Billy to get them. Instead, I gave Maggie a beseeching glance, and she stood up and followed me to the door. Much as she sometimes got on my nerves, Maggie had become a rock when it came to standing up to people.

The girl gave us both the once-over before turning her dark eyes on me. "What you messing with my cousin for?"

I pictured a second version of her and couldn't fathom who she was talking about. "You must have the wrong house."

"Are you Dixie?"

I matched her stance, my feet spread apart, my arms crossed. "What's it to you? I don't know you."

"Did you tell Vince you's having his baby?"

This was Vince's cousin? Ariana's words about the creep being his cousin came back to me. She had been right in everything she'd told me. I'm sure my surprise must have registered across my face for a second, but I forced myself to maintain an attitude. I'd dealt with girls like her at school. "What's it to you?"

Cindy came through the swinging kitchen door, stopped in her tracks, and screamed, then ran back into the kitchen.

I looked from the door, still swinging on its hinges, back to the two weirdos standing on the front porch. Was it the looks of them that scared her or what? I couldn't think of that at the moment.

Billy looked from Creep-o to Maggie. "That's the guy, I bet

anything," he said, and took off toward the kitchen.

A thought zipped through my mind—Maggie had said some creep had been hanging around Cindy's school; could it be the same guy?

Tony had come down the stairs and joined us.

"I'm Vince's cousin," the girl said, "and he don't want no baby."

Maggie stepped up to bat. "I guess he has a problem, then, because Dixie is having this baby."

The girl shoved an envelope at me. "He said to give you this to take care of it, and if you don't, he's going to come make you."

Tony took the envelope and flipped through the money inside. "Wow. There's a lot of money here."

Maggie snatched the envelope out of his hands and thrust it back at her. "You can give it back to him and tell him to stay out of our lives."

I expected Creep-o to leap at us or something, but he stayed positioned behind the mouthy girl, looking like some evil shadow.

"No doing," the girl said as she dropped the envelope at my feet, the money spilling out onto the floor. "You give it back yerself." She turned to go. "He don't take too kindly to nobody telling him no."

"Like that's news to us," Tony said.

As they drove off in the ratty blue 280Z, Maggie scrabbled around gathering the money back into the envelope; then I slammed the door shut and locked the deadbolt. "I can't believe that."

Maggie shook her head. "You sure can pick them."

Billy strode out of the kitchen. Cindy peeked out, her face

hung between the door and the wall, so pale it appeared like a ghostly apparition. "Are they gone?"

"Yes, they're gone. Did you know who they were?"

Billy nodded. "Just like I said. That's the guy that was hanging around her school playground, sitting on the swings and stuff."

Cindy stepped into the room. Her voice was shaky. "Mrs. Donaldson sent him away, but he showed up three more days until she called the police. I told you about it, remember?"

Maggie scowled at me. "That's right. They didn't know what he was up to, but I'm betting he's the guy you were talking about, isn't he, Tony?"

Tony nodded. "Vince sent him around. He was trying to bribe me with drugs to stay in the band. First drugs, and then he tried pushing me around that day at school."

"When that didn't work, he asked Tony if he would stay in the band if he got back together with you," Maggie said. "Like that made him family or something. Couldn't you see what a jerk he was?"

I didn't imagine her knowing much about drug use. Sure, everyone at school knew Asby and his friends were into drugs, but Asby wasn't creepy like this guy. In fact Asby was pretty cool. Not that I ever considered hanging with him or anything, but this guy in black was a totally different league, and I knew Ariana had been right about everything. Still, I couldn't believe he'd been messing with kids at the elementary school. "Did that boy say anything to you, Cindy?"

"No. I never let him get near enough to talk to me. I ran back into the school. That's what my teacher told us to do."

How could Vince have sent that creep to my sister's school or used him to bribe my brother? What a jerk! How had I ever been fooled into loving someone like him? Had everyone seen him for the loser he was except me? I pulled my shoes out of the closet. "I've got to go see him," I said to Maggie.

"Right now?"

"The sooner the better."

Tony counted the money, slid the wad back into the envelope, and handed it to me. "I think you better wait for Jessie and Dad to get home. One of them needs to go with you."

I got the keys from the hook by the coat closet. "Y'all may have planned out my future with the baby, but I have to fix the mess I made of my past, and I know where to find him."

Maggie wouldn't let me go alone. She grabbed a jacket and rushed out with me, yelling orders to Tony on her way out about letting my mama and Frank know where we were going, and to stay with Cindy till someone got home, as if he didn't know that already. But that was Maggie, responsible, always making sure all the bases were covered.

Strained silence filled the car on the long drive there. I had too many thoughts whirling through my mind to say anything, and Maggie must have understood that. She never once questioned me or spilled out advice, which she tended to do. Instead, she stared out at the road in front of us as I drove with the concentration of someone journeying down death row, with all the thoughts of life and death, heaven and hell, filling my head. I wondered at how God would judge me for all that had happened, for being with Vince, sleeping with him, deceiving my parents, denying the existence of His creation, this baby, and then wanting to kill it, and now driving down the road to face Vince one more time. Would God be with me now?

Forgive me, God, for all I've done. I'm trying to turn my life

*around, but I need Your help. I need You at my side to guide me
and keep me headed in the right direction. I want to fill my heart up
with You, again, to feel the happiness and peace, like You've given me
all my life through, and to raise my baby in Your light. Please, God,
help me through this. Help me to face Vince, to remain strong, and to
plant my feet firmly back on Your path once more. Amen.*

I know God heard my prayer. I felt stronger, capable of facing
what was ahead of me, whatever Vince might say or do.

I didn't knock. I barged into Vince's trailer with Maggie on
my heels.

I don't know who Vince was expecting, but not me. He lay
stretched out on the sofa watching television and didn't even turn
at my approach. "'Bout time you got here. Bring me a beer out of
the fridge, will ya?"

Me? Take him a *beer*? He hadn't drunk beer in front of me
before, let alone asked me to get him one. He must have been
expecting one of his buddies or maybe Pamela. I was tempted to
get a bottle just to pour on his head.

Maggie stopped just inside the door, but I continued across the
room. I walked up behind him, opened the envelope of money,
and scattered it across him.

He sprang up. "What the—?" His eyes were bloodshot and
his words were slurred. And his face turned cold at the sight of
me. "What are you doing here?"

"You're such a jerk; you can't even do your own dirty work.
You have to send some wimpy cousin and that creep that's always
hanging around."

Maggie laughed.

He looked toward her a moment then back at me, and I saw
the same hopeless look beneath the surface of his bravado that the

creep had—he was high on something. How had he kept it so well hidden from me all that time?

"I was doing you a favor," he said. "I figured if I gave you the money, you would take care of it, and we could get back to where we were."

"You just don't get it, do you? I don't want you anymore, and I sure don't want your money, Vince. I'm not having an abortion. This child, our child, isn't going anywhere. It's God's creation, a soul as worthy of life as you or me, and only God will determine when this child will die."

"Cut the Christian crap. It's a clump of cells, not a person."

"You are so ignorant." I had been ignorant, but I wasn't anymore. I'd been researching pregnancy online. "I'm ten weeks now. He has arms and legs and fingers and toes. He's a person. He's been a person since the moment he was conceived, whether you accept it or not."

"You better get that abortion. I'm warning you—"

He was so full of himself. Why hadn't I seen it before? Nothing but hot air and ego. "Warning me what? What do you plan to do? Murder me because I won't murder our baby? Tell me, Vince, did you sic those two creeps on my little sister? Are you really that low that you'd try to get to me through her?"

He shrugged. "They go where they want. I just offered them a bit of incentive to find some way to get to you."

"Like hurting my sister would make me go along with an abortion? That's the stupidest thing I've ever heard of. If they're spotted around the school yard again, I'll tell the police everything I've pieced together about you. I'm not afraid of you, Vince. I used to love you, or thought I did, but you know what? You're nothing. Pamela is welcome to have you all to herself."

He ignored everything but the one thing that was eating at him, the one thing he was powerless to stop. "You can't force me to be a father."

I laughed and used his own words against him. "I don't remember having to force you. In fact, you seemed pretty eager to me. What happened to all that love? What happened to all the sweet whispers? All those words sure evaporated when the chips were down. You never meant a word of what you said to me."

"Yes, I did." His voice slipped into that soft tone he'd used when he was trying to get into my pants. "Listen to me, Dixie. We had a good thing going."

I felt Maggie at my elbow. I squared my shoulders. "Let's not go this round again."

He would have shot fire from his eyes if he could have. "You've got to get rid of it. I'm not going to be a parent, and I'm not supporting a kid."

"No one is asking you to. My stepfather will be sending you papers to sign. It will totally release you from all responsibility, but you can't come make a claim on him, ever."

"Him?"

I shrugged. "The baby. Gut instinct. It's a boy. A son. Soon to be my son, and never yours."

Maggie couldn't stand it; she had to put in her two cents. "He won't even know your name."

Vince glared at her, then me. "You're going to regret this."

"Oh, believe me; I already regret everything about knowing you. I took our lovemaking to mean something, a vow of commitment. To you it was nothing. Nothing! I was just one more girl in a whole lineup. Just stay away from me, Vince." I took a step toward the door. "And if your creepy cousin shows up at my door again, I'll sic my dog on her."

"She was trying to help you out, taking the money to you."

"Really? Maybe no one's ever taught her to be civil. Not surprising, being she's related to you."

Maggie took my arm, but not without her own closing remark. "We just hope this baby takes after Dixie and not you, you loser."

"What's it to you?"

"Everything, jerk," Maggie said. "We're family — sisters — and we stick together."

It warmed me all over to hear her say it. It was good to have Maggie back at my side.

We walked out that way, arm in arm, giving each other a high-five outside the door before I crumpled into the passenger seat and lost it all to a bout of heavy-duty tears. Maggie took the wheel and spun the tires in the gravel getting us out of there.

"You didn't really want to get back with him, did you?" Maggie asked, as she turned at the first light, her neck craned forward to see beyond some overgrown shrubbery. "I mean, you can't really love someone like him?"

I'd given that a lot of thought. "No, not him. Just the idea of what I thought he was and what we were going to be together."

Maggie shook her head. "The sad thing is you don't really know him at all. Look in my pocketbook," she said. "There's an article I printed out for you just in case he came back and tried to hook his claws into you again."

I wasn't sure I wanted to read it; I had enough to deal with. But curiosity got the best of me.

I pulled her pocketbook into my lap and unzipped the center section. For such an organized person, her pocketbook was the opposite, a jumble of clutter. I leafed through a stack of coupons and pictures she'd clipped from flyers to remind herself of sale specials till I found the Internet printout.

It wasn't long, but very informative, a piece written a few years earlier and printed in his high school paper. He looked different in the photo—much younger and lacking the style and finesse he had now. In fact, he didn't look much better than his skuzzy cousin. And his name was Vince all right, but not Vince Evans, not that an alias was that big a deal. I could almost excuse him using an alias to protect his privacy as the band became more and more popular. But the more I read, the more I was convinced the fake name was more likely an attempt to hide his past. His real name was Vince Drummard, and at the time of the article, he'd been assigned to one year in a juvenile detention home.

I let the paper crumple under the weight of my hands as I turned to stare out the window.

We'd reached the interstate. Maggie concentrated on changing lanes before she spoke again. "Want to know more?"

I didn't answer. I wasn't sure how much more I could handle.

"His parents are divorced, and his sister wants nothing to do with him."

I couldn't blame her there. I was beginning to feel the same way.

"I haven't even started investigating his cousins, but I'm sure that would turn up a bit of interesting info. You just have no idea who you were involved with, Dixie."

A few weeks earlier, I would have had some smart reply to Maggie's remark, but I bit my tongue that day. She was right. I'd thrown my heart and soul away on someone I didn't even know.

The image I'd created of Vince in my head represented what I wanted, but he wasn't really that dream guy at all. And now I was going to give birth to a child that was half his. I have to say it scared me a lot, like an alien being taking over my body . . . but I focused on that little boy I'd seen in my dream and knew he was a creation of God's and someone totally separate from his father. He was his own person, unknown to anyone else yet, except me and God.

Which brought me to one more issue I had to face.

Chapter Thirty-Four

THAT SUNDAY, I got up and got ready for church with the rest of the family. When everyone headed for the door, I followed them out as if I'd been attending church with them all along.

Maggie stopped at the car door. "You're coming with us?"

I shrugged. "I thought I'd try it."

Tony slid the back door open and climbed into the middle seat of Mama's new minivan, then leaned forward to look in the rearview mirror as he slicked his hair down, and I realized with a pang that he'd started dressing better and his hair had been combed all week. It's like I registered the change but hadn't really noticed it.

Mama stood with her door open and fussed with the collar on her blouse. "But honey, you've been going to the other church since you were a little girl. You don't have to change."

Frank slammed his door shut and turned on the car. "Come on, we'll be late if we don't get a move on."

"Hush," Mama said. "We have plenty of time. You always get us there with twenty minutes to spare." She turned back to me. "Is this some gesture of goodwill or something?"

I gave Maggie a friendly push into the car and climbed past

her to join Cindy in the backseat. "Let's go."

"You're really coming with us?" she asked—with such enthusiasm I figured she ranked this as having saved my soul by getting me to go to the *right* church.

"Yes. Don't act so shocked."

As Billy dashed out of the house and climbed over Tony into the back with me and Cindy, Mama threw up her hands and slipped into the front. "I never understand you." She snapped her buckle. "What prompted this?"

I knew they wouldn't leave me alone if I didn't offer them an explanation. "I'm not going back to my church."

Maggie turned halfway around in her seat, her whole face turned into a question mark, wanting to know what had given rise to this change. "Really? Why not?"

As Frank backed the car out of the driveway and headed down the road, I thought about Mama's initial reaction to my pregnancy and how it wasn't all that different from our church. I sure didn't want to resurrect that argument, but how could I not explain what transpired with Mrs. Green and Reverend John? She was bound to hear it somewhere eventually, so I sucked in my breath and described my advice-seeking visit to the church.

Mama's face hung in the mirror slack-jawed and pale. "They kicked you out of youth group for being pregnant?"

I nodded.

She crossed her arms across her chest. "Wait till I get through with them."

I didn't have to wait long. She dropped off the rest of the family at home after church and headed straight over to our old church, striding around to the back entrance with determination driving every step. She only paused to pick up a handful of white rocks from the garden edging the walkway, which she dropped into her pocket without explanation.

We found Reverend John in his usual Sunday afternoon spot, finishing up coffee and sandwiches among the after-service lunch group. Heads turned toward Mama as if she were a bride entering a cathedral, but with expressions of alarm at her red face and pursed lips instead of awe at her beauty.

I thought the crowd would slow her down, but I was mistaken. She paraded between the tables and stopped at his side, towering over him with authority. "What do you mean by kicking Dixie out of the youth group?"

Reverend John gave his tablemates one of those weak, apologetic smiles that implied Mama was half-cracked. "I don't believe you want to discuss this here," he said, then took another bite of his sandwich. He switched to a more sly, knowing smile at Mr. Foster, sitting directly across from him, as if that dismissed me and Mama from his presence.

Mama wasn't about to be put off. "Actually I do want to discuss it, right here, right now."

Reverend John pressed his lips together as he looked first at Mama, then at me, and back to Mama again. "Are you aware of her *condition*?" He said it as if I had something that ought to be confined to a dungeon.

"She's pregnant, not a leper."

"Actually, leprosy isn't a sin. She'd probably be welcome to remain as youth leader if that were the case."

"Being pregnant isn't a sin! She's carrying a creation of God's. How can you hold that against her?"

I'd never noticed how pompous Reverend John was until that

moment, with his bottom lip puffed out and his eyes narrowed, trying to emphasize his authority—even though Mama stood over him with her hands on her hips, and he was sitting under her gaze with sandwich crumbs caught on his sweater where it swelled over his fat stomach. "Being pregnant isn't a sin, but the act that got her there is; she's not married."

"So who made you judge and jury that you decided that's enough to boot her out?"

His mouth was full of sandwich again, but he gave his table a closed-mouthed, smug smile while he chewed and swallowed. "I believe I am pastor of this church."

"Hmm." Mama scratched her cheek and tapped her foot, "Tell me, then, if she'd had an abortion, would everything be hunky-dory? She could stay on as youth leader?"

Reverend John swirled the ice tea in his cup before sucking some down. "Of course not. We don't promote pregnancy or abortion. What we want to maintain is a strict sense of propriety here, of abstinence for our youth."

"Ah," Mama said, "but if she'd had an abortion, who would have known? So in reality, although you want to enforce abstinence—with which I'm in total agreement, by the way—what you actually force the girls to do is sneak off quietly to have abortions without anyone knowing so they won't be persecuted for being pregnant."

Reverend John's face turned red with anger. "That's hardly the truth. We just cannot tolerate a girl in her condition holding a position intended as an example of purity, maturity, and wholesomeness for her peers. It contradicts everything we teach here."

All those long conversations with Maggie and the grace of God filled me with the words I needed. I stepped up by Mama and leaned forward on the table. "No, sir. What it does is blemish the image you try to project, but that's all it is—an image. What Jesus tells us is that God loves us, sins and all, and although He might open doors for us and guide our steps, we all have freewill to do our own bidding, and that's where we fail. But the glorious thing is that He will forgive even the worst sin. All we have to do is ask. And I've asked. In the end, that's all that matters—how God judges me, not you."

Mama walked around the table and plopped a dirty rock into the center of each plate, ending with Reverend John's, to the sound of groans and exclamations. "As Jesus said, *Let you who have not sinned cast the first stone.*"

That was enough for me. I turned toward the exit but stopped and faced them again. "The difference between me and half your youth group is that you have proof that I had premarital sex. Most talk the talk around you, but they don't all walk the walk."

Mama caught up with me, and we stormed out together, knowing we would be the talk of that church for a month of Sundays, but neither of us cared. We'd stood up for what was right, for what was real—the life within me—and the dark days of indecision faded to nothingness.

Chapter Thirty-Five

THINGS SETTLED DOWN after that. Graduation went without a hitch. Maggie was valedictorian and gave the perfect speech. I was just glad to graduate and shake off the dirt of high school to get on with life. I took a few summer courses at USC, which were tough, but I did well enough. Nesting instincts started kicking in, and I actually started hating piles of clutter as much as Maggie. So I cleaned up my act, got organized, and Maggie and I had a ball reorganizing the bedrooms and decorating the corner of our old room for the baby. I had an ultrasound, and even though that didn't tell me the sex, I kept that dream in mind and decorated for a boy with Pooh Bear stickers, sheets, and blankets. Maggie glowed with pride as much as me, and the two of us became as close as we'd been in our early years.

One fall evening, when my baby was kicking and squirming in my swollen belly; when Frank had gone up to bed early, and Maggie was off at university with Webb; when Cindy had fallen asleep on the sofa in front of a movie, Tony was out on a date with Gretchen, and Billy was spending the night with Jasper; I had Mama all to myself—and I knew it was time to find out the rest of the story about her, Frank, and Mallory. After all, I'd grown up a lot over the recent months, and I felt sure Mama would be more willing to share her past after all I'd been through.

We'd put off cleaning the kitchen earlier that evening with so many goings-on, so as the house quieted, I offered to help her clean up the supper dishes, knowing it would put her in a talking mood.

I set a mixing bowl into an upper cabinet as I broached the subject. "Mama, I was so sure that Vince was the right one. I wouldn't have slept with him if I hadn't. At least I don't think I would have. I was so caught up in the image of who I thought he was that I didn't think any of it through."

"I can see that. I'm just glad I got you free of him. Having a child at your age will be hard, but I know we'll love him and wonder how we ever lived without that little life entwined with ours."

I let that thought drift around us as I dried a pot and slid it into a lower cabinet. I dried the lid and took the next step. "At least Maggie's mama was a better judge of character than me. Frank married her."

Mama didn't respond, except to tackle a pan with a scouring pad.

"Do you think she did the same thing as me? You know, sleeping with Frank without really thinking about getting pregnant?"

Mama kept scrubbing a moment, even more furiously than before. When there was nothing left to scrub, she rinsed it under steaming water and laid it in the draining tray. Still she didn't respond. She pulled the plug from the sink, rinsed it with the spray nozzle, wiped the counters, dried her hands, and fixed herself a cup of hot tea, which she carried to the table with a half-empty box of doughnuts.

I wasn't sure what to do. I knew she'd heard me. I dried the pan, put it away, and hung up the towel, then joined her at the table, leaning forward on my arms, waiting to see if she would speak. It was like old times, back when the three of us—Cindy, Mama, and I—lived alone and I would sit up late at night talking to Mama about problems with friends or school. She always set out hot tea and doughnuts before we talked, saying it soothed the spirit.

"Don't you want some tea?" she asked.

"Has caffeine and depletes iron," I replied. I'd learned a lot about nutrition by then and was following a rigid diet to make up for those early months when I'd been too self-centered to consider the needs of my baby.

Mama nodded and sipped at hers.

I waited.

"Remember I told you that your daddy and I became engaged that Christmas before graduation, but I hadn't told Frank?"

I knew I'd been right, that there was more to the story. "Yes'm, I remember. You said Frank wouldn't talk to you about it."

She nodded and wrapped her hands around the tea cup, absorbing the heat. "I probably shouldn't tell you this."

"Please, Mama. Nothing you can say can be worse than all I've done."

She sighed. "It's just that for a while I wavered, thinking I was making a mistake. I'd been so in love with Frank in high school, I wondered if it was him I should be marrying and not your father. Richard, your father, was wonderful, and I loved him, but suddenly I was confused. I guess it was the pressure of really thinking about getting married and never having a choice again. And then, to make it worse, Frank showed up with Mallory."

"Where?"

"Oh, a double date your father hatched up. He could tell I was getting cold feet, and he intended to keep me at his side no matter what. He decided I needed to see Frank with his new girlfriend, so we all went out to dinner together." She sipped her tea again and let it slide down her throat as if it gave her strength to continue. "I couldn't believe it when they showed up. There she was, this peppy sixteen-year-old girl and Frank, twenty-two. I almost fell out of my chair. But I understood his attraction. She was gorgeous. Auburn hair so thick and beautiful, and green eyes that sparkled like an imp. She was like a leprechaun fairy come to life. Magic seemed to radiate from her, and Frank was so caught up by her that he couldn't walk and talk at the same time around her."

I'd seen pictures of Mallory and already knew how beautiful she was, but I let Mama prattle on about her anyway because it revealed more about Mama than Mallory—Mama had been jealous!

"Well, I can tell you it made me even more determined that Frank ought to be moping over me getting married, even fighting to get me to break up with your daddy, and I'm ashamed to say I flirted with him. I did everything I could think of, but whatever he'd had for me had fled when he met Mallory. The good thing was that he didn't resent me for marrying Richard anymore, and we became friends again, but I remained irked that he was so taken with her that he no longer wanted me, whether I was marrying your daddy or not."

I was sitting up straight listening at that point, even though it was uncomfortable in a kitchen chair with the weight of the baby pulling on me. I wanted to stretch out and relax, but I wasn't about to budge an inch till I'd gotten the full scoop. "And then Mallory got pregnant?"

Mama refilled her tea cup. "Oh, yes. Mallory could see what was what, and she wasn't about to let me come between them. Next thing I know, she's announced she's pregnant and the two of them are eloping. Of course, I have no proof, but I think she got pregnant on purpose to keep Frank from turning back to me."

Would Maggie's mother have been that manipulative? Would I have gotten pregnant on purpose if I'd thought it would make Vince marry me? I wasn't sure, but it didn't work out that way anyway, so I pushed the thought away.

Mama continued. "I kept on with my wedding plans, and your daddy and I got married a month later, which was all for the best." She reached across the table and touched my face. "Because I loved your father like no man before or after. I mean, I love Frank now, but your father and I had a wonderful marriage. And lucky for us, I conceived you six months after we married, and then Cindy later on. I wouldn't have changed that for all the world. You mean everything to me, Dixie."

I took her hand in mine. "I love you, Mama. And I'm so glad you shared all that with me. Strange, but it gives me comfort knowing you were as confused as me about love and marriage."

That made her laugh. "I guess maybe I was. Life is a tough puzzle to put together. Every step of the way is something new to figure out."

I touched my belly where the baby was kicking out an arm or leg. "It sure is."

I thought about our conversation for a long time after that, pondering the choices my mama and Mallory had made and the differences between my daddy, Frank, and Vince. What I figured out was too many of us go looking for love with our heads instead of our souls. And the reality is that I somehow equated love and sex as the same thing, but they aren't. Maggie was way ahead of me there; she knew that sex was meant to be a confirmation of a vow of love, not a path to finding love, and that it wasn't something to be entered into as lightly as prime-time television made it appear. I didn't even know *myself* at that point, let alone know Vince. It had taken me a long trek down a rocky path, but I was finally finding out who I was and who I wanted to be. I did a lot of soul-searching and a lot of praying as I pulled myself together. It gave me courage to keep facing each new challenge and each new day. I learned life was a great lesson, not one that can be taught in a classroom with one pattern for all, but one that God has to teach each one of us in a unique way, because it is His plan that prevails in the end.

I thought once more of that poem by Robert Frost, the one I'd thought of all those months earlier about the diverging paths, and how true the last verse was: *I shall be telling this with a sigh Somewhere ages and ages hence.*

Of course I shared all these thoughts with Maggie, along with Mama's story. Maggie and I had found our way back to being not only best friends but the best of sisters. Our lives may have diverged for a while, but even with different futures ahead of us, we were tied together for life, not just because we were family now, but because our hearts shared a common view and a love of God and life.

On November twentieth, not but a few weeks after that conversation with Mama, I awoke in the middle of the night, momentarily disoriented until throbs of pain hit my conscious body, and

I quickly remembered I was in the hospital.

A dim nightlight gave shadows to the room as my eyes adjusted. Everyone had gone. I was all alone.

I touched my belly. It felt like jelly, still swollen and far from normal, but not stretched out like a beach ball anymore. I'd given birth. My baby was out there somewhere in the nursery.

I'd held him for hours the evening before, as family and friends trooped in to admire him. Even Heather and Tammy stopped by to see him. So had Sam and Sophie, bringing along a teddy bear; they had both become dear friends, sticking with me even after graduation and carrying me out for ice cream through all the long hot months of summer.

As I lay there in the hospital bed, I feared it was all a dream, that my baby had disappeared, that someone might have snatched him away during the night. So I slipped from between the stiff white sheets, my feet hitting the linoleum floor with a soft thud, and reached for my bathrobe, a pretty silky blue thing my mother had brought me the night before. I sighed as I tied it around me, seeing how far I had to go to get back into blue jeans. But that would come.

I felt a little unsteady on my feet, but the nurse had assured me it was good to get up and walk around; I needed to get myself back in working order as soon as possible, and that meant pushing myself to walk and do everything else that needed doing.

I peeked out the door into the hallway. All was quiet. The nursery was down the hall and around the corner, so I stepped tentatively out the door, expecting someone to stop me, to tell me I couldn't see my baby. But no one stopped me as I ambled down the hallway, my steps almost silent among the hospital noises coming from some nearby nurses' station, and beeps and clicks from other rooms. I stopped to rest at the corner, one hand to the wall to steady myself as I took a breath.

Up ahead by the window of the nursery stood a guy in a T-shirt and jeans, staring at the babies, which seemed odd in the middle of the night. I watched him for a moment, first thinking he must have some ulterior motive. But he wasn't looking around nervously or anything—he was just staring in the window, as if deep in thought. I waited for that smile of recognition I knew would come when he finally spied whichever baby he was looking to find, but the longer I watched the more certain I was that he already knew which baby it was, and was studying it as if weighing out its entire future.

I stayed at the corner not wanting to disturb him, just watching him for a few minutes. I wasn't in any rush.

Maybe it was because I was so tired, or maybe it was because the drugs they gave me during delivery were still in my system making me groggy, but it wasn't till minutes later when he reached back and hooked his thumb into his back pocket that recognition began to dawn on me. Then he came to me like a picture. His posture, with his back slightly hunched in concentration, his feet planted apart like a batter. His hair had recently been cut so that it barely brushed the edge of his collar, but it was the same golden brown locks I'd run my fingers through so many times.

I gasped and grabbed at my stomach at the realization that it was him.

He shouldn't have been able to hear me from so far away, but maybe the movement caught the corner of his eye. He turned and looked at me. He knew it was me, yet he didn't smile. He didn't point to our baby and make some cute motion about this child we had created between us. Instead, he looked at Richie and back at me without an iota of change to his flat expression.

And then he turned and walked away.

He didn't wave. He didn't smile.

He just walked away.

I crumpled to the floor.

A nurse scurried up to help me back to bed, and as she tried to find out what had upset me so much, why tears flowed down my face like an unstoppable fountain, I managed to say I wanted my baby, and she hurried off to bring him to me.

Richie — Richard Graham Chambers after my daddy — was asleep in his bassinet, peacefully oblivious to the fact that his father had seen him face-to-face and walked out of his life. With a nod to the nurse, he was in my arms, the smell of his newness rising up to me and bringing tears to my eyes. His light fuzz of hair, so like my father's, felt softer than down. His face was still squished up and red, but I could see my father in his dimpled chin, and Vince in his long forehead. I would be seeing Vince in him all his life long, I knew, but that was okay.

His sweet little mouth found its way to my milk. I closed my eyes and relished the feel of him in my arms.

As love arced around us, I knew that life was going to be okay.

Richie stopped sucking and opened his eyes. I looked at him, this tiny being entrusted to me by God, and I wondered how I could ever have thought of his existence as a disaster. He was absolutely the most beautiful thing that had ever happened to me.

Acknowledgments

TO ALL THE folks at NavPress, my sincere thanks for pulling it all together, especially Kate Epperson, Kris Wallen, Arvid Wallen, and Reagen Reed.

Thanks to Jamie Chavez for her part in smoothing out the wrinkles.

My deepest gratitude to my family whose love, patience, and encouragement sustain me. Thanks to my teenagers, who kept it all real, and to my new little blessing, who reminded me how a sweet baby face makes all the nausea and exhaustion worthwhile.

In the end, I am naught without God. All glory be to the Father and to the Son and to the Holy Spirit.

About the Author

MICHELLE BUCKMAN has been a freelance writer for many years, but most enjoys writing fiction. She lives with her husband and children in the Carolinas, where she enjoys strolling along the beautiful beaches. She enjoys hearing from readers through her website: www.MichelleBuckman.com.

THE PATHWAY
COLLECTION

*Maggie
Come
Lately*

MICHELLE BUCKMAN

CHECK OUT THESE OTHER GREAT TITLES FROM THINK FICTION!

In Between

Jenny B. Jones
ISBN-13: 978-1-60006-098-4
ISBN-10: 1-60006-098-6

With her mom in jail and her dad a no-show, Katie Parker knows life isn't fair. Then she finds out she's being sent to live with a foster family and life sails right past bad to stinking. She's a temporary kid in a temporary home, and she definitely doesn't have ideas about making any of this permanent. God, on the other hand, may have other plans.

On the Loose

Jenny B. Jones
ISBN-13: 978-1-60006-115-8
ISBN-10: 1-60006-115-X

Life is looking up for teenager Katie as she adjusts to her foster family. But things turn chaotic when she's accused of stealing and she loses the lead in the school play, as well as her shot with a real-life Prince Charming. Then her foster mom is diagnosed with cancer, and she begins to doubt if God really does care.

Hollywood Nobody

Lisa Samson
ISBN-13: 978-1-60006-091-5
ISBN-10: 1-60006-091-9

Fifteen-year-old Scotty Dawn has spent her young life on the road. Scotty is wise beyond her years, but she struggles to find her identity. Complicating matters is a mother who offers no guidance and a father she's never met. She documents her journey on a "Hollywood Nobody" blog, but as she begins to find dark answers to tough questions, will her story have a happy ending?

To order copies, visit your local Christian bookstore, call NavPress at
1-800-366-7788, or log on to www.navpress.com.
To locate a Christian bookstore near you, call 1-800-991-7747.

www.thinkbooks.com